Annie's Secret

MARCIA CLAYTON

ISBN-13:978-1-0687456-2-1

Published by Sunhillow Publishing

In memory of my beloved son, Paul, who was
taken from us far too soon.

Also by Marcia Clayton

The Hartford Manor Series

Betsey: The Prequel

The Mazzard Tree

The Angel Maker

The Rabbit's Foot

Millie's Escape

A Woman Scorned

Annie's Secret

Acknowledgement

Thank you to my husband, Bryan, for his patience and encouragement and for being the first person to read this book to spot any serious plot holes!

Thanks to my talented daughter-in-law, Laura Clayton of LC DESIGNS, for producing yet another wonderful book cover which blends in so well with the rest of the series. Also, to my son, Stuart, for converting my files into PDFs.

Thank you to my sister, Gilly, my biggest supporter, who read the book in a day. If only I could write them as quickly as she can read them!

My heartfelt thanks to author Celia Martin for editing my book and providing me with so many valuable suggestions and excellent constructive criticism.

My thanks to author Shiv Saywack for checking that the routes I describe in London are feasible, or at least they were in Victorian England when there were no congestion charges or one-way streets.

I must also thank the many other authors and readers who have befriended me on social media and provided help, advice, and much-needed moral support. I appreciate it.

And last, but not least, my biggest thank you goes to you, my readers. I have received some wonderful feedback from readers, who have told me how much they have enjoyed my books. Their reviews and messages encourage me to continue writing. A simple message, particularly from a stranger, saying they loved my story, means so much to me.

The Main Characters of Hartford

The Carter Family

Edward Carter (b1812)
Married **Betsey Lovering** (b1814)

Their children:

1. **Eveline Carter** (b1837)

   Married **Charlie Chugg** (b1835)
   Their adopted children are:
   - Twins Joseph and Matthew (b1875) children of Eveline's late brother, William.
   - Amelia (b1876) daughter of Eveline's late brother, William.
   - Martha, (b1884) orphan, parents unknown.

2. **George Carter** (b1840)

   Married (1) Alice Brown (1840 – 1880)
   Their children:
   - Harriet (b1860)
   - Francis (b1862)
   - Alfred (1865 – 1869)
   - Theresa (b1868) married Louis Blaquiere

   Married (2) Mary Ann Brown (b1848)
   - Nellie (b1883)
   - Sophie (b1884)
   - Rosie Etheline (b1886)

3. **Frederick Carter** (b1841)

    Married (1) Lucy Fuller (1843 –1881)
    Their children:
    - Llewellyn (b1872)
    - Rosella (b1876)
    - Alfie (1877 – 1877)
    - Grace (1879 – 1879)
    - Eddie (b1880)

    Married (2) Charlotte Mackie (b1860)
    - Illegitimate daughter Doris (b1884)
    - Nicholas (b1885)

4. **Tom Carter** (1841 – 1880)

    Married Sabina Bailey (b1846)
    Their children:
    - **Annie** (b1864) married (1) Harry Rudd (1851 – 1881)
      Their daughter: Selina (b1881)
      Married (2) Robert Fellwood (b1863)
    - Mabel (1866 – 1866)
    - Willie (b1869) married Millie Grantley (b1870)
    - Mary (b1871)
    - John (1872 - 1880)
    - Emma (1874 - 1880)
    - Edward (b1876)
    - Stephen (b1878)
    - Helen (b1880)
    - Danny (b1880)   Foundling (Son of Charles and Eleanor Fellwood)

5. **William Carter** (1845 – 1881)

    Married (1) Lottie Chang (1850 – 1880)
    Their children:
*   Identical twins Joseph (b1875) and Matthew (b1875)
    (now adopted by Charlie and Eveline Chugg)
*   Amelia (b1876)   (now adopted by Charlie and
    Eveline Chugg)

    Married (2) **Sarah Martin** (b1845)
    Their son:
*   Bentley (b1882)

The Lovering Family

Adam Lovering (1780 - 1824)
Married (1) Ellen Richardson (1784 -1821)
Their children:

*   Barney (b1810) married Bronwen Evans
*   **Betsey** (b1814) married **Ned Carter** (b1812)
*   Norman (1817 – 1821)

Married (2) Greta Thompson (1784 – 1825)
Their daughter:

*   **Emily Lovering** (b 1823)
    Married Lenny Gibbs (1815 – 1872)
    Their daughter:
*   **Rosemary Gibbs (1843 – 1885)**
    Her children:
*   **Millicent** (b1870) married Willie Carter (b1869)
*   **Jonathan** (b1880)

The Fellwood Family of Hartford Manor

Ephraim Fellwood (1770 – 1840)
Married Helena Thompson (1775 – 1820)
Their children:

a) **Joshua Fellwood** (1803 – 1868)
Married Marianne Simpson (1805 – 1825)
Their son;

• **Charles Fellwood** (b1825)
Married: **Eleanor Chichester** (b1838)
Their children:

1. David Fellwood (1861 – 1881)
2. Lily Fellwood (1862 – 1864)

3. **Robert Fellwood** (b1863)
Married **Annie Rudd** (b1864) nee Carter
Their children:

• Selina (b1881) (Annie's daughter)
• David and Thomas (twins b1885)

4. **Victoria Fellwood** (b1863)
Married Frank Eastleigh (1863 - 1885)
Their children:
  • Caroline   (b1882)
  • Joshua (b1884)
  • Francis (b1885)

5. **Sarah Fellwood** (b1870)

6. **Danny** (b1880) (Adopted by Sabina Webber)

b) **Thomas Fellwood** (1805 – 1823)
Married Gypsy Jane (b1805 – 1841)
Their son:

• **Sam Fellwood** (b1821) married Gypsy Jenny (b1824)

Their son

- **Marrok Fellwood** (b1840) married Laura Smith (1842 – 1885)
  Their children:
- Jinnie and Elizabeth (twins) (b1876)
- Martin (b1880)
- Paul (b1882)

c) **George Fellwood** (1807 – 1833)

d) **Margery Fellwood** (b1814)
   Married Clarence Montgomery (1810 – 1870)

The Hammett Family
   Isaac Hammett (1806 – 1880)
   Married: **Liza Jones** (b1810)

The Chugg Family

Alfred Chugg (b1815)
Married Jane Watts (1820 – 1884)
12 children - one son still living at home: Jimmy Chugg (b1855)

Charlie Chugg (b 1835) (Alfred's brother)
Married: **Eveline Carter** (b1837)
Their adopted children:

- Identical twins Joseph and Matthew (b1875)
- Amelia (b1876)
- Martha (b1884)

The Webber Family

Peter Webber (b1815)
Married Mary Jane Watson (1818 – 1866)
Their son:

Arthur Webber (b1836)
Married (1) Drucie Reynolds (1840 – 1866)
Their children:
- Christopher Webber (b1856) married Clarice Gubb
- Dudley Webber (b1858)
- Elsie Webber (b1863)
- Maria Webber (b1866)

Married (2) **Sabina Carter** nee Bailey (b1846)
Their child:
- Katel Webber (b 1885)

The Cutcliffe Family

John Cutcliffe
Married (1) Hannah Matthews (1846 - 1880)

Their Children:
- Daisy (b1873)
- Mary (b1874 - 1880)
- Rachael (b1876)
- Tommy (1879 - 1880)

Married (2) **Noeleen Gubb**
Her children:
- Clarice (b1867) married Christopher Webber (b1856)
- Ruth (b1869)
- Susanna (b1872)

xiii

CHAPTER 1

The old man sitting in his wheelchair looked considerably older than his sixty-two years, for Charles Fellwood was not a well man. The light breeze ruffled his wispy, grey hair as his carer pushed him to a sheltered spot on the terrace outside his ground-floor bedroom. Disabled several years earlier by a severe stroke, one arm lay uselessly across his lap, and he could no longer stand unaided. Even the smile he raised in thanks to his nursemaid was lopsided, but his eyes were bright enough as he surveyed the attractive gardens surrounding him.

Charles, and many generations of his family before him, had been born in Hartford Manor, and he knew he would end his days in the elegant building. He and his wife, Eleanor, now lived in the west wing, having given up the main residence to their son, Robert, his wife, Annie, and their family. Charles was content with the arrangement for as long as he could stay at Hartford Manor; he didn't mind which part of the house he occupied. Indeed, since moving a few months earlier, the couple has been pleasantly surprised at how comfortable the west wing was since its refurbishment, and they loved the convenience of the new fitted bathroom - an absolute luxury, which they remarked upon most days.

It was a warm day in mid-May, and Charles enjoyed listening to the birdsong and watching some honey bees buzzing lazily around the fragrant honeysuckle that scrambled across one of the low walls surrounding the terrace. A few early roses bloomed, among them a vigorous pink rambler loaded with opening buds, which would be a picture in a week or two.

A movement to his left alerted his attention, and he noticed Eleanor strolling around the garden. A sad expression crossed Charles's face, for he knew exactly where his wife was heading and why. The wind carried children's voices from the central garden, just beyond the fence, and he could hear them squealing in delight as they played their innocent games. When he heard the words 'coming, ready or not,' he guessed they were playing hide and seek and remembered how, as a child, he had played the same game in that garden.

Eleanor stopped to sniff a fragrant cream rose before continuing her walk through the garden and towards the shrubbery. As expected, for he had witnessed this scene several times before, she pushed her way into the undergrowth and crept to the far hedge. She was dressed in a bright blue dress, which was clearly visible through the trees, and she came to a halt, keeping very still.

When he first noticed her doing this, he was puzzled, for why would the lady of the house push her way into the dense foliage and risk damaging her fine clothing? Then he noticed that she only did this when the children next door were playing outside and realised she was spying on them. Charles knew his wife was unhappy and that many of the reasons for her discontent were of her own making, but he felt sorry for her nonetheless.

Against his parents' wishes, their eldest son, David, had foolishly gone off to fight in the Boer War and perished within months of being sent to the front. That was some seven years ago, but Charles knew that he and Eleanor would grieve for the boy to the end of their days. Next in their family were the twins, Robert and Victoria, now twenty-four years old and both with children. Until recently, Victoria had been living in the Manor House with her parents, for following the tragic murder of her husband, Frank, and the birth of her third child, she was grateful for their support. Now, however, she had bought a splendid house in Lynton and was enjoying renovating it to her taste and moving on with her life. Although she missed her husband, she and Frank had not been on good terms, and, given the chance, Victoria would have left him, for he was repeatedly unfaithful. Nevertheless, his murder had been a terrible shock, and the police were no nearer to finding the culprits. Charles and Eleanor missed Victoria's children, Caroline, Joshua, and Francis, whom they had grown close to during their time living together. They were looking forward to visiting their daughter in the next few weeks and staying for a few days.

Victoria's twin brother, Robert, lived in the main part of Hartford Manor and managed the estate. Upon his father's death, he would become the next Lord Fellwood. Robert and Annie also had three children. Selina, from Annie's first marriage to Harry Rudd, and two-year-old twins, Thomas and David, who were now quite a handful and into everything. Unfortunately, Eleanor refused to acknowledge her daughter-in-law, for she had been a servant at the Manor before her marriage, and the lady viewed the union as unsuitable. So it was that neither of Robert's parents was acquainted with the three grandchildren who lived next door. Charles's thoughts were disturbed by his youngest daughter, Sarah, as she joined him and settled into a comfortable chair.

"Hello, Papa; what a glorious day. Isn't it nice to feel the sun? Rosie told me you were out here; do you mind if I join you?"

"No, of course not; I'd be delighted if you did. What have you been up to today?"

"I've been riding with Mabel; we had a wonderful gallop over the moors; it was so exhilarating. Sorry, Papa, you must miss riding; I know you loved it."

"Yes, I did, but I'm afraid my riding days are long over, more's the pity. Anyway, are you looking forward to your trip to London next month?"

"Oh yes, I am. I love London, and joining the celebrations for Queen Victoria's Golden Jubilee will be an amazing experience. It will be quite a spectacle, I think. Are you sure you and Mama will not come? I think you would be comfortable staying with Uncle Percy; his house is so luxurious."

"I know it is, and I'd love to come if I were well, but I can't face the journey. It would simply be too much for me. No, I'm content here in my own surroundings, but I look forward to hearing all about it when you return. I'm hoping to persuade your Mama to accompany you, though, for a change of scenery would do her the world of good, and I'll be fine here."

"That would be nice. I'll try to persuade her as well. Where is Mama? Have you seen her? I couldn't find her in the house."

"I think she might have gone for a stroll, but I'm sure she'll be back before long."

Charles hoped his wife would not reappear from the undergrowth for a few moments and arouse Sarah's curiosity, for he had no wish to explain. They chatted for a few more minutes, and then Sarah left, saying she wanted to relax in a nice hot bath before their evening meal.

Returning his attention to the garden, Charles saw a flash of blue as his wife emerged from her hiding place and rejoined the path back to the house. Feeling his gaze, her face reddened with discomfort at being caught snooping, and, with a subdued smile, she waved and walked towards him.

"Hello, Charles. Are you enjoying the sunshine?"

"I am. Did you enjoy your walk around the garden?"

With some embarrassment, she tackled the matter head-on.

"I did, but I presume you saw me enter the shrubbery?"

"Yes, and not for the first time, I believe. What is so interesting amongst the undergrowth, my dear?"

"I think you know, Charles. I was watching Danny play. He's such a sturdy little boy now; you'd barely know he was so deformed at birth. I know it's stupid, but I can't resist going to see him. He closely resembles David at that age, and I wish it were possible for us to spend some time with him. Do you think that woman would let us have him back if we paid her enough?"

Charles took her hand in his and squeezed her fingers. "Oh, my dear, you must let this go. It's far too late for that. You didn't want the child when he was born, and it wouldn't be fair to disrupt his life now. He has no idea that he's our son, and it would be cruel to take him away from Sabina after all she's done for him."

"If we couldn't have him back, perhaps he could visit and let us get to know him."

"Now, how could we achieve that when you won't even meet Annie because of her upbringing, and Danny has been raised as her brother? No, I'm afraid what's done is done, hard though it is. At least we know he's happy, well cared for, and wants for nothing."

"Yes, I know all that, but when I asked you to arrange for him to be adopted, I asked that it be with someone far away. I didn't expect him to end up living on our estate and regularly visiting Robert and his family next door. If I'd never set eyes on him again, I could have put it all behind me, but as it is, his presence is a constant reminder of the child I lost. Two children, in fact, for he's the spitting image of David."

"It wasn't possible to find someone far away to take him, and I don't want to be cruel, Eleanor, but you didn't lose him; you chose to give him away, and now I think you must accept it."

Eleanor snatched her hand back from her husband's and rose angrily to her feet.

"Well, thank you so much for your understanding and those few kind words, Charles! How typical of you to point out this is all my own fault."

CHAPTER 2

In the main part of the Manor House gardens, Annie was entertaining some of her family and was blissfully unaware that her mother-in-law was spying on them. Since her marriage to Robert, her mother, Sabina, had lived in the Lodge House, a quarter of a mile away at the end of their driveway. Having lost her first husband, Tom Carter, to consumption a few years earlier, Sabina was now happily married to Arthur Webber, and they were delighted by the arrival of their daughter, Katel, who was now eighteen months old.

Annie's daughter, Selina, loved having other children to play with, and it was she who had organised the game of hide and seek. The little girl faced a tree, covered her eyes, and counted to one hundred before shouting the words 'coming, ready or not' that Charles Fellwood had overheard, and then raced off to find Sabina's children, Stephen, Helen, and Danny.

The five women sitting on the terrace in the sun enjoyed watching the antics of the older children whilst Annie's two-year-old twins, David and Thomas, toddled around the terrace playing with Katel. As well as her mother, Sabina, Annie was joined by Liza Hammett, an old lady who had lived with the Carter family for several years, her granny,

Betsey Carter, and Matilda Rudd, the mother of Harry, Annie's deceased first husband. The women met regularly and frequently remarked how lucky they were now, compared to their previous existence living in extreme poverty, which they had endured for many years.

"Look at Danny; it's amazing to see him now compared to that poor little mite I took in all those years ago. The doctors have done a wonderful job, and you'd never believe he was so disabled as a baby. I must admit, I never thought he'd survive; it was so difficult for him to feed with his cleft palate."

"It's all thanks to you, Sabina. I don't know how you coped back then, what with raising your own family, working on the farm, and breastfeeding Helen and that little boy. He was so lucky to be taken in by you."

"Thanks, Matilda. It was a difficult time, but I couldn't turn a vulnerable child away when Annie found him abandoned in the woods, and now I wouldn't be without him. I love him every bit as much as my own."

"Does he know he's a foundling?"

"No, and I see no need to trouble him with that information."

Sabina glanced at Annie, and they exchanged a brief smile, for although Liza knew the truth about Danny's parentage, Betsey and Matilda were unaware that he was the child of the noble Fellwoods living next door, and the brother of Annie's husband, Robert. When Sabina agreed to raise the child, she was sworn to secrecy by Charles Fellwood, a promise she did not take lightly, for she knew she would be evicted from her cottage and lose her job if she ever let him down. Although no longer dependent on the influential man, she still kept her secret and always would.

"How do you like living in Hartford Manor, Annie? You must have so much more space than you did in the west wing."

"Yes, we do, and I love it, though I'm still surprised Robert's parents agreed to swap accommodation with us. I think they're enjoying living in the west wing, though. We'd had it refurbished, and it was so comfortable; I certainly miss our new bathroom."

"How are your renovations going? I know Robert has grand plans to take in visitors for fishing and shooting weekends."

"The building work on the guest bedrooms is finished, so now our accommodation will be modernised. I can't wait for it to be finished, for despite the staff working hard, there has been dust everywhere. It's going well, though, and we had our first visitors at Easter. They seemed to enjoy themselves, and many said they would be back, which is encouraging. Robert says we're fully booked until the end of the summer, which will recoup some of the money he's had to spend. Unfortunately, I barely see him these days as he's so busy. By the time he discusses the management of the estate and the farms with Jack Bater and attends seemingly endless meetings with the banks and solicitors, he's barely at home, and when he is, he's exhausted. Still, I mustn't grumble. No doubt it will all settle down eventually. Anyway, Gran, do you have any news of Emily, Hubert, and the others? How are they getting on in Brampford Speke?"

"All right, as far as I know. Emily writes to me about once a week and says she and Hubert have settled into Grantley House with Jonathan, though reading between the lines, I think they're finding it difficult. Some of the staff there, particularly the housekeeper and the butler, are loyal to their former mistress, Lady Lilliana, and are not making life easy for their new owners. Emily and Hubert lack the confidence to issue orders, and the staff are taking advantage. I think Jonnie's miserable too, as he misses all of us and especially the other children to play with. Millie wrote to me a few days ago and said she and Willie have settled into Bramley Cottage. It's called a cottage, but it's a large house and not the two-up, two-down cottages we're used to. She's invited Ned and me to visit, so if Ned's feeling up to it, we're going next week. Millie will send their carriage to pick us up, so the journey will be fairly comfortable despite the state of the roads. I'll feel happier when I've visited them and see where they are, and I love spending time with Emily. It's so nice to find I have a half-sister after all these years, and it's surprising how much we have in common."

"Oh, that's good, Gran. It will be nice for you and Grandad to have a little holiday. How is he?"

"Ned's not too bad, thank you. He has to rest a lot with his weak heart, but fortunately, he can do that now that we've left the inn and we're enjoying living in Sunset Cottage. Oh, here comes Danny, and he's looking upset about something."

The little boy ran to Sabina and whispered something in her ear. She stared at him in surprise. "Are you sure, Danny?"

He nodded. "Yes, and the lady put her finger to her lips when I saw her, like it was a secret."

"What's the matter, Danny? What's wrong?"

"He says a lady was watching him through the hedge, and when he saw her, she smiled at him and put her finger to her lips."

"How strange. Was it one of the maids, Danny, from when we lived in that part of the house?"

"No, it was a lady. I think it was that lady who doesn't like us."

"What, Lady Eleanor? Papa's mother? No, I wouldn't think so. She never gives any of us the time of day."

"Well, it was her!"

"Oh well, perhaps she was walking in the garden and noticed you playing. Don't worry about it; at least she smiled at you."

Annie made light of the matter, but later wondered about it and resolved to mention it to Robert, as it was so out of character for her mother-in-law.

With some difficulty, Betsey rose to her feet and unhooked her walking stick from the back of her chair.

"Anyway, my dears, I've enjoyed myself this afternoon, but I'll love you and leave you now, as I want to call on my friend, Nancy Brookes, on my way home. We've known each other for so many years, she's almost like a sister to me, and she's been a bit under the weather. I like to check that she's all right most days."

"Hold on then, Betsey, I'll come as well; I mustn't outstay my welcome. I'm so glad you still let me be a part of Selina's life, Annie. It was awful losing Harry like we did, and he'd be so proud if he could see her now."

"Yes, I know he would, Matilda, and you're welcome here anytime. You never know; Francis might make you a grandmother one day."

"Aye, he might, but he's been so busy rebuilding the business since the smithy burnt down that he's had no time for romance. Things are improving, though, and he's beginning to turn a profit, so I hope he might find a young lady to settle down with."

"How about Jacob? Is he all right?"

"Aye, as you know, he's not too bright, but he works hard, and Francis keeps an eye on him. It's a comfort to me that they get on, for I know Francis will always take care of him after I'm gone."

Betsey and Matilda strolled back to the main village and parted at Nancy's cottage, where they embraced.

"Bye then, Matilda. I'll see you again in a day or two. Take care."

Betsey saw Nancy looking out of her window and waved to her before walking around to the back door, which was wide open.

"Come in, Betsey, and leave the door open, please. It's warm today, and I like to feel the breeze. How are you, my dear?"

"Oh, I mustn't grumble, Nancy; not too bad. How about you?"

"Yes, I'm all right, thanks. Now, tell me all your news. Did you enjoy your afternoon at the Manor House? I still find it hard to believe you spend time there these days. It's a far cry from our childhood, isn't it?"

The two old friends enjoyed chatting with each other and sharing all the village gossip until Nancy struggled to her feet and said she would fetch them a glass of lemonade and a piece of the cake she had made that morning.

"That would be lovely, thank you. I saw your cake cooling on the table and I thought it looked delicious."

Nancy hobbled to the kitchen and then exclaimed in surprise.

"Well, would you believe it! My cake's gone!"

"Gone? How can it be gone?"

"I don't know, but it's gone. I'm glad you saw it, or I'd think I was losing my mind."

"Well, it was there when I came in, so someone must have stolen it. What a cheek in broad daylight. Who would do such a thing?"

"No matter, I have some biscuits I made yesterday; we'll have some of those instead. It's a bad job to be robbed from your own kitchen, though."

CHAPTER 3

Later that day, Robert called on his parents, which he tried to do at least once a week. However, his mother had retired early due to a headache, and he entered his father's study somewhat reluctantly, as the pair had not been close for some years.

"Hello, Papa, I'm sorry to hear Mama's feeling unwell; is it anything serious?"

"No, I don't think so, but she's prone to migraine attacks and finds it best to rest as soon as she feels one coming on. She got upset about something this afternoon, and I think I probably made matters worse."

"Oh, what upset her?"

"As unlikely as it seems, she's pining for the child she gave away. If Danny had been adopted miles from here as we hoped, this wouldn't have happened, but unfortunately, the way we live now, she sees him nearly every day, and it's upsetting her."

"Well, she was adamant he should be adopted when he was born, and but for Sabina's care, I'm sure he would have died."

"I know that, and so does she. Nevertheless, it doesn't make things any easier for her. She's missing Victoria's three children now that they've moved to Lynton, and she refuses to acknowledge yours, which I know is a sore point."

"How did you upset her?"

"I said what's done is done, and that the child was not taken from her; she gave him away. I should have chosen my words more carefully, even if they were true. It was a little harsh."

"So, what does she want to happen? I mean, I can't see a solution, and you're right, what's done is done."

"Well, I know this is impossible, but she wondered if Mrs Carter, or Webber, as I think she's called now, would let her have the child back."

"You can't be serious! Of course, she wouldn't let her have Danny back. He doesn't even know he isn't her son, and it wouldn't be right to upset him. What was she thinking?"

"I know, and I agree with you, but she's taken to watching him through the hedge when he plays with your children. I've told her she's only torturing herself and should put it behind her, but naturally, that's easier said than done."

"If she weren't so stubborn about accepting Annie as one of the family, this wouldn't be a problem. You could get to know our children, and maybe Danny too, in time, but I know that will never happen."

"A month ago, I would have agreed with you, but now I'm not so sure. Eleanor is lonely and dreads her old age, particularly as it's likely I'll go first. She feels she has little to look forward to."

"Rubbish! She still has Sarah living at home, and soon she can accompany her to London for her coming-out season. Mama lives a life of luxury and has nothing to complain about; many people are far worse off than she is."

"You're right, of course, but things haven't been the same since David died in the Boer War. Then there was my stroke, and your marriage to a kitchen maid. What with Frank being unfaithful to Victoria and then getting murdered, it's not difficult to see why she's melancholy."

"Things have been difficult, it's true, but as I say, we're so fortunate compared to many. Do you think Mama might accept Annie and the children? It would be marvellous if she would, but how would you feel about it?"

"Well, after the way I treated your wife when she was a maid here, I hardly have the right to judge, do I? I'm so ashamed of my behaviour now, but I have no excuses, and I understand that she will never forgive me for what I did. How is the child, anyway?"

"Selina is a joy and full of life. She can be a handful sometimes, but she's a kind little girl and has no idea I'm not her father. Again, like Danny, we can't see that there's any point in telling her the truth and at her age, she wouldn't understand."

That evening, Robert joined Annie in the study for their customary glass of Madeira wine. They sat in front of a roaring fire, for although the day had been hot and sunny, the evenings were still chilly, with a hard frost some mornings.

He stretched out and rested his feet on a footstool, then put his arm around her and drew her close, enjoying the warmth and fragrance of her skin.

"What have you been up to today?"

"I had tea in the garden with Mum, Liza, Matilda, and Gran. It was a warm afternoon, and Selina enjoyed having all the children here to play. They had a wonderful time. It's so nice that they live just down the driveway and can see each other often. How about you?"

"Oh, busy as usual. I met with Jack this morning for our daily meeting about the farm and the estate, and everything is in order. Having Marrok as the tenant at Sugworthy Farm now is a godsend, for we know it's in safe hands and we can rely on him."

"Has he replaced Willie and Edward yet?"

"Yes, I believe he's taken on three new farmhands because they're growing more crops this year and increasing the herd of cows and flock of sheep. According to Jack, who visited Marrok a few days ago, Sam and Florrie have hit it off, and he thinks romance may be in the air."

"How wonderful; it would be so nice for the pair of them to find a partner in their later years. Sam's marriage, many years ago, was unhappy, and Florrie never married. Oh, I must tell Mum and Gran that bit of news when I see them next. What about this afternoon? Did you go into Barnstaple?"

"Yes, I had to visit the bank to check on our finances."

"Was it all right?"

"Yes, Mr Billery is satisfied that our finances are improving now that we've had a few weeks of visitors to the estate. It will be a year or two before we see any significant profit, but the shooting and fishing breaks are popular, and the meals we provide for the guests and their spouses generate additional income. I think we should plan a few activities for the women to enjoy, such as a ball or two, a hunt, or a treasure hunt on horseback. What do you think?"

"Yes, if you want, as long as I don't have to participate."

"Why not? You're an excellent rider, and no one would know you weren't born a lady; you've adapted so well."

"Maybe, but I'm happier with my own people; it's still an effort for me to act the lady, and some of the guests will know of my background and look down their noses at me. No, it's better I take a back seat, and I'd prefer that, anyway."

"As you like, but I think you have more friends than you think."

"Did you see your parents today?"

"Yes, well, I saw Papa, but Mama had retired with a migraine. Papa told me about a surprising development that could be good."

"Oh, what's that?"

"Mama's finding it difficult knowing Danny plays here with Selina. After all, he is her son, even if she did reject him at birth because of his deformities. Papa says if he'd been adopted miles from here, which was what Mama wanted when he was born, she wouldn't have seen him again, but now he lives so close it's a constant reminder. Apparently, she's taken to spying on him through the hedge when she hears the children playing in the garden."

"Ah, that explains it then; Danny came running up to Mum earlier and said a lady was watching him. He said it was that lady who doesn't like us. He said she smiled and raised her finger to her lips like it was a secret. How dare she! After giving him away, she should mind her own business and keep her nose out."

"That's a bit harsh, my love. Surely, as a mother, you can understand her feelings?"

"I understand I would never have parted with any child of mine, however much disabled they were. She even had the money to employ all the help she needed, but she abandoned him without a second thought."

"I'm sure it wasn't without a second thought, and she even told Papa she'd like him back."

"What! No way! I hope you realise that's impossible. Danny has no idea of his parentage or even that he's a foundling, and there's no need for him to ever know. Think how upset he'd be, and it would hardly make him fond of Eleanor and Charles, knowing they gave him up. Mum and his brothers and sisters would be so upset."

"I agree, and so did Papa, but I have encouraging news. Papa thinks that because Mama wants to see Danny so badly, she might accept you, Selina, Thomas, and David, and you could all get to know each other. Wouldn't that be wonderful?"

Annie stared at her husband in disbelief and removed herself from his embrace.

"I do hope you're joking?"

"Well, no; I hate this terrible enmity between us all. Surely, it would be better for everyone to get along?"

"There was a time when I might have tried to get on with them to keep the peace, despite what your father did to me, but I would have always found it difficult. Now, given how they've continued to treat me over the years, I feel differently, and that's something you've conveniently overlooked: my feelings. Have you forgotten that your father raped me and left me pregnant? And that your mother continues to despise me for becoming pregnant before I was married. I will never, ever spend time in their company, just as I will never, ever forgive your father for what he did. You seem to think this is all about your parents accepting me; well, the way I feel about them now, I will never accept them, so you can forget that idea."

Leaving her husband with no chance to reply, Annie stormed off to spend the night in the spare bed in the nursery.

CHAPTER 4

It was a busy morning at Hollyford Farm, as it was market day in Barnstaple, and Eveline Chugg was getting ready to travel there with her husband, Charlie, his nephew, Jimmy, and their adopted children. The twelve-year-old twins, Joseph and Matthew, and Amelia, their eleven-year-old sister, were the children of Eveline's late brother, William, and Martha, now three, was an orphan who had joined their family when only a baby.

"Will you please get a move on, Joe, and you, Matthew; we're already running late, and you two aren't helping matters. Get your shoes on quickly, and then help Martha with hers. Hurry, or we'll be late. Amelia, have you taken all the eggs out to Charlie to put onto the cart?"

"Yes, they're all loaded up, and Charlie says he's ready to go."

"Right, is Jimmy with him?"

"Yes, he's putting the milk churns on the cart, and he says there'll be enough room for us to ride at the back."

"Good. Now, Alfred, are you sure you'll be all right here on your own if we all go to town?"

Her brother-in-law sneezed into his handkerchief a few times before he was able to answer, and was then interrupted by a lengthy bout of coughing. He waved his hand at her dismissively.

"Go and sell your produce; you've worked hard, now make some money. I would have liked to come today because I believe there's a Gigglet Fair on as well as the usual market, and we could use a new worker, but I'm sure Charlie and Jimmy will choose wisely if there are any suitable candidates. And anyway, I'm not on my own; I've got Maria here to keep me company and cook my dinner, so I'll be fine. Go on, now, I'm looking forward to a bit of peace and quiet with you lot out of the way."

"All right then, but I think I'll call on Doctor Luckett and ask him to visit. I don't like the sound of that cough."

"You'll do no such thing. I'm on the mend, and even if I'm not, there's not much he can do about it. It would be a waste of money."

"All right, then, we'll give it a few more days, but you take it easy. Charlie and Jimmy have taken care of the animals, and anything else can wait until we're home again. Is there anything I can get you from Barnstaple?"

"Aye, a couple of ounces of baccy, and some barley sugar, please. You can get the children some as well, and I'll pay you when you get home."

"Very well, I'll see you later. Maria, make sure he puts his feet up and gets some rest."

Eveline kissed the elderly man on the cheek and patted him on the back, then took Martha by the hand and led her outside to the waiting cart.

Charlie, the three older children, and Alfred's son, Jimmy, were already on the cart, and Eveline lifted the little girl up to Charlie so that she could ride between the two of them.

"Are you sure you're all right back there, Jimmy?"

"Aye, I'm fine. Right, Charlie, I think we can go now."

Despite Eveline chivvying her family to make haste and grumbling that they would be late, it was still only half past seven. The journey to Barnstaple would take over an hour, and she wanted to arrive at the market early to set up her stall in the Pannier Market and sell as much produce as possible. Eleven-year-old Amelia was looking forward to her day out, as her Aunty Eveline had promised she could serve the customers and take the money.

Eveline put her arm around Martha and wondered how the little girl would get on with sitting in the market all day. It was the first time she had brought the child on a Friday, for normally she stayed at the farm with Maria, their kitchen maid. However, Maria was suffering from the same cold that was troubling Alfred, and Eveline thought she would have enough to do looking after the old man while she was still not too well herself.

"I hope you'll behave yourself for me today, Martha. You can sit on the bench beside me and watch what's going on in the market. You mustn't wander off."

The little girl nodded her head and clutched her rag doll tightly to her chest as the cart bumped violently over a large rut in the road.

"What about us, Aunty Eveline? Can we go off and explore the town?"

Eveline knew Matthew and Joseph would soon be bored sitting in the market.

"Yes, but don't go near the river and keep out of trouble. You can help to unload the cart and then go off for a couple of hours. Come back to the market when you're hungry. Mind you, I don't suppose that will be long the way you two eat."

"Oh, good, we want to climb to the top of Castle Mound near the cattle market. Is that all right?"

"Yes, I remember doing that as a child. You'll have a nice view from there and be able to see everything that's going on in the cattle market."

"Was it a castle once?"

"I'm not sure, but I know it's been there a long time, and it's known as Castle Mound, so I expect so."

The threatening rain, thankfully, held off, and they arrived in Barnstaple, dry, and in plenty of time. Charlie tethered the horse and cart in Butchers Row, and for the next twenty minutes, they were busy unloading the farm produce and helping Eveline to set up her stall for the day.

"There, I think that's the lot. Will you be all right now if Jimmy and I get off to the cattle market? We want to buy some goslings and ducklings to fatten up for Christmas. The Gigglet Fair will be held there too, so we'll see if there's a suitable farmhand. I'd like to take on an extra pair of hands and stop Alfred from doing so much. It's time he took a back seat and put his feet up."

"I'm fine, now, thanks, Charlie, and yes, I agree. We could use more help around the house, too, so if a married couple is looking for work, that would be ideal. I'll see you later."

The two men walked through the market, passing the time of day with several stallholders, and as they neared the exit from the market onto the High Street, Jimmy hesitated.

"You go on to the cattle market, Charlie, and I'll catch you up in a little while. There are one or two things I want to buy while I'm in the town, and the auction won't start for an hour or so. You suss out the best birds, and then we can bid on them together."

"Yes, all right; see you later."

Jimmy set off down the High Street in the opposite direction to his uncle as he wanted to visit a couple of shops in Cross Street. At the junction of High Street and Cross Street, he noticed a youth grab the basket of a young woman. She was having none of it and put up a fight, but the teenager gave her a hard slap that sent her sprawling to the ground, and snatching her basket, quickly legged it down the High Street. Jimmy was furious and immediately gave chase. The street was crowded with shoppers, and Jimmy dodged and weaved, uttering apologies as he tried to catch the culprit.

"Stop him! Stop that thief!"

A burly man, chatting to his friends, saw what was happening and helpfully stuck out his foot, tripping up the boy and sending him hurtling to the ground. Jimmy grinned.

"Nice one, mate. I'll take it from here."

He hauled the thief to his feet, gave him a shake, and pulled the basket away from him.

"I should take you to the police station for what you did. How dare you knock a poor woman down like that? You should be ashamed of yourself."

The boy trembled as Jimmy held him by the scruff of his neck.

"Oh no, don't do that, mister. I'm sorry, but I'm starving and I need to eat."

Jimmy observed the miserable individual that he held in his grasp, for the boy was nothing but skin and bone. Dressed in filthy rags, he looked about fifteen, but could have been older.

"Well, I can see you're desperate, but that's no excuse for hitting a woman. I'll let you off this time, but if I see you do it again, you won't be so lucky." He reached into his pocket and withdrew a sixpence. "Here, buy yourself a pasty and find a better way to make some money."

"Aw, thanks, Mister. I haven't eaten for a couple of days, and I'm so hungry."

The boy ran off, and Jimmy gazed after him, wishing he could do more to help, but knowing there were far too many in the same sad predicament. Hooking the basket over his arm, he retraced his steps to the High Cross junction, where the young woman was being comforted by a few people.

"Are you all right, ma'am? Oh dear, your nose is bleeding, and you've skinned your hands and knees too. I wish I'd given that young whippersnapper a hiding now; I let him off too lightly. He was starving, though, the poor wretch. I got your basket back, anyway, and I don't think you've lost any of your shopping."

"Oh, thank goodness. I'm so grateful; you've saved me from a lot of trouble."

"You're welcome. I'll tell you what, my shopping can wait, and I've got half an hour to spare, so why don't I take you into The Three Tuns for an ale or a cup of tea, and you can get cleaned up? I know the landlord and his wife, and I'm sure they'll attend to you in the parlour if you're uncomfortable with going into the bar."

"'Tis kind of you, sir, but I need to get back home or my Uncle Noah will not be best pleased."

Jimmy studied the young woman. She was shabbily dressed, her garments patched, but clean, and she had a winning smile. Her auburn hair tumbled in disarray over her shoulders, and she regarded him with warm brown eyes. He guessed her to be around thirty and wondered if she was talking about Noah Berryman, the landlord of the notorious brothel, The Tucker's Arms. Jimmy's family had fallen foul of that scoundrel in the past, and he was intrigued to know what connection she could possibly have to the infamous rogue, if indeed it was the same Noah. He fervently hoped she was not one of his prostitutes.

"Well, look, we need to stop that nosebleed, and there's blood soaking through your skirt, so that wound on your knee must need attention. That will surely give you a plausible excuse for being late returning home. I'm Jimmy, by the way, Jimmy Chugg."

He held out his hand, and she grinned, showing even white teeth, and dimples appeared in her rosy cheeks. Jimmy, a confirmed bachelor, was suddenly desperate to know more about this girl. She took his hand and then winced as the wound on her hand smarted.

"Well, all right then, thank you. I don't suppose half an hour will matter when I show my injuries. My name is Nell, Nell Patterson."

CHAPTER 5

The Three Tuns was crowded with farmers and revellers looking forward to the Gigglet Fair with all its attractions, and Nell hesitated at the door when she saw how busy it was. However, Jimmy took her arm, led her past the entrance to the bar and down a corridor, where he knocked on a door on the right. It was a few minutes before a red-faced woman answered.

"Oh, hello, Jimmy, lad. I haven't seen you for a while; how can I help?"

"Hello, Winnie, I'm sorry to bother you when you're so busy, but this poor lass was attacked by a young ruffian and her nose is bleeding, and she's grazed her hands and knees. I wondered if we could go into your parlour so she can clean herself up a bit? It's so crowded in the bar, there's barely room to move."

"Oh, dear, you poor maid; yes, of course, Jimmy, come in and I'll fetch some warm water and a cloth for you to clean yourself up."

The portly woman led them through the kitchen to the parlour and indicated a comfortable chair.

"Sit yourself down there, my love, and I'll be right back. Can I interest you in a pint, Jimmy? And what about you, my dear? I expect a hot cup of tea would help to calm your nerves."

"That would be most welcome, thanks, Winnie."

It was only a few minutes before Winnie returned with a bowl of warm water and a clean cloth on a wooden tray, which also held a pint of ale, a teapot, a cup and saucer, a sugar bowl, and a small milk jug.

"There we are. Now, I'm afraid I must leave you to it, but take as long as you like, and I hope you feel better soon."

"That's so kind of you, Winnie; I appreciate it."

Jimmy pressed some coins into the woman's hand as she rushed back to continue serving behind the bar. Picking up his tankard and moving to the door, he said, "I'll go to the bar for a few minutes to give you some privacy to clean up your knees, and by the time I return, your tea will have brewed, and we can have a chat."

Ten minutes later, Jimmy knocked on the door, and Nell bade him come in. She was still dabbing at her nose but had washed her hands and face, bathed her knees, and was looking calmer.

"Thank you so much for this, Jimmy, but I must be going. Noah would be furious if he knew I was here with you."

"Well, at least drink a cup of tea before you go. It would be a waste now that I've paid for it. Here, let me pour you a cup. Do you like milk and sugar with it?"

"Yes, I do, though it's seldom we have any. But yes, thank you."

She took the cup gratefully.

"Are you feeling better now?"

"Yes, thank you. I can't believe I allowed a young lad to steal my basket; I should have put up more of a fight."

"Well, he took you by surprise and gave you a hefty slap; it's no wonder he got the better of you. You mentioned your Uncle Noah, and it's not a common name. Is he the Noah Berryman that keeps The Tucker's Arms?"

The woman's cheeks flushed, and she looked embarrassed.

"I'm afraid so. Do you know him?"

"I know of him, but no, fortunately, I've not had the pleasure of meeting him. He has a terrible reputation in the town, as I'm sure you know. Have you always lived with your uncle?"

"No, and I wouldn't be living there now if I had any choice. He's not my blood relation; it's his wife, Meg, that I'm related to. She's my late mother's sister. I'm from Landkey, and until a few months ago, I lived there with my husband, Roy, in a tied cottage. He was a farm worker, but he died from consumption in January and me and my two daughters had to leave. My parents are both dead, and I had nowhere else to go, so Aunt Meg said I could stay with them."

"Oh dear, I'm sorry to hear about your husband; consumption is an awful disease. Had he been ill long?"

"Quite a while, but he caught pneumonia in December, and he was too weak to fight it. The farmer he worked for didn't want to turn us out, but he needed the cottage for the new worker and his family. It's what happens."

"Yes, unfortunately. How old are your daughters? You seem young to have a family?"

"Well, thank you, I certainly feel old enough. Jane's five, and Laura's three. I don't like leaving them at the inn when I go shopping, but Noah insists. He never lets me bring them both out with me, in case I don't return. They're his insurance against me leaving."

"That's terrible. Do you want to leave?"

"I'd love to leave, but I've nowhere to go and I have to nurse my Aunt Meg. She's only in her fifties, but she's ill with something and can't leave her bed. She's a big lady and she's losing the use of her legs, so it takes me all my time to try to keep her clean, not that cleanliness is high on her list of priorities."

"I hardly like to ask, but does Noah make you do anything else?"

"I know what you're thinking, Jimmy, but thankfully, no, I've not had to work as a prostitute. My Aunt Meg's not much better than her husband, but so far, she's made sure I haven't had to do that. They used to have a woman called Cissie who lived there and did all the drudgery, but somehow she escaped with her son, Mickey. I met her once, and she was a kind woman, so I'm pleased for her, though if Noah ever finds her, she'll rue the day. I work morning, noon, and night, doing everything around the place. I cook all the meals, do the cleaning, washing, and shopping, as well as nurse Aunt Meg. It's no life for Jane and Laura, but at least we have a roof over our heads and food to eat. I worry that if Aunt Meg dies, and I suspect she doesn't have that long left, that Noah will force me onto the game, and I dread the thought. I worry about my girls, too, for Noah and his sons, Abe and Reggie, have no morals where children are concerned."

Jimmy took her red and calloused hand and cradled it in his, taking care not to touch the nasty graze.

"I'm sorry to hear that, Nell. My family had a run-in with Noah and Abe Berryman a while back when they abducted my Aunt Eveline's niece, Theresa Carter. Abe duped her into visiting the inn and then held her prisoner for weeks, and I'm afraid your Aunt Meg had a hand in it. A gentleman from London had seen her on a previous visit and wanted her for himself when he next visited Devon. Fortunately, my Uncle Charlie and a few others rescued her before that could happen, as well as Cissie and Mickey."

"Oh, my goodness; don't tell me anymore, Jimmy. Noah's still furious about the whole matter because the gentleman in question refused to pay for all the weeks that Noah had kept the girl, so he was out of pocket. He's determined to find her, Cissie, and Mickey, and if he does, they won't be seen again."

"Well, Theresa's married now, and hopefully safe, but no, I won't tell you where Cissie and Mickey are, though I think I can trust you."

"You can, especially after your kindness today, but I'd rather not know; he can't get the truth out of me then. Anyway, Jimmy, I must go. I worry about leaving the girls for too long, though they stay in the bedroom with Aunt Meg. I think they're safer there, though I don't fully trust her either, and she sleeps a lot of the time."

"Can I see you again, Nell? I've enjoyed talking to you. I'll be in Barnstaple again next Friday."

"Don't you have a wife to go home to, Jimmy?"

"No, I've never met the right woman; I'm still single. I live on my Dad's farm in the middle of nowhere, and I'm not one to socialise much."

"I like you, Jimmy, but no, I don't want you to have anything to do with The Tucker's Arms and my uncle. You're better off steering clear of me, especially as your family was involved in the other matter, but thank you for helping me today."

Nell rose to her feet and gathered up her basket. She kissed Jimmy on the cheek before quickly leaving the room and hurrying into the crowds.

Knowing he had taken far longer than he intended, Jimmy hurried along the High Street and headed for the cattle market in Tuly Street. He pushed his way through the crowds until he found the poultry section, but Charlie was nowhere to be seen. Realising the auction had begun and Charlie had gone to bid without him, he made his way to where he could hear the auctioneer's voice singing out the bids at an impossible speed. He spotted Charlie next to the ring, where a dozen goslings were on display. The young birds, their soft yellow down gleaming in the sunlight, were unhappy with the proceedings and squeaking loudly, clearly distressed. Jimmy apologetically shoved people out of the way until he was at his uncle's side and in time to hear Charlie make the final successful bid.

"There you are, Jimmy. I had to go ahead and bid, so I hope you approve of my choice; I thought you'd have been here long before now. Did you get the things you wanted?"

"No, I didn't get anything as it happens, but there's nothing that can't wait until next week. I'll tell you about it later when we're on our own."

Charlie stared at him curiously, but didn't pursue the matter.

"Very well. I've earmarked a dozen ducklings that I want to bid for, and I think they'll be dealt with next. After that, we'll visit the Gigglet Fair and see if we can hire some new workers. There are two married couples in the line-up, and I'd like to get it sorted today because the next fair won't be for a year, and we need the help now, coming into summer."

There were several batches of ducklings on offer, and Charlie was outbid on the first two lots, but, determined not to go home empty-handed, he paid rather more than intended for the third batch and arranged to collect all the birds later in the day.

The two men hurried to another part of the market, where a line of men and women stood on a platform, hoping to be hired.

"See the two married couples? The pair on the end are a bit older, but they probably have more experience, or there are the two youngsters in the middle. The older ones aren't so likely to start producing children as soon as we hire them, but which do you think would be best?"

"Blimey, I don't know, Charlie; can we have a word with them and hear what they have to say?"

"Yes, I think we should do that. While we're here, you could find yourself a wife, Jimmy; it's about time you settled down with someone. You know the old custom, don't you?"

"I'm not sure that I do, but I don't suppose I can stop you from telling me."

"At a Gigglet Fair a young man is allowed to claim a kiss from any young maid that takes his fancy, but better than that, he can buy himself a wife, and if he leads her all the way home with a halter around her neck, they're considered man and wife; he doesn't even have to trouble himself with a church service. I remember old Alfie Cook doing that when I was a boy. Led poor Susie twelve miles, he did, with a large crowd following them, me included. The squire and the vicar made such a fuss about it, and folk didn't think Alfie would be allowed to get away with it. He did, though, and they lived together for years and had a long string of children."

"Poor woman; how degrading. Didn't she mind?"

"I don't think she had much say in it. Her first husband sold her for half a crown, and she had to do as she was told. I think Alfie treated her well, though, you'd hope so by the number of children they produced."

"No, I am certainly not buying myself a wife today, Charlie. If, and when I marry, I'd like the woman to be willing, and to have some feelings for me."

His uncle chuckled. "Just as you like, and I don't blame you. Come on, let's get this sorted, and then we can have some dinner at The Golden Fleece; I'm hungry."

By the end of the day, Eveline had sold most of her produce in the Pannier Market. Amelia had enjoyed being in charge of the money while her aunt dispensed the goods and chatted with her friends. The little girl had a quick mind, and the customers were impressed with how quickly she added up the amount they owed in her head. Eveline, listening carefully in case Amelia made a mistake, was delighted to find her so reliable. Joe and Matthew had explored not only the Castle Mound but also a large part of the town. They returned at intervals throughout the day as their stomachs dictated the need for food, and their aunt wondered, and not for the first time, where they put it all. Poor Martha was exhausted and nearly asleep when, at four o'clock, Charlie and Jimmy arrived to reload the cart, ready to travel home. They were accompanied by the older married couple who carried their few belongings in two sacks.

"Eveline, I'd like to introduce you, would you believe, to Jack and Jill Crosby, our new helpers. I still think they have made up their names, but I've agreed to give them a month's trial."

Eveline smiled and held out her hand. "I'm pleased to meet you, and we can certainly do with your help, but Charlie, I don't think we'll all fit on the cart with the two wicker baskets of goslings and ducklings as well. The poor old horse can only cope with so much."

"No, we won't; I've only brought Jack and Jill here to meet you and say hello, but I've arranged for them to travel back with old Mr Smith. He's got room on his cart and will drop them off at the farm on his way home."

A few minutes later, Charlie flicked the reins and the horse set off for the farm. This time, Eveline travelled with the children on the cart, for Martha was fast asleep within minutes, and it was easier to let her stretch out with her head resting on her aunt's lap. Jimmy sat up front with Charlie and, at last, had the opportunity to tell him about Nell Patterson and her connection to Noah Berryman.

"You should steer clear of that particular young lady, then, Jimmy, though I feel for her. We want nothing more to do with that rogue and his family, especially if he still bears a grudge about Theresa and Cissie. He's a dangerous man and best avoided."

Jimmy looked thoughtful but said nothing.

CHAPTER 6

Dawn was breaking in the village of Hartford, and the first slivers of light crept through the tiny windows of Sunset Cottage and glinted on the snowy white hair of the woman sitting at the kitchen table.

"Ned, are you sure you feel up to this trip?"

"Aye, I'm fine; don't fuss, woman. You want to see Millie and Jonnie and everyone, don't you?"

"Yes, of course, I do, but not if it's too much for you."

"I'll be fine; I've only got to sit in the carriage after all. Fancy us travelling all that way in style? We've gone up in the world, my love."

"That we have, but it will still be tiring, being jolted around for hours. I'm looking forward to seeing Emily and everyone, though. Oh, look, here's the carriage now. It's earlier than I expected, and I believe I see Millie and Jonnie inside. How kind of them to come."

Betsey greeted Millie and Jonathan with a big hug.

"I'm so glad to see you; are you well? I didn't know you were coming to fetch us."

"Hello, Aunty Betsey. Yes, we're fine, thank you. I thought it would be nice to travel with you; we have so much to share with you. Are you ready?"

"Yes, we are, but would you like a cup of tea or something to eat before we start back to Brampford Speke? It's such a long way. How did you get here so early? You must have travelled overnight?"

"No, we're all right, thank you. We wanted to surprise you, so we travelled here yesterday and stayed the night at The Red Lion. It gave Jonnie a chance to see Bentley, Rosella, and Eddie. He misses the other children to play with, don't you, Jonnie?"

"I do. I wish we still lived here with you, Aunty Betsey, as long as Granny could come as well."

"Oh, dear, don't you like it at Grantley House?"

"No, it's boring, and I've got no one to play with."

"Oh, well, you'll have to come and stay here for a week or two in the summer holidays, then. How about school? Have you made some new friends?"

"One or two, but I'd rather go to school with Bentley and Danny like I used to."

"You can tell me more about it in the carriage, but we'd better get going; the driver won't want us to keep him waiting, for it will be a long day. I'll be having a word with Fred and Charlotte, too, not telling us they were expecting you yesterday."

The driver, however, was an elderly man who liked his new employers, for they treated him far better than the previous ones, and nothing was too much trouble for him. He loaded their luggage and helped Betsey and Ned up the three steps and into the carriage, ensuring they were comfortable. The journey would take all day, for it was over fifty miles to Brampford Speke and might necessitate an overnight stop if they encountered any problems.

Betsey smiled happily at her newly discovered great-niece and nephew. She reflected that until six months ago, she didn't know they even existed, nor, for that matter, their granny, her half-sister, Emily.

Betsey's father, Adam Lovering, had deserted his three children many years earlier when Betsey was a little girl. At the time, her eldest brother, Barney, was no longer living at home, and with their mother recently deceased, the little girl and her brother, Norman, were found in a sorry state, suffering from malnutrition and hypothermia when their neighbours finally discovered them. Betsey had pulled through, but sadly, three-year-old Norman perished. Unbeknownst to Betsey, her father had moved to Exeter with a girlfriend and had no intention of ever returning to his family. Before long, he remarried and had another daughter, Emily.

When, a week or two before Christmas, Emily's daughter, Rosemary, died of typhoid, and with Emily too suffering from the awful disease, she sent her grandchildren, Millie and Jonnie, on their way in search of relatives in Hartford whom she hoped would offer them a home. Their quest was successful, for as soon as they saw Betsey, the youngsters knew she must be related to their granny, as they were so much alike.

It was common knowledge in Brampford Speke that Rosemary Gibbs had been the lover of Sir Edgar Grantley for many years and that he had fathered two bastards, Millicent and Jonathan, though the pair had no idea who their father was. When he, too, died of typhoid, on the same day as his lover, Emily was distraught, for she knew his wife, Lady Lilliana, would seek revenge for the years of humiliation his affair had caused her and would, no doubt, evict them from their cottage. So it was that in the dead of night, Emily insisted that her two grandchildren set off on the long journey to Hartford despite the fact that it was in the midst of winter.

In yet another twist of fate, a surprising truth came to light a few weeks later. Sir Edgar Grantley was a bigamist, and when he wed Lady Lilliana in a union long-arranged by their families, he had already married Rosemary Gibbs in secret. This meant, much to the fury of Lady Lilliana, that Millicent and Jonathan Gibbs were not illegitimate as everyone thought, but the entitled heirs of the rich man.

Six-year-old Jonathan Gibbs was now Sir Jonathan Grantley, and the little boy had inherited Grantley House, much land, and a small fortune. His sister, Millicent, lived in a cottage on the estate and was rich in her own right. The one drawback was that the will specified Jonathan must live in Grantley House, something he was not enjoying, although he was cared for by his grandmother, Emily, and her new husband, Hubert March.

With the youngsters chattering nineteen to the dozen, Betsey was surprised when they arrived in Barnstaple, and the carriage stopped at the Royal and Fortescue Inn in Boutport Street.

"This is a grand place; are we stopping here, Millie?"

"Yes, and the food is delicious, so we thought we'd stop here for a bite to eat and refresh ourselves before continuing our journey. This is where Jonnie and I spent a night on the way to Hartford when Sir Roger Everson and his wife gave us a lift in their carriage from Kings Nympton."

"How on earth did you afford to stay here? It must cost a small fortune."

"Oh, we didn't pay, Uncle Ned. We arrived here late at night, and as it was so bitterly cold, Lady Jasmine insisted we be given a bed. We stayed in the servants' quarters and ran away at first light in case they decided to hand us over to the police. We stopped here for an hour on the way to Hartford yesterday and thought we'd do the same on the way back. Come on, they're expecting us and should have a meal ready."

Betsey and Ned wondered at Millie's confidence as she led them into a comfortably furnished room, where they were shown to a dining table and served a delicious meal.

"My goodness, Millie, I'm impressed with how quickly you've become accustomed to your new life, and I can't believe we're sitting in such fine surroundings, but tell me, how are Willie and Edward getting on? I hope my grandsons are enjoying their new life."

"I think they are. It's been strange for all of us moving to the Grantley Estate and living in Bramley Cottage, but we love it. Although it's called a cottage, it's big, and we even have maids to do all the cleaning and a cook to provide our meals. Edward found it strange at first because, being deaf, we couldn't explain things to him, but Willie thought he'd rather come with us than stay at Sugworthy Farm on his own."

"What are they doing with their time? They've always worked hard for a living, and I can't see them wanting to be idle."

"They're working on the estate, but things are a bit awkward. As we're married, the solicitor who's been handling everything insisted Willie should become the Estate Manager rather than a farm hand, but the other workers resent him, though they have to be respectful, or they could lose their jobs. The existing manager was given excellent references and paid handsomely to leave, but it's a difficult situation."

After an hour or so, with the passengers feeling refreshed after a rest, the carriage continued on its journey, making two more stops at Chulmleigh and Crediton before arriving at Brampford Speke at ten o'clock. As it was too late for Jonnie to travel the short distance to Grantley House, he, too, stayed at Bramley Cottage, and all the travellers were relieved to get to their beds.

The next morning, Betsey and Ned were delighted to be reunited with their two grandsons. Willie hugged them both, and eleven-year-old Edward clung to Betsey, causing a few tears to appear in her eyes. She surveyed her grandson keenly, wishing he could speak and tell her how he was feeling, for she was unsure he had settled into his new surroundings. She thought he looked a bit under the weather and resolved to keep an eye on him and, if necessary, take him back home to Hartford.

At breakfast, Willie clasped Millie's hand and asked if she had told the visitors their news. She shook her head, smiling widely.

"What are you two grinning about?"

"We have wonderful news, Grandad. Millie is expecting a baby, and we're thrilled. I can't believe I'm going to be a father, and you two will have another great-grandchild."

"Oh, I'm so pleased, lad. Congratulations, Millie; how are you keeping?"

"Not bad, thanks. I've had a bit of morning sickness, but it's better now than it was."

"When's the baby due?"

"Not until November, so I'm about four months gone."

"You seem young to be bringing a child into the world, but I'm delighted for you."

CHAPTER 7

The next morning, Millie and Jonnie accompanied Betsey and Ned on the short stroll along the drive to Grantley House. It was a pleasant walk in the warm May sunshine, with the vibrant green of the newly opened leaves evident on the trees, and the hedgerows covered in a haphazard profusion of bluebells, foxgloves, and red campion. As the enormous mansion came into view, Ned exclaimed out loud.

"Goodness me, I didn't realise it was such a large house. It must be nearly as big as Hartford Manor."

"Yes, I think it is. Jonnie and I have explored some of it, but we keep getting lost, don't we, Jonnie?"

The little boy nodded. "Yes, it would be a great place to play hide and seek, but part of it's a bit scary because in some rooms everything's covered in sheets, and I'm worried there might be ghosts."

"Perhaps when you've made a few more friends, they could come and play with you, Jonnie. You would feel safer with lots of people around, though I doubt there are any ghosts. Where do you sleep?"

"I was a bit frightened in a room of my own, so Gran let me have one that leads off the one she shares with my new grandad."

"I see, and how do you get on with Hubert? Is he a kind grandad?"

"Yes, I like him. He plays cards and draughts with me."

"That's good. Here we are then; which way do we go in?"

"The front door, of course, Aunty Betsey. It seems strange to do so, but Jonnie does own the place, though it's still hard to believe. Oh, there's Gran now, looking out of the window."

Millie waved, and they saw the woman rise from her seat. By the time they reached the steps leading up to the front door, Emily and Hubert were waiting to welcome them.

"Hello, Betsey and Ned; it's wonderful to see you."

Emily hugged her half-sister, and then Ned, and Hubert shook Ned's hand warmly and kissed Betsey on the cheek before leading the way inside. The front door opened onto an impressive hallway, and their eyes were drawn to the elaborate and colourful ceiling patterns as they followed their hosts across the flagstoned floor. The walls were panelled in oak and covered in paintings; some depicting portraits of the Grantley family, while others featured scenes of the grounds, and a few showcased beloved horses and dogs. There was also a mounted head of a magnificent stag, and one or two of foxes. Hunting was a popular pastime for this well-to-do family.

With Emily and Hubert leading the way, the visitors were led into an opulent drawing room where, despite the warm sunshine outside, a cosy fire was burning merrily in the inglenook fireplace. Again, the guest's eyes were drawn to the colourful ceiling and the splendid, intricately carved furniture that graced the room. Betsey ran her hand lightly across the top of an ornate cabinet, marvelling at the sleek veneer of the wood, and, peering inside, admired a rare collection of ceramics.

Emily rang a bell-pull on the wall, and within minutes, a maid appeared, asking how she might help. Emily asked her to bring coffee and cakes.

"I don't think I shall ever get used to having servants, but we enjoy being waited on, don't we, Hubert?"

"We do, but there are one or two I haven't taken to. The younger ones are all right, and I think they appreciate being spoken to nicely, but if I have my way, the housekeeper and the butler will be looking for new jobs before too long."

"We shouldn't rush into anything, my love; we need their help to run a house this size, even if they are downright rude."

"They shouldn't be rude to you, surely? You're the new owners."

"I know, but Mr and Mrs Watson have been here for many years, and they seem to have favoured Lady Lilliana rather more than her husband, Sir Edgar. In fact, I wonder if they moved here with her all those years ago when she was a new bride, or so she thought, poor woman. From what I've heard, she was a nasty piece of work, and she caused so much trouble for Millie and Jonnie, but Sir Edgar did treat her disgracefully. I mean, she knew about his affair with Rosemary for many years, and that must have been embarrassing enough, but then to find she was married to a bigamist. Well, she does have some right to be aggrieved."

"That's true, but I think you need to nip this in the bud and make Mr and Mrs Watson aware that unless they are respectful and the service improves significantly, then they'll need to find other jobs. I'm sure new staff could be found. Would you like us to ask Robert if he could help? He knows about these things."

"Thank you, Ned, that would be wonderful. We lack experience in handling such matters and need support from those who do. We don't want to sack the pair of them and then find everything starts to go wrong, because, despite their attitude, they know what they're doing."

Betsey suddenly chuckled. "I've had a much better idea, and I know the ideal person for this job. Did you meet Margery Montgomery, Robert's Aunty Margery, when you were in Hartford?"

"Yes, she came to the joint wedding for Millie and Willie, and Hubert and me. Why?"

"You don't know her well, but I can assure you this is a job she would relish. She does not suffer fools gladly, and having been born a lady; she can make the best of servants shake in their boots if she is in any way displeased. Would you like me to ask if she'd be willing to visit you? Trust me, this is a job she would excel at. Maybe Annie would keep her company. She was talking about visiting you the other day when she called in to see us."

"Yes, please, that would be helpful, thank you. Maybe if the housekeeper and the butler need to go, she could help us appoint suitable replacements."

After they had enjoyed the coffee and cakes, Hubert offered to show Ned the grounds and the stables whilst the women and Jonnie explored the house. Jonnie was thrilled to have the attention of not only his beloved granny, Emily but also his Aunty Betsey. He was looking forward to a further treat that afternoon, for Willie had arranged for Edward to give Jonnie another of several riding lessons that the pair had been enjoying for some weeks. Edward was a natural with any animals, but horses in particular, and his presence seemed to have a calming influence on not only the pony but the little boy as well, and Jonnie was quickly becoming a proficient rider. An essential skill for a young gentleman.

Emily led the way around the old house, enjoying the exclamations of surprise from Betsey as she gazed in wonder at such wealth and luxury. The library, in particular, took her breath away; a comfortable room with a luxurious deep blue carpet and plenty of comfy armchairs and settees to lounge in. The walls were lined with bookshelves to a height of around eight feet, all filled with ancient and precious tomes. Above the shelves, the walls, adorned with red and gold embossed wallpaper, were hung with yet more portraits of the Grantley family. Again, a cosy fire was burning in the vast fireplace and around the walls, several cabinets displayed priceless collections of china, ceramics, and treasures brought home from many overseas holidays and excursions.

"My goodness, there's a small fortune held in this one room alone. I didn't realise Jonnie and Millie were now so rich. It's rather overwhelming, isn't it? Do you like it here, Emily?"

"I won't lie, Betsey. It's taking some getting used to, and there are times when I long for my little cottage, but, of course, there are benefits too. We certainly don't have to worry about having enough coal for the fire or if there's any food left in the pantry, but we're not quite at home yet, and I'm not sure we ever will be, but we're making the best of it. We have to for Jonnie's sake. This is such an amazing opportunity for both him and Millie that we're determined to make it work as best we can."

Ned and Hubert had not known each other long but found they had a lot in common. Having walked around and admired the extensive gardens, they sat on a comfortable bench in the warm sunshine, enjoying their pipes together. Having been brought up in the workhouse, Hubert was no stranger to hardship. He was sent to his first job as a farmhand at the age of twelve, and luckily for him, his employers were kindly folk, and he fared far better for the next few years than he ever had as a younger child. Ned, too, although an innkeeper by trade for most of his life, had from time to time worked as a farm labourer in his younger days to earn extra money, and so they had plenty to talk about.

After a while, they decided to return to the house and rejoin the ladies. As they walked through the first stable, they could hear raised voices and the sounds of a scuffle. Ned put his finger to his lips to warn Hubert to be quiet, and they peered around the doorway to see what was going on in the yard. At the sight before them, Ned turned a dark shade of red and stormed forward to grab one lad by his hair, whilst Hubert manhandled the larger youth, pulling him away from a smaller boy, whose head they were holding under the water in a long trough. The boy rose from the water, red in the face, coughing and spluttering, and Ned's anger increased significantly when he realised it was his grandson, Edward. He pulled the lad he was holding around by the hair and wielded a hefty blow, cuffing him on the ear.

"You little buggers! What the hell do you think you're doing to my grandson? I'll see to it that you're flogged for this, and then you'll be down the road. You see if you're not. You pair of cowards, picking on a younger boy, especially one who can't hear you coming or call for help. By God, you're going to suffer for this."

Ned suddenly clutched his chest, his face white, and Hubert released his hold on the young man, who was trembling with fear and threw him to one side to help Ned.

"Quick, fetch help from the house. Tell them to send for the doctor and someone to carry this man to his bed. Go on now. Run! If I have to tell you again, you'll be sorry."

The two youngsters ran off to the main house to fetch help, while Edward knelt on the ground, cradling his grandad's head in his lap, tears running down his face.

CHAPTER 8

Although it was early afternoon, the heavy curtains in the guest bedroom were partially drawn, and the occupant of the bed was fast asleep. The old man's face was heavily lined and his hair white, a colour closely matched by his pasty complexion. The sun shining through the bay window cast dappled patterns on the far wall, which danced and rippled as the light breeze rustled through the trees outside.

Betsey watched her husband's chest rise and fall, her wrinkled face wearing an anxious expression. If she were one to pray, now would be the time, but she had long since come to the conclusion that God helped those who helped themselves, and she had no faith in assistance from any higher being. It was not surprising, given the difficulties she had overcome in her lifetime. A light tap on the door drew her attention, and she bade whoever it was to enter.

"I've brought you a cup of tea, Betsey, and a piece of cake; you must eat, my dear, to keep your strength up. You'll be of no use to Ned when he awakens if you're poorly as well."

"Thank you, Emily. 'Tis kind of you, but I'm not a bit hungry. I don't think I can face food until Ned wakes up and I know he's all right."

"I'm sure he'll wake up soon; it's just the effects of the sleeping draught the doctor gave him, and that was to make sure he had complete rest. Why don't you try a couple of mouthfuls of cake and drink your tea, and then get your head down for a couple of hours? You can lie beside him while I sit here, and I promise I'll wake you straight away if he stirs."

"Thank you; maybe I will; I don't think my eyes will stay open much longer. This reminds me of when I used to sit with him when he was severely burned after being struck by lightning. That was donkeys years ago, and I never thought he'd live then, but he pulled through. I wish he would wake up, because I want to try one of my herbal remedies on him, and I can't do that while he's asleep."

"Are you sure that's wise? The doctor's already bled him and put a mustard plaster on his chest to improve his circulation, and at least with the laudanum, he's getting some rest now."

"I know, but I've never thought bleeding folk helps, or at least not in my experience. No, I've confidence in the ancient remedies that an old lady called Gypsy Freda taught me when I was but a child, and I know if Ned were awake, he'd want me to try them, even if it did no good. It was my herbs that saved him from his burns all those years ago, and they certainly won't harm him."

"Do you have everything you need to make the medicine?"

"Yes, because Ned has heart problems, I always keep a bottle of my cure with me wherever we go. I need him to wake up and have a couple of spoonsful, and I'm sure it will help. It did the last time he was sick like this."

"What's in it?"

"It's a powder made from dried foxglove leaves, and it can be poisonous, so you have to be careful to get the dose right, but I know what I'm doing. The last time he had one of these attacks, Doctor Luckett thought he'd got him through it, but Ned didn't improve until I dosed him up with my medicine. I didn't tell the doctor, though, because they like to think they know everything. When the laudanum wears off and he wakes up, I'm going to give him my potion, and we'll see what happens. That's if Ned is willing, and I know he will be."

Having eaten a few mouthfuls of cake and drunk her tea, more to please Emily than from desire, Betsey stretched out beside her husband and closed her eyes. Emily observed them both fondly, thinking how lucky she was to have found them this late in her life, and fervently hoped they would be around for many more years to come.

Below them in the parlour, the atmosphere was less tranquil. The two farmhands responsible for upsetting Ned and bullying his grandson stood before Willie and Hubert, shaking in their boots. Both boys were fifteen years old and feared a beating, and indeed, if Hubert had his way, that was what they would have received. Willie, however, was not of a violent nature, and in that they were fortunate, for most landowners would have seen them soundly whipped for far less. Standing beside Willie stood Edward, looking slightly perplexed and more than a little anxious. With no way to communicate with his brother about what was happening, Willie decided it was best for him to watch and figure it out for himself. He knew his brother was intelligent, despite being deaf and mute.

The two boys had their few belongings with them, and after giving them a sound telling-off, Willie sacked the pair on the spot and sent them off without a reference. He knew this would be more of a punishment than any beating, for they would find it difficult to find work without one, and would, in all probability, have to travel far enough that no one knew them or where they had worked, to secure new employment.

A few days later, with Ned seemingly out of any immediate danger, Millie and Jonnie were allowed to visit.

"Oh, Uncle Ned, we've been so worried. How are you feeling?"

"Not too bad, thank you, Millie, and that's thanks to your Aunty Betsey here. She always puts me right with her lotions and potions, don't you, my love?"

"Well, fingers crossed, and not a word to the doctor, you two. He thinks his care has brought Ned round, but I will always think differently. No point in stirring up trouble, though, and you still need to take it easy, Ned. On that, I do agree with the doctor."

"Yes, I know, and for once I can't argue, for I feel that tired. Still, Hubert and Emily have said we can stay as long as we like, and I'm content to rest here for a few weeks. You don't need to stay here all the time, minding me, though. Go out and enjoy yourselves; I'll still be here when you get back."

"If you feel like a little trip out, Aunty Betsey, we're going to visit Vivian and Angela at Hilldale Farm this afternoon, and you could come with us. Would you like that?"

Betsey glanced worriedly at her husband, and he answered for her. "Yes, she'd love to come, Millie. No arguments, my dear. I'll be fine here, smoking my pipe and enjoying a glass of brandy while I admire that fantastic view from the window. What stunning gardens there are. I can't wait to regain my strength and finish looking around them."

A couple of hours later, the Grantley carriage, carrying Betsey, Hubert, Emily, Millie and Jonnie, travelled the short distance from Brampford Speke to Newton Sy Cyres and entered the gateway of Hilldale Farm. Before his marriage to Emily, the farm was Hubert's home, and he missed his son, Vivian, and his family, though they were not far away.

Being a Saturday, Hubert's grandchildren, Gertie, Albert, Rosie, and Walter, were at home from school, and they gathered around the carriage, excited to have visitors. Being the same age, Millie and Gertie soon disappeared upstairs to enjoy some time together, and the younger children ran off to play, while Vivian walked his father around the farmyard, seeking his advice on various matters.

Angela made a cup of tea for Betsey and Emily, then sat down contentedly to feed eight-month-old Jessica and enjoy some rare female company.

"How do you like living at Grantley House, Emily? I bet you're leading a life of luxury now."

"I am, but to be honest, I was much happier here with all of you. The butler and the housekeeper are so snooty, looking down their noses at me and Hubert. You'd think they were the owners of the place rather than the hired help."

"Don't worry about them, Emily. They don't know what's in store for them. As soon as I can arrange for Robert's Aunty Margery to come, they won't know what's hit them. I've seen her in action when something displeases her, and I can tell you, it's pretty scary."

"I hope you're right, Betsey, because it's getting me down. It's not just me either; I don't think Jonnie is at all happy, poor little lad. He might have inherited a fortune, but he hates it at Grantley House; it's so stupid that he has to live there. He goes to see Millie every day, but it's not the same as having other boys of his age to play with. He'll certainly enjoy his visit here today."

"Where do your children go to school, Angela?"

"Albert, Rosie, and Walter all attend Newton St Cyres School, Betsey, though Gertie has left now; why do you ask?"

"I was thinking that now Jonnie's rich, surely he can go to whichever school he likes. It's not far from Grantley House to here, so maybe the carriage could take him to and from Newton St Cyres School, and then he'd be with your children. That might help a lot. He hates the school where he is because everyone knows he's rich, and they're giving him a hard time."

"What a wonderful idea, Betsey. How stupid we haven't thought of it before. When Millie comes down, we'll see what she thinks, but I reckon Jonnie would be over the moon to do that."

"Yes, I agree. Walter and Jonnie get on so well, and they'd be in the same class. In the past, all the children from Brampford Speke attended Newton St Cyres School anyway. It only changed when they built a new school at Brampford Speke about ten years ago. Seeing as he has a carriage at his disposal, it would be easy for him to go there."

CHAPTER 9

A few days after Ned's heart attack, Robert received a telegram from Hubert March. He and Annie were eating breakfast together, but there was an uncomfortable atmosphere in the room, and for the last few days, Annie had insisted that Selina eat her breakfast in the nursery instead of with them. Normally, the couple were devoted to each other, but Annie remained furious with her husband for even thinking she would spend any time with his parents, particularly his father, after what he had put her through. Robert understood her feelings, but was weary of all the unpleasantness surrounding his family and was hopeful that, through Danny, some peace could be achieved. The household staff had noticed the tension in the air but were unaware of the reasons for the rift and were careful not to do anything to upset their employers. The butler, Ethan Bater, presented the telegram to his master on a silver tray, along with the other mail, and Robert tore it open and exclaimed in dismay.

"Oh, Annie, I'm so sorry, but this telegram is from Hubert March, and it says Ned is ill and suffering from cardiac distress. It doesn't give much detail, but says he collapsed and will have to stay at Grantley House for some time to recover."

As Annie's face blanched, her husband hurried to her side and tried to draw her into his arms to comfort her. However, she remained stiff in his embrace and, holding out her hand, merely answered, "May I see?"

"Yes, of course."

"It says not to worry, but how is that possible when we know Grandad has heart trouble? I'll have to visit. I can't travel all the way to London and enjoy the Queen's Jubilee celebrations, not knowing if Grandad is all right. Maybe I won't go at all. I'd rather spend the time with him until he's better, and Gran will be so worried."

"Ned wouldn't want you to miss your trip to London. Why don't we bring our plans forward by a few days and call into Brampford Speke en route to London? We could stay at Grantley House and catch up with everyone at the same time. The only problem is I have a meeting at the bank on Wednesday with a group of businessmen from London, and it's too late to rearrange now. I'll visit Jack this afternoon, and if his back is better, he can go instead of me. I can tell him what to do."

"No, it's all right; you attend your meeting, and I'll travel to Grantley House. I'll stay for a few days and check that Gran and Grandad are all right, and then, if they are, I can join you on the train to London."

"Are you sure?"

"Yes, I know you'd rather attend the meeting yourself, so that's what I'd rather you do."

"Annie, this meeting is important for it's likely to provide us with a lot more business which we need, but I'll send Jack if you'd like me to come with you; I don't mind."

"No, I called in to see Jack yesterday, and he's in a lot of pain and can barely stand. I don't want you to ask him because he'll feel obliged to help, and the last thing he needs is to be jolted around all the way to Barnstaple. Anyway, I think we'd benefit from a few days apart. I'll make the arrangements."

Annie exited the room swiftly, leaving her husband distraught and wishing he could turn the clock back and handle matters differently. The trouble was that he could see no solution to the dilemma they faced. He understood Annie's feelings about his father and realised he was wrong to assume she would set them aside for a quiet life, but it was difficult living next door to his parents and trying to keep everyone happy. He also agreed with Annie that his mother had willingly given up her son because of his deformities and should now live with that decision. However, he was a warm-hearted man who hated disharmony and wished everyone could get along with one another. The question was how to achieve that?

Another family get-together was scheduled for that afternoon, but this time at The Red Lion Inn, where Charlotte would be the hostess. Annie had arranged to call for Sabina and Liza at the Lodge House and walk with them and the children to the village. She left early to allow enough time to talk to her mother about Eleanor's desire to spend time with Danny before meeting everyone else, for few knew the truth about the boy's parentage.

With Selina skipping ahead, Annie pushed the twins in their pram, for although they were nearly two and would have preferred to walk, it was a bit too far to the inn. She knocked lightly on the back door and let herself in.

"Hello, Mum, hello, Liza, it's me, Annie."

"Hello, love, you're early, and we're not quite ready. I'd like to wash these dishes before we head to the inn. Do you want a cup of tea while I finish up?"

"No, it's all right, thanks. I came early because I wanted to talk to you about something while we're on our own. "How are you, Liza?"

"I'm fine, thank you, Annie. Sabina, I'll finish the dishes and you chat with Annie."

"It's something you should hear as well, Liza, so I'll sit here and explain while you both finish getting ready. Selina, why don't you go outside and play with the others until we're ready to go?"

The little girl scampered off to the back garden to find Helen, Stephen, and Danny, and Annie took the twins from their pram and let them play on the floor with a box of toys.

"Now, what is it you need to talk about, Annie?"

"There are two things I need to tell you. The first is that we had a telegram from Hubert March this morning, telling us Grandad's been taken ill and is suffering from heart trouble again. He and Gran will stay at Brampford Speke for a while until he's fit to travel home."

"Oh dear, poor Ned; Betsey will be so worried. Was anything said about Willie or Edward?"

"No, as far as I know, they're fine. Anyway, I'm going to leave tomorrow to visit Grantley House on the way to London, to make sure everyone is all right. If they're not, I shall stay there for a while and not go to London. It would be a pity to miss the Jubilee celebrations, but I wouldn't enjoy them if I were worrying about Grandad."

"What about Robert? Is he going with you?"

"No, he has an important business meeting later in the week, and I know he doesn't want to miss it. He'll join me in a few days, and we'll travel to London on the train together if all is well. A little time apart will be no bad thing for us at the moment, and he's so busy these days organising all these hunting weekends that I barely see him, anyway."

"That doesn't sound too good, love. You and Robert are usually inseparable."

"We had words a few days ago, and I'm still angry with him. When I tell you, you'll understand why."

Annie explained how Eleanor had spied on Danny while he was playing in the Manor House garden and how Lord Fellwood had confided to Robert that she would like him back.

"What! I hope Robert told him no. I'm not giving Danny up now after raising him since he was a few hours old. The blooming cheek of that woman! Does she think that now the child has had all his deformities put right, she can turn the clock back?" Sabina glanced anxiously at her daughter. "She can't, can she? I mean, I know she's a rich lady, but surely Robert wouldn't let her take him from me?"

"No, he won't let that happen, Mum, and even his father told her that was impossible, but the alternative is almost as bad."

"Why, what's the alternative?"

"Eleanor realises it would be difficult for Danny to leave the only home he's ever known, but she wants to spend time with him and get to know him. Robert thought this might be one way to solve the problem, but then he infuriated me when he suggested it could be a good thing, because surely then Eleanor would have to accept me too and allow me into the family. How dare he assume that I would want to spend time with either of his parents? His father raped me and allowed me to be thrown out on my ear from the Manor House, and his mother regards me as if I'm a nasty smell. Well, he can think again. Longer ago, I might have considered it to keep the peace, but as they have continued to shun me over the years, I don't want anything to do with them. As far as I'm concerned, they're not good enough to meet with me, not the other way around."

"Oh, Annie, I'm so sorry to hear all this. You're right, of course, and it would raise a lot of questions if Lady Eleanor took a sudden interest in Danny, and what about the rest of us? Would she still walk by with her nose in the air and ignore us? This is an awful situation, and one we could never have seen coming, for we never expected you to marry Robert, or for us to live in the Lodge House, but I was afraid it might cause trouble one day."

"Well, we can't turn back the clock, and now you know why we need a little distance between us for a day or two. We're both angry and need time to cool down. I hope his mother will give up on the idea because I can't see a solution. Now, are you ready? Shall I round up the children, and we'll walk to The Red Lion? I'm looking forward to seeing everyone, but can we keep this between ourselves for now? I take it Danny still doesn't know he's a foundling and not your child?"

"Yes, we will, love, and no, Danny doesn't know that he wasn't born a Carter. Oh, what's that noise?"

Sabina went to the kitchen to investigate and found Stephen looking dishevelled and trying not to cry.

"Are you all right, Stevie?"

"I fell over and hurt my knees and my arm."

"Let me see. Oh, yes, you have some nasty grazes; I'll wash them clean for you; it might sting a bit, but it's best to get the dirt out of the wounds."

"Aw, that looks sore, and you are brave not to cry. Do you think one of Liza's cakes might help you to feel better?"

The boy nodded, and Annie went to fetch him a cake.

"There you are; a cake always made me feel better if I'd hurt myself. Who's coming this afternoon, Mum?"

"Well, not Betsey, because she's away, but Aunty Eveline is coming with the children, and Aunty Margery, and Aunty Charlotte will be there too, of course, so there will be seven of us, plus lots of children, as usual."

Annie allowed Liza to push the twins in the pram as she said it helped her along. The old lady was in her late seventies and was becoming frail. It had been over seven years since she moved in with the Carter family, and the arrangement had worked satisfactorily for all concerned. At that time Liza was recently widowed and soon to be homeless, and she had volunteered to mind Sabina's children to allow her to work on the estate and keep her tied cottage after the death of her husband, Tom. Times were so hard back then, and a far cry from the privileged life they had led since Annie's marriage to Robert Fellwood. Although the union had brought its fair share of problems, there were considerable benefits too, and Sabina pondered Annie's worrying news as she pushed Katel's pram.

CHAPTER 10

As it was a sunny afternoon, the ladies decided to sit in the private section of The Red Lion's garden. Fortunately, the inn had plenty of land at the rear, and Fred had erected a fence to afford his family some privacy from the ever-increasing number of guests that visited the area. Since Robert Fellwood had closed the canal, built many years before by his grandfather, Ephraim, the barges, which had once transported limestone and coal, now carried holiday makers and were proving to be a lucrative venture.

The meadow, which sloped down to the canal, was furnished with picnic tables, swings, a seesaw and a slide. There were also four swingboats, all of which were appreciated by the many tourists to such a picturesque part of the country. A jetty afforded access to the three barges, which were towed by two shire horses and one donkey, and carried the passengers to the next village and back on pleasure trips.

Annie, Sabina, and Liza were the last to arrive at the inn and found Sarah Carter, the widow of Annie's late Uncle William, minding the bar. She told them where to find the other ladies.

"If you'd like to make your way through to the garden, Charlotte, Eveline, and Lady Margery are already there. I'll bring you some refreshments if I get a chance, but it's quite busy here today."

"Don't worry, Sarah; you have more than enough to do. We'll see to ourselves when we want something."

They received a warm welcome from their hostess and the other guests and were soon chatting. The older children raced off to play with their cousins, leaving the babies, David, Thomas, and Katel, to spend some time with Eveline's adopted daughter, Martha, and Doris and Nicholas, the youngest children of Fred and Charlotte. As this part of the garden was enclosed, the toddlers could wander where they liked without coming to any harm.

Annie told her family about Ned's illness, and all were concerned, particularly Eveline.

"Oh no, will Dad be all right? I was worried this trip would be too much for him, but as you know, he never complains and assured me he was up to it."

"I don't know, Aunty Eveline, but I'm going there tomorrow to see for myself because the telegram didn't say much. I'll send a postcard to each of you to let you know how he is, before I travel on to London, that's, if I go at all. How's Charlie and everyone at Hollyford Farm? I haven't seen him for ages."

"He's fine, thanks, and Alfred's getting over a nasty cold. We're a bit concerned about Jimmy, though."

"Why, what's wrong with Jimmy?"

"Oh, there's nothing wrong with him, but we fear he's fallen for the wrong woman. At one time, he barely left the farm, and we were always encouraging him to socialise and find a wife; and now he's visiting Barnstaple every week and more often if he can."

"Well, that's good, isn't it? It would be nice to see him married."

"Yes, it would, but the woman he's taken a fancy to lives at The Tucker's Arms, and we all know what a den of thieves and rogues that place is. Look what happened to Theresa."

"Oh, my goodness, is it a prostitute he's fallen for? No good will ever come of that."

"No, fortunately, that's not the case. It's a woman called Nell Patterson, and she's the niece of Fat Meg, Noah Berryman's wife. You know, the innkeeper. Jimmy says Nell is respectable and is only living there with her two young daughters because she had nowhere else to go when her husband died earlier in the year. Apparently, Meg is seriously ill and bedridden, and Nell is nursing her and doing all the skivvying that Cissie used to do before she was rescued."

"Oh, well, that's not quite so bad."

"No, it sounds as if the woman is respectable but has fallen on hard times. The trouble is, Nell's worried that if Meg dies, and she thinks she will, Noah will force her onto the game; it's only her aunt who's protecting her from that. She's concerned for her two children as well, for although they're only young now, we all know that Noah has no morals."

"What an awful situation to be in. How did Jimmy meet her? Surely he doesn't frequent The Tucker's Arms."

"No, he doesn't, or rather, he didn't. He met Nell when she was knocked over in the High Street by a young lad who tried to steal her basket. Jimmy gave chase and got the basket back and then took her into The Three Tuns to get cleaned up. He's taken quite a liking to her and has been visiting The Tucker's Arms to see if he can get her away from there. He's never been one for alcohol, but now he struggles to get out of bed some mornings, and he was always such a reliable worker in the past. Alfred thinks he's gambling too, though he denies it. There's not much we can say because he's in his thirties and old enough to do as he likes."

After commiserating about Jimmy's worrying behaviour, Charlotte excused herself for a few moments to fetch them all a cup of tea or a glass of cold lemonade and promised to return with freshly baked pasties and cakes.

Sabina accompanied her to help. However, both ladies returned looking puzzled.

"Honestly, you have to nail things down these days if you don't want them stolen. I baked a dozen pasties this morning and two of them have vanished, as well as a couple of cakes, and this isn't the first time food's gone missing from my kitchen."

"Perhaps Sarah's sold them? It was busy in the bar when we arrived."

"No, she hasn't; I checked, and I'd already stored the food for the inn in the larder."

"Mum was saying something similar happened when she visited her friend, Nancy, in the village a week or two ago. She had a cake stolen. I wonder who's doing it? It's risky, going right into people's homes like that, and stealing food from under their noses. Whoever it is must be desperate, for the law would take a dim view of it."

"Never mind, there are more pasties in the oven that are nearly ready, so we'll let the children have these and we can wait a little longer. Now, Aunty Margery, tell us your news. Have you visited Sam and Marrok at Sugworthy Farm lately?"

All of Annie's family had taken to calling the old lady Aunty Margery, and she loved it. Although one of the aristocracy, Margery Montgomery called a spade a spade and had friends from all walks of life. She explained that she, too, would be visiting London to attend Queen Victoria's Jubilee celebrations and then surprised them by announcing she had invited her nephew, Sam Fellwood, and his friend, Peter Webber, to join her. She had even arranged for Christopher, Peter's grandson, to accompany them to care for the disabled artist. This news was met with some amusement, for none of the men had ever visited a large city before, and a trip to London would be quite an adventure for them.

"I visited Sugworthy Farm last week and also invited Marrok to join us, but he declined to take me up on my offer. He's enjoying himself too much getting the farm to his liking, and he's missing Willie and Edward now that they've gone to live at Brampford Speke with Millie. He's taken on new workers, but feels it's too early to leave them in charge for any length of time. He's certainly turning things around there, though. It was in such disrepair when Tommy Houle died, but with Sam's and Robert's help on the financial side, he's made huge improvements. You'd hardly recognise the house from the leaky, dilapidated dwelling that it was. The housekeeper, Florrie, is now in her element, as the house is worth keeping clean, and she has some new maids to help her. Speaking of Florrie, I suspect romance is in the air. I'm sure she and Sam are developing feelings for each other."

"Really? Florrie's been an old maid all her life and always swears she's never wanted to marry."

"That's as may be, but I've seen the way she and Sam look at each other, and I'm sure I'm right. Perhaps she never met the right man until now. I thought he was going to turn down the offer to visit the capital, but I think the fact that I invited Peter persuaded him, because they enjoy each other's company and have missed each other since Sam moved to the farm. I'll tell you another thing, too. A new family has moved into Kerscott Farm, and I think Marrok is taking an interest in a young woman there."

"Goodness, love must be in the air. Still, it would be lovely if Marrok did meet someone. It was sad that he lost Laura in the workhouse, but he's a young man with his life to lead. His family would benefit from a new mother, too. Florrie looks after them well, but she's never had children. How old is this young woman?"

"Oh, about Marrok's age, I think. I've only seen her once. The family is from Wales, and I understand she's a widow with two children and is living with her parents. I'm trying to think of her name; it was unusual. Oh, I know, it was Eirlys, Eirlys Williams, that was it. I remarked on it, and she said her name means 'snowdrop' in Welsh. When she was born and her father first saw her, he said she was a Fair Maid of February, which, as you may know, is another name for the flower."

"Is the farm part of the Hartford estate, or does her family own it?"

"Yes, it's part of the estate, so Robert owns it, and they're the new tenants."

It was not often that the Carter family cousins were all together, but since it was a Saturday and there was no school, they made a large gathering. Selina, Stephen, Helen and Danny were joined by Fred and Charlotte's older children, Rosella and Eddie, and Charlie and Eveline's adopted family, twins, Joseph and Matthew, and Amelia, all children of the late William Carter, Eveline and Fred's brother.

They were playing a game of hide and seek, and Stephen had climbed into the tree-house that Fred had built in the meadow for his family and guests to use. The carpenter had done a magnificent job, and the children loved the new addition to the attractions. A wooden ladder provided access to the room, which had a hole in the floor with a pole to slide down, or for the more nimble to climb up. Windows faced across the garden and meadow, providing a scenic view of the canal as it meandered out of sight. Along one side were cupboards containing blankets, cushions, and a few toys. Stephen crept into the first one and left the door slightly ajar, thinking it was the perfect hiding place.

Sitting there waiting for Matthew to find him, Stephen was suddenly concerned when he heard a slight noise from the next cupboard. He thought it was a sneeze, but was sure none of the other children had got to the tree house before him. Just as he was beginning to think he had imagined it, he heard another sound as if someone had changed position, something he could understand as it was cramped in the tight space. He debated whether to investigate or slide down the pole and risk being caught when Matthew's face appeared at the top of the ladder. Seeing the cupboard door ajar, he prised it open with relish and grinned at the other boy.

"Ha! There you are! Got you! Come on, you're the last one. I've found all the others. Come and have some food that Aunty Charlotte's brought for us."

However, Stephen put his finger to his lips and whispered. "I think there's someone in the next cupboard."

Matthew was puzzled and wondered if he had missed someone. The two boys stood in front of the cupboard until the older boy decided to take action.

"Only one way to find out."

Matthew pulled open the door, discovering that the catch was broken, and peered inside. Curled up as small as possible was a skinny boy who was terrified of being discovered.

The boy timidly exited from the cupboard. He was barefoot, dressed in rags, and a stranger to soap and water. As the other children appeared one by one at the top of the ladder, they stared at their unexpected guest in surprise, and the boy grew increasingly concerned. Matthew handed out blankets and cushions for everyone to sit on, including the boy, and the others fetched the food.

When everyone was seated, Matthew looked expectantly at the boy.

"Go on then, tell us why you were hiding in the cupboard and then you can share our food if you like. Where do you live?"

"I've been living here for the last few weeks, because I haven't got anywhere else to go. I'm sorry, but it was mostly dry here unless the wind blew in the rain, and it was warm in the cupboard with the blankets. It's still quite cold at night."

"You must have come from somewhere? Where did you live before you came here?"

"I'm from Barnstaple, but I can't go back there. My mother died, you see, and her husband, Jem, has always hated me, but now, Ma's gone, it's even worse. I got fed up with being beaten black and blue for nothing and getting no food, so I reckoned I was better off out of it. I've walked and hitched lifts on carts to get here, cos I want to find me real father."

"Who's your real father?"

"I never knew it wasn't Jem, but on her deathbed, Ma told me it was a man called John Cutcliffe. She told me he lived on the Hartford estate and she hoped he would take me in. Do you know him?"

The other children glanced at one another in surprise until Rosella spoke up. "There's a Rachael Cutcliffe at school, and I think her father might be called John, but I'm not sure, and they don't live on the estate. They have a cottage on the edge of the village. I think he works on the estate, though. I know his other daughter, Daisy, too, but she's left school and is working somewhere now. Are you hungry?"

The boy nodded. "I'm always hungry, but I stole a couple of pasties earlier and I was going to eat them later."

"Well, you can share ours for now, and save yours for later."

"Could you tell me how to get to John Cutcliffe's cottage? I need to find out if he'll help me."

"Yes, we can, but it might be best to stay here for a day or two and let us find out a bit more. I think his wife's a bit of a dragon, so you need to be careful, or she'll hand you over to the law without a second thought. What's your name?"

"It's Eli. Eli ... Cutcliffe, I think."

CHAPTER 11

As the train pulled into Paddington Station in London and came to a halt, Christopher, Peter, and Sam immediately rose to their feet to disembark. However, their companion lazily waved her hand at them, indicating that they should resume their seats.

"No need to go anywhere for the moment, my friends. We'll sit here comfortably whilst my footman and maid locate our luggage and get it transferred to the carriage for our journey to my townhouse. The platform will be crowded, so we'll wait here awhile."

The train journey was a revelation to the three men, for none had been on a train before, or travelled in such luxurious surroundings. The first-class carriage, furnished with deeply cushioned velvet seats, carpets on the floor, and thick curtains at the windows, had ensured their long journey from Devon was as comfortable as it could possibly be.

The men had watched in amazement as the train flew past fields, hillsides, and valleys, and from time to time, the hustle and bustle of many stations along the way. Now, they felt distinctly uncomfortable and out of their depth in the capital itself.

"Oh, Margery, thank goodness we have you with us. Look at all the people. I didn't know there were this many people in the world. Don't lose us, for we would not know where to go or what to do."

"Don't worry, Peter, I'll take care of you, and my carriage should be waiting for us. Ah, here comes Simmonds now."

The footman advised that the luggage had been transferred from the train to the carriage, which was waiting at the station entrance. As the passengers followed their guide, the three men looked about them in awe, admiring the architectural marvel created over thirty years earlier by Isambard Kingdom Brunel. They gazed in wonder at the three-span arched glass and iron roof of the train shed, its platforms bathed in natural light, and the polished brass fittings gleaming in the shafts of the late afternoon sunshine. Porters in uniform bustled to and fro, shouting out destinations and loading luggage, and the station smelled of smoke, hissing steam, and hot metal. All around them, they could hear the clanking of the porters' trolleys as they trundled across the flagstones.

Upon reaching the carriage, the footman assisted Lady Margery inside, and the three men joined her, the maid travelling outside with the footman. The carriage, too, was luxurious and unlike anything the men had ever seen.

"Is it far to your house, Margery?"

"No, it's only a few miles to Belgravia, Sam. Our journey should take us less than an hour, if there are no delays. I first lived in Montgomery House after marrying Clarence, and I had some happy times there, but I was always relieved to return to Devon after a couple of months. I'm a country girl at heart, though I must admit I enjoy the distractions and pastimes the capital has to offer. The house is not far from one once owned by my Aunt Genevieve, and my brother, Joshua, and I stayed there the first time I came to London for my coming-out season. The area was a little different back then, as many buildings have been erected since. I remember Joshua telling me that the area was originally called the Five Fields and was once used for grazing sheep and cattle; it's hard to imagine that nowadays."

As they travelled along the busy streets, Lady Margery allowed her companions to marvel at the scenery from the windows, whilst she studied each of them. A slight smile hovered around her mouth at the amazed expressions on their faces. She had known London would come as a shock to them.

Sitting next to her was Sam, who, although not much younger than her, was her nephew and the son of her late elder brother, Thomas. Sam had spent much of his life as a beggar and a tramp until his true parentage was revealed a few years earlier. He had inherited a fortune from his late father, and his life had changed forever. To his delight, he had also been reunited with his son, Marrok, from whom he was parted many years earlier, and they now lived together at Sugworthy Farm.

Sitting on the opposite side of the carriage were Peter Webber and his grandson, Christopher. Peter was the father of Sabina's husband, Arthur, and over the years, he had worked as both a farm labourer and a miner in the silver mines of Hartford. Sadly, a terrible accident had robbed him of both his hands, and he was in the depths of despair for a long time until Sabina invented a harness which, strapped to his body and equipped with various tools, allowed him to feed himself and paint surprisingly good pictures from which he now made a comfortable living. Through this love of art, he and Lady Margery had struck up an unlikely friendship, and he now lived in Primrose Cottage on her Enderby estate in Devon, with his grandson, Christopher and his family.

Her attention moved from the two older gentlemen to their younger companion, and she watched him with amusement as he took in the bustling London streets. Christopher was a handsome young man, married to Clarice, and the father of a little boy named Peter after his grandfather. Christopher worked on the Enderby estate and also cared for his grandfather, attending to all his personal needs, which was why he was included in this trip. The lady's thoughts were interrupted when she realised they had arrived at Eaton Square.

"Here we are, gentlemen; our long journey is at an end. Welcome to Montgomery House."

The passengers alighted from the coach to find themselves in pleasant surroundings and outside an impressive white stucco-fronted house. Built in the 1830s and standing five storeys tall, the house was accessed by a flight of steps, bordered on either side by black cast-iron railings. The impressive front door was also black with a shiny brass doorknocker and a lantern-shaped gaslight above it.

Lady Margery had planned her visit to London carefully, allowing herself and her guests a week to rest before attending the Queen's Jubilee celebrations on the twentieth of June. She knew they would need a few days to recover from the long journey, which, though undertaken at the height of luxury, was still tiring, particularly for a lady of her advanced years. However, after a couple of days, she offered to take her guests sightseeing and discussed this with them at breakfast one morning.

"There are so many wonderful sights to see in London that it's difficult to know which ones to show you first. Is there anything in particular that you'd like to see today?"

"I think it's best we leave it to you, Margery, though I have heard Robert and Annie talk about Buckingham Palace and the Houses of Parliament, and I believe Robert took Sabina to the Tower of London on one of her visits. Speaking of that, do you know when Robert and Annie will join us? I believe they're going to stay here as well."

"Yes, they are, but I don't think they'll arrive for a few more days, as Annie wanted to visit Betsey and Ned in Brampford Speke en route. She wants to make sure Ned is recovering from his heart troubles before travelling to

London. She and Robert usually stay with his cousin, Percy. However, as Eleanor is also coming to London with Sarah, and they will stay with Percy, I've invited Robert and Annie to come here. As you know, Eleanor does not recognise Annie as Robert's wife, and it would be awkward. I wondered if Eleanor might arrange for Sarah to be presented to the queen as a debutante this year, but she's decided to leave that until Sarah is eighteen next year.

"Anyway, yes, the places you mention are all worthy of a visit. I suggest we take the carriage, drive past Buckingham Palace and the Houses of Parliament, and then perhaps visit the Tower of London after the Jubilee celebrations. I think it will be mayhem there during the festivities. One place I think you may enjoy is Madame Tussaud's Waxworks. Have you heard of it?"

"No, what would we see there?"

"It's an exhibition of replicas of real people made out of wax, and they're incredibly lifelike. I've been a few times and find it fascinating. There will, no doubt, be a model of Queen Victoria and the late Prince Albert, and the last time I visited, I enjoyed seeing Horatio Nelson and William Shakespeare, but probably the most fascinating of all was the Chamber of Horrors."

Having had their curiosity piqued, the men agreed on a visit to Madame Tussaud's, and they left in the carriage an hour later. On the way, Lady Margery entertained her guests with a little more information about the exhibition.

"I'm looking forward to this just as much as you are, as I've not visited the new premises. The last time I went to Madame Tussauds, it was situated in Baker Street, but the exhibition moved to a larger site in Marylebone Road a few years ago."

"It's a strange name, Madame Tussaud's. Was she a real person, or is it a made-up name?"

"She was a real woman, a French artist who, if I remember correctly, created death masks during the French Revolution and later brought her collection to Britain. I think she's dead now, but she had sons to continue the business. Anyway, here we are; oh, I see the prices have increased again. A shilling each now. I expect they raised the prices for the Jubilee celebrations."

"Goodness, a whole shilling each; that's a lot." Sam rummaged in his pockets. "I have some money here, somewhere."

"Don't worry about it, Sam. I've already given the Simmonds some money, and he'll purchase the tickets for us. Come on, I think you'll enjoy this."

Margery led the way inside, and the men followed eagerly. They were not disappointed, for the life-sized figures were incredibly convincing, particularly in the mellow glow of the numerous gas lamps. As she led the group, Margery pointed out many famous people and provided snippets of information, though some of the names meant little to the three uneducated men. However, when they reached the Royal Room, they were intrigued to see an elaborate model of Queen Victoria and her late husband, Prince Albert, and wondered at the costumes and jewellery they wore.

They stopped before a statue of Florence Nightingale, and here the men took more interest, for they had heard of this famous lady, and it was an impressive scene. The nurse was shown standing in a hospital ward and surrounded by wounded soldiers. Her face wore a calm and serene expression, and she was dressed in a long-sleeved, full-length gown of deep blue, featuring a white lace collar and a white apron. In her hand, she held aloft a small lamp, and the inscription on the sign read, 'Florence Nightingale; The Lady with the Lamp.'

"What a kind lady to nurse the British soldiers in the Crimean War. If I were injured, I'd want someone like her to look after me."

"Yes, she was an inspiration and is quite rightly fondly remembered. She was born into a wealthy English family and had no need to work. She was born in Florence, which is how she got her name. I believe she's still alive, but suffering from ill health. Anyway, come along, gentlemen. I think you will enjoy the next part of the exhibition."

Lady Margery had a gleam in her eye as she led her companions into the Chamber of Horrors, for she suspected they would enjoy the macabre exhibits.

"Oh, my goodness, Margery, this is a bit bloodthirsty. Look, that lady has had her head chopped off!"

Lady Margery chuckled. "Yes, Sam, that poor soul is the French queen, Marie Antoinette, and she had her head chopped off by the guillotine, as did many of the nobility in that country a few years ago. Thankfully, that madness did not reach this country, or it could be my head lying in that basket. Come on, I'll point out a few more notorious rogues you may have heard of. Look, this is Jack Sheppard. Have you heard of him?"

The three men shook their heads.

"Oh, well, he was a thief back in the last century, but he became famous because he was so clever at escaping prison. The story goes that he escaped from one using a rope made from bedsheets and climbed over the wall, and on another occasion, he broke through a ceiling and made his escape disguised as a woman. However, his most famous escape was from Newgate Prison, the most secure penitentiary in the country. There, he allegedly sawed through irons and somehow got away. I believe the law caught up with him eventually, though, and he was hanged at Tyburn when he was still a young man. He was a popular figure, for I don't think he was a violent man, and his escape tricks amused folk.

"Here's one you must have heard of. This is Guy Fawkes, who was responsible for the Gunpowder Plot more than two hundred years ago. Do you remember having bonfires in November on Bonfire Night, and burning a 'guy' on the top?" The men nodded. "Right well, that was Guy Fawkes, and he and his gang tried to blow up the Houses of

Parliament and King James with gunpowder because they wanted to replace the Protestants with Catholics."

"Were they successful?"

"No, the gunpowder was found and the plot foiled and Fawkes and all his men were hanged, drawn and quartered, but the matter is remembered on the fifth of November each year by burning an effigy of the man on a bonfire."

"You're so clever, Margery. You make me realise how little I know."

"We've led such different lives, Sam, for all we come from the same family. I was educated from an early age, whereas you were not. However, if I had to live rough as you have, I would be like a duck out of water and have no knowledge of how to catch a fish or a rabbit to feed myself or keep myself warm. We all have our strengths and knowledge, but sharing some of mine with you today is a pleasure."

CHAPTER 12

Despite her protestations that she would be fine on her own, Robert insisted that a maid accompany Annie to Brampford Speke, for it was not the done thing for a lady to travel alone. He replied promptly to Hubert's telegram advising that Annie would be travelling to Grantley House on the train and asking that a carriage be sent to collect her from Thorverton station.

Annie's emotions were in turmoil, and she longed to allow her husband to take her in his arms as she knew he wanted to do. However, he had not backed down from his request that she accept an invitation to visit his parents, in the unlikely event one were issued. She was determined never to set foot in the same room as his father, and so their farewell was stiff and awkward, leaving them both unhappy.

Following Annie and Robert's move to the main part of Hartford Manor, their housekeeper, Mrs Potts, and Maisie, the cook, had gone with them, though Maisie, now married, would soon be leaving her post to start a family. Both members of staff knew their mistress well, having worked with her before her prestigious marriage when she was just a kitchen maid. They were puzzled by the obvious rift between her and her husband, for they were normally so devoted to one another. They watched Annie leave from a window, and the old lady shook her head.

"I don't know what's amiss, but something serious has upset the pair of them, and neither seems keen to talk about it. Normally, they confide in me about whatever is troubling them, but not this time. Can you shed any light on it, Maisie?"

"No, I'm as much in the dark as you, and it's strange because I'm close to Annie. When she came for a cup of tea and a chat the other day, she wouldn't be drawn, though she admitted she was cross with Robert about something. It's a shame, and I hope they sort it out soon, though with Annie going away on her own, that won't help matters. Anyway, I'd better get back to work, for the lunch won't cook itself. How is your rheumatism today, Mrs Potts?"

"I've been better, and that's a fact. My mother used to say that old age doesn't come alone, and she wasn't wrong. Still, I suppose it's better than the alternative. Arthur and I are thinking of retiring when you leave to have the baby. I was going to mention it to Master Robert the other day when he came to the kitchen, but he seemed so troubled that I decided to leave it for another time."

"Where would you and Arthur live? You'd have to leave your rooms in the house, wouldn't you?"

"Yes, we would, and that's one of the things we'd need to discuss with Master Robert. John Cutcliffe's cottage in the hamlet has lain empty since he married Noeleen Gubb and moved into her cottage. Jack Bater didn't need to employ another labourer, as John's still working on the estate, so we're hoping we might live there, though we couldn't afford to pay much in the way of rent once we stop earning a living. We have a little put by, but it won't last long. Anyway, that will have to keep for another day. Now, I'd better do my house rounds and ensure everything is in order."

In the carriage that was taking her and her maid, Ruth, to Eggleston station, Annie was secretly glad to have a companion, for despite her bravado to her husband about not needing one, she had never travelled alone on a train. Ruth was the daughter of Noeleen Gubb, whom Mrs Potts had been talking about, and she had been Annie's maid for only a couple of months, but was proving to be a reliable worker.

The train journey passed without incident, and Annie enjoyed watching Ruth's face as she gazed in wonder out of the window at the scenery flying by, for the girl had never been on a train before. When they arrived at Thorverton station, they were relieved to find Hubert March waiting for them. After a warm welcome and having assured Annie that Ned was making good progress, he loaded their luggage onto the phaeton, and they set off for Grantley House.

Annie and Ruth alighted from the vehicle and were delighted to see Betsey and Emily waving to them from a window. Having entered the grand hallway, a servant escorted Ruth to the kitchens, leaving Annie to greet her relatives with a big hug.

"Oh, Gran, I'm so pleased to see you, and you too, Aunty Emily. Uncle Hubert says Grandad is improving; can I see him?"

"He's doing well, thank you, Annie, and yes, he'll be better still for seeing you. We were delighted to receive Robert's telegram, saying you'd visit on your way to London. Is he not with you? I thought he would be?"

"No, he has a business meeting in Barnstaple later in the week, but he'll travel here over the weekend. He's so busy with this new venture of the fishing and shooting weekends that I barely see him these days."

"How's that going? Is it a success?"

"Yes, I think so, though it's early days. It's a bit strange having guests we don't know staying in the Manor, but the alterations to the house mean we don't have to mix with them; our accommodation is private."

"That's good. Now, would you like some refreshment first or see Ned?"

"I'll visit Grandad, please, for I can't wait to see him. Perhaps we could have some tea brought to his room? I am a little parched."

"Yes, of course. Come this way."

Ned's wrinkled old face lit up, and his blue eyes twinkled as he feasted his eyes on his eldest granddaughter.

"Oh, Annie, hello, my love. Thank you for coming all this way to see me. I feel a bit of a fraud lying here and being waited on, for I'm fine now, and I wish they'd let me out of bed."

"You must stay there until the doctor says you can get up, or you'll have me to reckon with."

Betsey glanced at her husband sternly, but the love in her eyes belied her tone.

"Aye, I know, don't nag, woman."

"What happened to make you have another funny turn, Grandad?"

Ned relayed the story of the two boys who had been bullying his grandson, and Annie was furious that her brother had been treated in such a way.

"Oh no, poor Edward. And he couldn't even tell anyone about it."

"No, and, of course, being deaf, he couldn't hear the pair of them creeping up on him. I was that angry when I saw what was going on that I wanted to give the pair of them a good thrashing."

"Aye, I know you did, Ned, but you must remember you're not twenty-one anymore and have a weak heart. Still, I can understand it, for I would have felt the same. I didn't think Edward looked too happy when we arrived, but I didn't know why."

"So, what's happened? I hope the boys were punished."

"They certainly were. Willie sacked the pair of them with no pay and no reference, and he did it in front of Edward to make sure he understood what was happening. I still think they should have been flogged, but Willie's too soft-hearted for that."

After they had finished their tea, Betsey insisted that Ned take a nap, and Emily and Hubert left Betsey for some time alone with her granddaughter. The two women decided to take a stroll around the extensive gardens, and they walked slowly, arm in arm, admiring the beautiful peonies, azaleas, and rhododendrons, some of which were enormous, having grown there for many years. They each caught up on the news of all members of the family, and then Betsey paused for a moment, and her eyes explored Annie's face.

"Is everything all right, love? You don't quite seem yourself."

"Oh, Gran, you know me so well. I'm fine, but Robert and I have had a bit of a quarrel, and we didn't part on the best of terms. I thought a few days apart might help, but now I'm not so sure."

"In my experience, it's best not to sleep on an argument, but admittedly, some things are more difficult to reconcile than others. I don't want to pry, but I'm a good listener if you want to share it."

"Robert thinks his parents may be coming around to receiving me, and he assumed I'd be grateful and willing to meet with them. He didn't stop to think that I may not want to."

"I can see how that would be annoying, but would it be such a bad thing to try to get on with them? I can see that this enmity puts Robert in a difficult situation, and that he'd like it resolved."

"Yes, but there are things you don't know, Gran, and some things I can't tell you, but they did sack me as soon as it became known I was pregnant with Selina."

"I'm afraid that's what always happens when a maid gets in the family way, my dear, and I don't suppose Lord and Lady Fellwood even knew about it; it was the housekeeper, Miss Wetherby, that sacked you, wasn't it?"

"Yes, it was, but she knew it wasn't my fault. It wasn't as if I slept around; I was taken against my will by one of the gentlemen in their house, but she wouldn't believe me."

"Did you ever find out who it was?"

Annie hesitated. "I did, but if I tell you, Gran, will you promise to keep it to yourself? I wouldn't want you to even tell Grandad, because he'd be so angry and it's not advisable for him to get upset."

"Well, I never normally keep anything from Ned, but I won't put his life in danger, so if it would ease your mind to tell me, then yes, I promise to keep it to myself."

Annie took a deep breath.

"Only Robert, Mum, and Liza know this because we've kept it a secret, but it was Charles Fellwood who raped me!"

Betsey's face registered disbelief, then shock, followed by intense anger.

"The dirty old sod! How can you be sure? I thought you couldn't see your attacker because it was dark."

"I couldn't, and I didn't know who it was for a long time, but then one day, I was at Mum's house and Robert called about some repairs. He saw me undressing Selina and noticed the birthmark on her shoulder. It's similar to one that his sister, Victoria, has, and apparently, it runs in the family."

"Does Lady Eleanor know? Is that why she refuses to acknowledge you as Robert's wife?"

"No, she doesn't know. She refuses to accept me because I was a servant, and she's a snob. It is why Robert and I were allowed to marry, though. Robert tackled his father and showed him Selina's birthmark and said that if he didn't give his permission for our marriage, then he would show Eleanor."

"Oh, my goodness. I always wondered why the wedding was allowed. But what's changed? Why would Lady Eleanor have had a change of heart and be willing to receive you now?"

Annie hesitated again, but then gulped and continued.

"There's more, Gran, but you might as well know everything. Do you remember how I found Danny in the woods when he was a newborn baby and everyone thought he'd been abandoned because of his disabilities? Well, that much was true, but what no one knew was that he was Eleanor and Charles Fellwood's child. Danny is Robert's brother."

"Oh my God! You couldn't make this up. Why did the Fellwoods give him up? They had enough money to look after him better than anyone. Everyone thought it was some poor soul who couldn't cope with his disabilities."

"Eleanor rejected him at birth. She had a half-witted and disabled brother who suffered badly and died young, and she thought the same would be true of Danny. She wanted him sent far enough away that she would never see him again, but then Robert asked Mum if she would have him because she'd recently given birth to Helen and had breast milk and could feed him.

"All was well until Lady Fellwood recognised Danny when Mum moved to the Lodge House after my marriage to Robert. She's even taken to spying on him when he comes to the Manor to play with my children, and it seems she wants him back. She misses Victoria and her family, since they moved to Lynton, and Sarah is all but grown up, but it's an impossible situation. When Mum took Danny in, she was desperate for money to feed all of us after Dad died, and Charles Fellwood paid her well but threatened her with eviction from her cottage if she ever told anyone. Only she and Liza knew the truth, and me and Robert, of course. Now that Robert has taken over the estate, there's no fear of her being evicted, but it's still something that no one involved would want to be known. Even Victoria doesn't know Danny is her brother, although Aunty Margery guessed some time ago. You won't tell anyone, will you, Gran? It would cause so much trouble and must always remain a secret."

"No, my love, I promised I wouldn't tell anyone, and I won't, especially Ned. I don't like keeping anything from him, but you're right; if he knew all of this, he'd be so angry at how you've been treated that it could bring on another attack. What's going to happen, though? Presumably, Sabina doesn't want to give Danny back. I mean, he's one of the family now, and he'd be miserable to be parted from all of us. We're the only family he's ever known. I don't think he even knows he's a foundling, does he?"

"No, and Robert won't let him be taken away from Mum, but he thinks his mother might agree to receive all of us so that she can get to know Danny. He was even pleased at the thought. He never considered how I might feel being expected to socialise with the man who raped me. I'm so angry with him."

"Oh, my love, come here. A cuddle won't solve this lot, but it won't do any harm."

And, as she had done so often in times of trouble, Betsey wrapped her arms around her granddaughter and held her close as she tried to comfort her.

CHAPTER 13

The next day dawned bright and clear, and Annie decided to walk the short distance from Grantley House to Bramley Cottage, the new home of her brothers, Willie and Edward. She felt a little better for sharing her problems with her granny, though slightly guilty for burdening Betsey.

As she neared the cottage, she spotted Edward carrying some hay to the stable. A wide grin of delight spread across the boy's face, and he stopped what he was doing to hug his sister. After a few seconds, Annie held Edward away from her at arm's length and observed him. He smiled when she stood beside him, comparing their height, and then indicated that he had grown considerably and was now nearly as tall as she was. She patted him on the back and pointed to the cottage to show that she was going to see Millie. The boy nodded his understanding, waved his hand, and heaved the hay back onto his shoulder.

Annie had never visited Brampford Speke before, and she surveyed the magnificent countryside as she walked along the stony track to the front door of the cottage. The sides of the path were bordered by bluebells, white wood anemones and primroses, and somewhere she could smell the distinct aroma of wild garlic. She knocked on the back door and was delighted when Millie herself answered.

"Annie, I'm so pleased to see you. How are you?"

"Hello, Millie. I'm well, thanks; how about you? I hear congratulations are in order."

"Yes, Willie and I are thrilled about the baby, though we didn't expect it to happen quite so soon. It would have been nice to have a few months to get used to living here, but with Gran and Hubert a stone's throw away, I'm more than content. You've timed your visit well, for Willie, and Edward will be in shortly for their mid-morning snack. They start work at the crack of dawn, and by this time, they need some sustenance."

"I've just seen Edward, and he's shot up several inches; you must be feeding him well."

Millie led the way into a comfortable parlour, and the two women chatted away, catching up on all the gossip until they heard the back door creak as Willie and Edward entered the kitchen. Grinning widely, Annie feasted her eyes on her eldest brother, and he hugged her tightly.

"Goodness, Willie, I'm sure you're bigger than ever and look at those muscles. It's a pity you missed the arm-wrestling against Francis Rudd at the May Fair this year; I reckon you'd have beaten him again. How are you?"

"I'm very well, thank you, Annie, and all the better for seeing you. How is everyone back in Hartford?"

The siblings spent a pleasant half an hour chatting while Willie and Edward demolished a large plateful of bacon, sausages and eggs. Willie pushed his plate away contentedly.

"Ah, that's better. That will keep us going until dinner time. I'll have to get back to work, Annie, but perhaps we could catch up again later. I know I'm the farm manager here, but I like to set a good example. How long are you staying?"

"Robert will arrive over the weekend, and then we'll catch the train to London, probably on Monday. How are you getting on working here? Have the men accepted you?"

"One or two are a bit resentful of my position, for they think I only achieved it because I'm married to Millie, but it's getting easier. I think now they can see that I know what I'm doing; they're beginning to respect me. It will take time, but I think it will come right in the end. I hope so, for I need something to do. Did Gran tell you what happened to Edward?"

"Yes, she and Grandad were so angry, and so am I. I'm glad you sacked the two lads; they deserved to be punished. Grandad would have given them a thrashing if he'd been able to."

"Yes, I know he would, and it's a pity he was the one to catch them bullying Edward, for it caused him to have a relapse. Still, I'm glad they were caught in the act. I could tell something was bothering Edward, but I didn't know what it was. He's much happier now."

Robert arrived from Hartford on Saturday afternoon, and Annie went with Hubert to collect him from the train station. Hubert shook his guest's hand firmly, and Robert hugged Annie, but their embrace lacked its usual warmth. Later in the day, after all the pleasantries were exchanged between the families, Robert suggested to Annie that they stroll around the grounds.

Normally, on such an occasion, the couple would have been chattering nineteen to the dozen and seizing every opportunity to embrace and kiss, but beyond Annie pressing her husband for news of their children, a stony silence hung over them. They wandered along a woodland path to the lake, where several swans had cygnets following them, and there were a few broods of moorhens and mallards.

"Annie, I hate this atmosphere between us. We must sort things out."

"Yes, I hate it too, but I can't think of a solution. I've told Mum everything, and she's worried that Danny will be taken from her. Have you spoken to your parents since I left?"

"Not Mama, as she and Sarah left for London several days ago, but I hope you've put Sabina's mind at rest? I would never let Danny be taken from her. Mama and Sarah travelled in the carriage, which took much longer than the train, and Mama wanted time to rest before attending the Jubilee celebrations. They're staying with Percy, so he'll take care of them. I spoke to Papa again, and he thinks Mama is so desperate to have Danny back in her life that it's likely she'll be willing to receive you and your family, and that's something I never thought would happen. Surely, it's worth a try, Annie? I know how you feel about my father, but he's an old man now, and so sick he can never harm you again."

"See, there you go again. You're as much a snob as your parents. You assume that just because I was a kitchen maid from a poor family, I should be falling over myself with gratitude that the mighty Lady Eleanor Fellwood would deign to receive me. Well, you're wrong. She's treated me like dirt for years, and now, because she wants something, she assumes I'll fall in with her plans. Well, she can think again. And as for your father, the very sight of him makes my skin crawl, even if he is old and sick. Have you conveniently forgotten that he raped me? I wonder what your precious mother would say about that if I told her. Perhaps I will. That would give her something to think about and take her mind off the son she so readily gave away."

Annie stormed off, leaving Robert to find his way back to the house. He had always teased her that her vivid red hair did not come alone, for she had a formidable temper when something displeased her. However, he had never seen her so angry and was at a loss for how to put things right.

On Monday, after a difficult couple of days during which their relatives could sense the tension between them, Hubert ferried Robert and Annie to Thorverton station to catch their train. They had not discussed the matter of

Danny again; in fact, they had barely spoken. Apart from anything else, Annie was feeling slightly under the weather and wondered if she was coming down with something. As a usually healthy young woman, she decided an ailment was the last thing she needed at the moment.

Having said their goodbyes to Hubert, the young couple boarded the train for the short trip to Exeter St David's station, where they would change for their onward journey to Paddington Station in London. They travelled in first class and appreciated the velvet seats and heavy curtains at the windows, keeping out the sunlight and the dust. They were also glad of their carriage's privacy, for neither was in the mood for conversation. As they sank into the comfortable seats, a porter blew a piercing whistle, and the great engine emitted a hissing sigh of steam as it pulled out of the station. The journey was one of the quickest possible, stopping at only a few stations and the train was expected to reach London within six hours.

As they neared their destination, the green fields gave way to soot-streaked, gloomy buildings and the sprawl of the London suburbs. Eventually, the mighty iron arches and the bustle of the crowds at Paddington Station came into view, and with some relief, they left the train and the oppressive silence that had dominated their journey. Robert hailed a cab and instructed the driver to take them to his Aunty Margery's house in Belgravia.

Despite her troubles, Annie was intrigued to see all the bunting and flags hanging in the streets. On every street corner, stalls were selling memorabilia to commemorate the Golden Jubilee of Queen Victoria. She wished she felt more like participating in the celebrations that would usually have filled her with joy, but the estrangement from her beloved husband weighed heavily on her, and she was deep in thought, wondering how to resolve their differences.

CHAPTER 14

Following his discovery by the many children of the Carter family, Eli Cutcliffe was better looked after than at any time in his short life. Rosella, Eddie, and Bentley provided him with ample food as they lived at The Red Lion Inn and could easily smuggle it to the tree house in the garden without raising suspicion. However, the number of visitors to the inn was increasing steadily with the better weather, and particularly with the upcoming festivities planned for Queen Victoria's Golden Jubilee, and the children tried to think of a safer place for the runaway to hide.

One Saturday, a week or so before the Jubilee celebrations, Stephen, Helen, and Danny joined their cousins, Rosella, Eddie, and Bentley in the garden of the inn and, having begged a picnic from Charlotte and Sarah, climbed the ladder to the tree house to join Eli. The children were enjoying the subterfuge of looking after the boy and had tried to find out more about his alleged father, John Cutcliffe. Their cousins, Matthew, Joseph, and Amelia, would have liked to be more involved, but living at Hollyford Farm, a couple of miles outside the village, made it difficult.

"I talked to Rachael Cutcliffe at school the other day, and her father is called John, and he still works as a farm labourer at Hartford Manor. She was curious why I wanted to know, but I said I wondered why they didn't live in the tied cottages in the hamlet any more. She said she remembered they used to live there, but after her mother, Hannah, died of diphtheria, John married Noeleen Gubb, and she had her own, better cottage, so they moved there. I think Rachael's brother and sister died as well. Anyway, she likes her new step-mother, though she's strict and religious and makes them attend church twice on Sundays. Rachael said that's a bother, but Noeleen is an excellent cook and feeds them well, so she doesn't mind. She said her dad used to drink a lot of cider too and was often drunk, but Noeleen won't have alcohol in the house and he seems to keep to her rules, though I think he has a lapse occasionally."

"Could you point him out to me?"

Stephen and Rosella said they could and thought the best place to spot him might be at the Jubilee celebrations, when there would be a lot of folk roaming around and Eli could safely mingle.

"It's not safe to stay in the tree house any more, though, Eli. There are lots of visitors around, and there will be even more next week. Their children will also play here in the garden, and in the tree house, and you may be discovered. We've been chatting about it, and we think the best place to hide would be in an old pigsty at the bottom of the garden at the Lodge House where I live with Stephen and Danny."

"Thanks, Helen. Would you be able to bring me food there?"

"Yes, that would be easy enough, and no one ever goes there. Me, and Stephen and Danny, have been playing in there for the last few days and have asked Mum and Liza if we can make it into a den. They don't mind, and so they've given us old blankets, mugs and things to take there, and we've cleaned it out a bit. I think you'll be more comfortable there, and we can keep an eye on you until you get things sorted out. You can move there tomorrow morning when we're all at church. The service starts at eleven o'clock and lasts over an hour. You'll hear the church clock strike, so you'll know when it's the right time."

The next morning, the children were excited as they got ready for church and enjoyed having a secret. They knew their cousins, Joseph, Matthew, and Amelia, would also attend the service with their parents, Eveline and Charlie Chugg, and they hoped might come back to the Lodge House afterwards and be able to go with them to see Eli.

In the garden of The Red Lion Inn, Eli listened for the church clock. Having had no schooling, he could not count or tell the time, but the other children had told him that when the clock struck many times, it would be safe to walk to the Lodge House, where they would leave the garden gate open.

Unfortunately, it was difficult for the boy to know whether the church clock striking nine, ten, or eleven o'clock counted as lots of times, and so he arrived at the gate to the Lodge House far too early at nine thirty. Luckily, Stephen was playing in the garden and saw the gate open slowly and Eli's frightened face peer around it. Stephen glanced around and, seeing no one, beckoned the boy inside and led the way to the abandoned pigsty at the bottom of the garden.

Although much work had been undertaken in the large garden when Sabina and her family moved into the house, the tumbledown structure was ignored, as she had no desire to keep pigs. Constructed of cob, a mixture of mud, straw and sand commonly used as a building material in Devon, and with a thatched roof in desperate need of repair, the building had a dilapidated and abandoned appearance. However, it was largely dry inside, with two windows that let in some light. Although not glazed, they were small enough not to let in too much rain.

Stephen quickly led the way inside and proudly showed his guest the old straw-stuffed palliasse he had begged from his mother, so they had something to sit on. The floor was roughly swept, and any smell from the previous inhabitants had long since dispersed.

"What do you think? Will you be all right here?"

"Yes, I think so; thanks ever so much. I brought one of the blankets with me from the tree house, but I'm glad to see there are some here too because some nights are bitterly cold; it was even frosty this morning."

"Right, well, I've left you some bread and cheese over there, look, but I must get ready for church or I'll be in trouble. We'll come and see you later and bring you some more food."

The boy hastened back inside the house and confided in Helen and Danny that Eli had arrived early and was already ensconced in the pigsty.

The church service seemed even more tedious than usual that morning, and afterwards, there was no opportunity to visit Eli as Sabina had invited Charlie, Eveline, and their children to join them for roast chicken and all the trimmings, followed by apple pie and custard.

Charlie Chugg pushed his plate back contentedly. "Mm, that was delicious, Sabina; thanks for inviting us."

"You're welcome, Charlie. It's a pity Alfred and Jimmy couldn't come with you."

"Aye, well, Alfred's a bit poorly at the moment. He still has an awful cough, and Jimmy didn't come home last night. Alfred's not best pleased with him, but he has a mind of his own. I hope he's all right."

"Jimmy's a sensible man; I'm sure he will be. He's courting, isn't he?"

"Yes, and normally we'd be delighted for him, but he's taken a liking to a young woman at The Tucker's Arms. We've warned him to steer clear of her, but he's not taking any notice. It sounds as if she's respectable enough, but she won't stay that way living there. He'd like to help her escape Noah Berryman's clutches, but she won't leave her Aunt

Meg while she's so ill. I'm worried that he stayed out all night."

"Yes, that is concerning. I do hope he's safe and sound."

"Mum, can we go out to play now? I want to show Mattie and Joe our new den."

"Yes, that's fine; we adults can enjoy a peaceful cup of tea together."

"Can we take some of Liza's biscuits and some lemonade for a tea party?"

"Goodness, Stephen, you've only just finished your apple pie. You can't be hungry."

"Well, we don't have to eat them straight away."

"Yes, all right. They're in the blue tin in the larder."

On the way through the kitchen, whilst Stephen sought out the biscuits and lemonade, Helen quickly scraped the leftovers from the dinner plates into a dish, whilst the maid was busy clearing the table. She grinned at her brother as they quickly made their escape to the bottom of the garden, where they proudly showed off Eli's new dwelling to their cousins.

Eli was delighted to have the remains of a roast dinner, for he had lived for several weeks on pasties and cakes, and whilst grateful for anything, he was glad to have a change. The children stayed with him as long as they could, for though he didn't complain, Eli found the long hours alone tedious. However, when they heard voices in the garden, they quickly left the pigsty as they didn't want any adults entering Eli's new home.

"We'll see you tomorrow, Eli, and next week, it will be the Jubilee celebrations, and we'll point John Cutcliffe out to you."

CHAPTER 15

Jimmy Chugg was nursing a hangover brought on by far too much cider the night before. It was an experience he was unused to, for he was not a heavy drinker. He awoke with a parched throat and a severe headache, and wondered where he was. Then he groaned with embarrassment as he remembered knocking on the back door of The Three Tuns in the early hours of the morning. He was lucky that Winnie, the innkeeper's wife, was an old friend of his father, Alfred, and she had taken pity on him and given him a bed for the night.

He slowly put his feet over the side of the bed, pulled on his boots, and walked gingerly down the stairs, for any jarring movement made his head throb. He hoped he looked better than he felt and knew he would have to explain himself before he could make his escape. Winnie glanced up from the soup she was stirring as he shamefacedly entered the kitchen, and she grinned at him.

"Feeling a bit fragile, lad? You were full of the joys of spring last night."

"I'm so sorry for disturbing you, Winne; it was unforgivable. I should never have got into that state."

"Ah, don't worry about it; I couldn't turn you away to get into even more trouble. I've known your father and mother since we were at school together, and I can remember you as a babe in arms. Is everything all right, though, Jimmy? It's not like you to get so drunk. Sit down there, look, and I'll fetch you a cup of tea and a slice of bread and dripping; it will help to soak up the cider."

"Thanks, Winnie; 'tis kind of you. I got a bit carried away last night, I'm afraid. Do you remember that young woman I brought here a few weeks ago? A lad had tried to rob her, and she'd grazed her hands and knees and had a nosebleed, and I brought her in here to clean herself up."

"Aye, I remember; she was a friendly lass. What of it?"

"Well, I took to her that day and wanted to get to know her better. I've tried to see her several times since then, but it's been difficult. You know Fat Meg, who lives at The Tucker's Arms?" Winnie nodded, a frown on her face. "She's Nell's aunt, and she's ill, so Nell's looking after her."

"Eh, Jimmy, you should steer clear of that place even if you do fancy the lass. Noah Berryman is pure evil, and from what I hear, his two sons are no better. Is that where you were last night?"

"Yes, I'd arranged to meet Nell yesterday afternoon on top of the Castle Mound, but she didn't turn up and I was worried, so I went to the inn last night to try to see her."

"Aw, Jimmy, she's not for you. If she lives there, she must be on the game, and though you could pay to spend time with her, there would never be any future in it. Noah never lets his girls escape until they're so old no one wants them, and by that time, they're in a sorry state. No, lad, move on and find yourself another decent maid and forget her."

"No, it's not like that. Nell's only living there because her husband died earlier in the year, and she had nowhere else for her and her two daughters to go. Her Aunt Meg is bedridden, and Nell's nursing her and doing all the skivvying jobs that Cissie used to do. Fat Meg doesn't have many principles, but she's refusing to let Nell be used as a prostitute, for now, anyway, though Nell is worried that if Meg dies, it might be a different matter."

"I can assure you, it will be if Noah has anything to do with it. What's wrong with Meg? She isn't that old, but I haven't seen her out and about for a long time."

"I don't know, but Nell says she's getting worse all the time, and reckons she's on her way out. It's hard work looking after her, for she soils the bed, and it takes Nell all her time to keep her clean. Noah's too mean to pay for a doctor."

"So, what happened last night for you to get into such a state?"

"I went to The Tucker's Arms to see if I could have a word with Nell, but although I was there all night, I didn't see her. That's why I got so drunk. I had to keep ordering cider to be able to stay, and I think I ended up playing cards too."

"Oh, Jimmy, have you any money left?"

Jimmy sank his hands into his trouser pockets and then those of his coat, and felt around for some cash. Winnie could tell by the expression on his face that there was nothing left.

"Did you have much money on you?"

"Aye, a few pounds for I brought some piglets to market yesterday, and I had the money from selling them. Dad will be furious with me."

"Well, as long as that's all you've lost, you've been fortunate. You could have gambled away far more; you didn't, did you? Can you remember?"

"No, I had nothing else on me to gamble with. As luck would have it, I forgot to pick up my pocket watch yesterday morning, and I missed it all day. I'm glad I left it at home now, or I might have lost that as well, and it was my grandad's."

"That was lucky, but Jimmy, do listen to me and give up on this girl. I feel for her, I do, but if your dear mother were still with us, she'd tell you there are plenty more fish in the sea and to walk away from this one. Dear Jane is no longer here, so I'll say it for her as I know she'd want me to."

"Thanks, Winnie; I'll be careful, I promise, but I must make sure that Nell is all right. We've met a few times recently, and I've become fond of her. It's only been a few months since her husband died, but he used to raise his hand to her, and she feels safer without him, although she's been left homeless. She's never failed to show up before, and I'm worried about her. She usually goes into the town each morning to fetch bread and things, so I'll see if I can find her and put my mind to rest."

"You must do as you see fit, but take care, lad."

"Thanks again for letting me stay last night, Winnie; it won't happen again."

Jimmy left The Three Tuns and wandered down the High Street to the bakery, where he had seen Nell purchase bread before. However, she was not in the shop, and so he turned back towards Butchers' Row, where he thought she might be buying meat.

He strolled along the street where the thirty-three small shops were all occupied, as the name suggested, by butchers. It was an impressive thoroughfare, built of Bath stone, with elegant wrought iron supports and an elaborate archway at each end. However, Jimmy was in no mood to admire the impressive architecture as he checked one shop after another, searching for Nell. In the fifth shop, he was delighted to see the back of her black bonnet and hear her driving a hard bargain with the butcher, but when she turned to face him, his smile vanished, for she had a black eye and a swollen lip. Quickly, he approached her and took her arm.

"Nell, I was so worried when you didn't meet me yesterday. What happened? Who did this to you?"

Impatiently, Nell pushed him away and removed her arm.

"Jimmy, I've told you before, you must stop seeing me. It's dangerous, and Noah doesn't like it. His son, Abe, saw me with you last week and told his father. Noah confronted me yesterday and told me that if I met you again, he'd see to it that you, as well as I, would suffer for it. He hit me to make sure I got the message and said if I valued my children's lives, I'd do as I was told. Now, please, go away, Jimmy. I like you, but I can't risk any harm coming to the children."

"I went to The Tucker's Arms last night, hoping to see you. I was worried about what had happened to you."

"Well, that explains why he was so angry this morning. He must have been making enquiries about you, Jimmy, and somehow he knows your family was involved in rescuing that girl, and Cissie and Mickey. He warned me that if I desired male company, he could soon find me some, and you know what that means."

"How's your Aunt Meg?"

"Getting worse by the day, unfortunately, and I don't think she's long for this world. It's strange, though, because she's done some terrible things in her time, but she seems determined to see that I come to no harm. I know she was close to my mother years ago, before she died, so perhaps it's that, or she's trying to make amends before she meets her Maker. Folk tend to do that when they know they haven't long left. She even hinted that she has something that she will give me when the time is right, that will keep me safe from Noah, Abe, and Reggie."

"Do you know what it is?"

"No, and it may be the laudanum talking, for she takes ever bigger doses. It worries me that she'll overdose and die, but without it, she's in terrible pain, so I can't blame her. How long did you stay at the inn last night?"

"Too long. I drank far too much cider and lost a lot of money playing cards; I should know better. My father is going to be furious with me when I get home, but I kept staying a bit longer, hoping to see you."

"I never go into the bar if I can help it; I don't want to tempt fate."

"I wish I could get you away from there. If I found a way, would you come and live at Hollyford Farm? In fact, will you marry me, Nell? I've fallen in love with you, although we see little of each other."

"Oh, Jimmy, I'd love to, but I can't leave Aunt Meg while she's so ill; maybe, if I can get away after she dies, but then I'm afraid Noah will have other uses for me. I must go, Jimmy, and please don't come to the inn again; promise me? You'll make matters worse and probably get beaten."

Reluctantly, Jimmy agreed and stayed in the shop long enough for Nell to be on her way before he exited. He was thrilled to think she hadn't turned down his offer of marriage, for the more he thought about it, the more he liked the idea. He found it strange that since he first set eyes on Nell, he had known she was the one for him, and he was hopeful that she felt the same way about him. However, there was the small matter of getting her and the children away from the despicable Noah Berryman.

CHAPTER 16

The weeks leading up to Queen Victoria's Golden Jubilee had been a busy time in Hartford, and indeed in most towns and villages throughout the country. Never before had a monarch of Great Britain reigned for such an extended period of time. The people in the capital were looking forward to seeing their queen, who had observed such a long period of mourning following the death of her beloved Prince Albert in 1861.

In Hartford, many events were planned. There was to be a cricket match held in one of the meadows close to the centre of the village. This would be a match to remember, for there was intense rivalry between the Hartford team and that of the nearby village of Warkley. The Hartford team included Dudley Webber and his father, Arthur Webber, both market gardeners, Charlie Chugg of Hollyford Farm, Fred Carter, the innkeeper of The Red Lion, as well as Eli's alleged father, John Cutcliffe. The men had practised for weeks and were confident of victory.

Fred wondered whether he should participate in the cricket match, for he knew the inn would be incredibly busy that day. However, Charlotte persuaded him to play, insisting she could manage with Louis Blaquiere, Sarah, and the many additional staff they had employed. The other members of the team were delighted when he agreed to join them, for Fred was their star player and a demon bowler.

However, although Charlotte had boasted confidence to her husband, she was nervous about the day ahead, for there was much to organise. In the meadow at the rear of the inn, additional picnic tables were erected for the many visitors who were expected to flock to the village to enjoy trips on the canal barges.

In the centre of the village itself, a street party was to be held, and flowers, bunting, and flags adorned the main street, wafting gently in the light breeze, and many heaved a sigh of relief that the weather was favourable. Stalls selling everything imaginable from pigs' trotters to paper windmills, toffee apples, and commemorative coins drew the crowds.

Other events planned included a fancy-dress competition for the children, the traditional arm-wrestling contest, the selection of a Jubilee Queen, and a tug of war to be held across the small brook that ran down one side of the village street.

In Betsey's Kitchen, another food outlet of The Red Lion Inn, a free meal was to be offered to the poor of the village, and this was one of the many things on Charlotte Carter's mind that morning. She served on the committee organising the event and had begged contributions from all and sundry to cover the cost. A whole oxen was to be roasted, served with hot potatoes and crusty bread, and followed by plum pudding and clotted cream.

Apart from the absence of Robert and Annie, who were in London, and Betsey and Ned, who were still in Brampford Speke, the whole Carter family was to attend the celebrations. That morning, Sabina and Liza collected Selina, Thomas and David from Hartford Manor, determined that the children would not miss anything in their parents' absence. Having walked around many of the attractions, Sabina and Liza selected a bench on which to rest whilst they watched the judging for the Jubilee Queen.

They were pleased when the late George Carter's widow, Mary Ann, asked if she might join them.

"Yes, of course, Mary Ann; how are you?"

"I'm well, thank you, Sabina. Are any of your children in the contest for queen?"

"Yes, Helen and Selina, and their cousins, Rosella and Amelia. Oh, and I see Marrok's twin daughters, Jinnie and Eliza, are also in the lineup. I've not seen Marrok yet today, but I thought he'd be here. In fact, I think the whole village is here. Thank goodness the weather is fine. It's a pity that Betsey and Ned are missing this; they would have loved it."

"How is Ned? Have you heard?"

"Doing well, I believe, and in safe hands, I'm sure. How about you, though? Having lost Tom, I know how difficult it is to bury a husband."

Mary Ann's eyes suddenly glistened with unshed tears.

"I'm coping, thank you, but you're right, it is difficult. I miss George terribly, for although he wasn't popular with everyone, I loved him and he always treated me kindly. His death was unexpected, too, for although he'd been ill for some time, he worsened and died within hours, and it was such a shock."

"That must have been awful for you. I'm glad you have Cissie to help you with the little ones, and Harriet working in the shop. Are you looking for an assistant to help her, now that Theresa has married Louis?"

"We will be, yes. Theresa will continue working for the time being, but I expect there will be babies on the way before too long; that's usually the case. She and Louis have settled into Bluebell Cottage, and I know she longs for a child. I must confess I'll enjoy being a step-granny when the time comes."

"Oh, look, I think they will announce the winner; I wonder who will be the Jubilee Queen?"

The lucky winner was Rachael Cutcliffe, a popular winner, for she was a kind and pretty little girl. Beaming from ear to ear, she dipped her head to allow the judge to position the homemade crown on her head, and accepted her prize of a whole shiny shilling, before leading all the contestants down the main street for everyone to admire.

Just down the road, Harriet Carter, Mary Ann's stepdaughter, was enjoying watching the arm wrestling. As usual, Francis Rudd drew a huge crowd as one after another he despatched his opponents with ease. He was not sorry that Willie Carter had moved away, for the young man had overcome the blacksmith in the previous year and spoiled his reputation for being unbeatable. He smiled widely as, after quite a tussle, he forced Marrok Fellwood's arm to the table for the second time and pocketed the cash lying on the table.

As he raised his eyes and enjoyed the praise from the crowd, he noticed Harriet watching him. The warm sunlight glistened on the red highlights in her long tawny hair, and her eyes were a startling blue. At twenty-seven, Harriet had all but despaired of finding a husband and accepted that she was destined to be an old maid. However, when she noticed Francis gazing at her, she smiled back at him, and not for the first time, wondered why he had never married.

The truth was the young man had never had time for courting. A few years earlier, the smithy had burned to the ground, and he had lost both his father, Ben, and his elder brother, Harry. The tragedy had left him as the head of the family and responsible for caring for his elderly mother, Matilda, and younger brother, Jacob, who was mentally impaired. Francis spent every waking hour rebuilding the business and had no time for distractions. In that moment, however, he wondered how he had never noticed how attractive Harriet Carter was, and determined to seek her out later and endeavour to get to know her better.

Having seen the Jubilee Queen elected, folk wandered the short distance to the meadow where the cricket match was underway. Among the spectators was Eli, enjoying being out and about and not lingering in the pigsty alone.

He sat on the grass with Stephen, Danny, and Bentley and watched as John Cutcliffe went in to bat.

"That's him, that's John Cutcliffe. Do you think he's your father?"

"I don't know, do I? Do you think I should try to speak to him today?"

"Perhaps it would be best to catch him when he's walking to work. That's his wife, sitting over there, and she's not one to cross. If he accepts he's your father, he might not want her to know, or at least want to pick the best time to tell her. Now you know what he looks like, I'd speak to him on my own if it were me. At least you can sit here and watch him."

"I think I'll do that. Do you think I look like him?"

"No, but you look a bit like his daughter, Rachael."

They turned their attention back to the match, which was drawing a large crowd. The Hartford team had gone into bat first and accumulated a respectable total of two hundred and nineteen runs. A score that many thought was unlikely to be beaten. However, the Warkley team were on form and determined to surpass that score. When they had amassed two hundred runs with their last batsman in the crease, the atmosphere was tense as Fred Carter, Hartford's star bowler, took the ball. The batsman hit the first ball cleanly for six, and the Hartford supporters groaned. Amidst shouts of encouragement, Fred aimed again and this time took the wickets out cleanly to a huge cheer from his teammates and most of the crowd of onlookers.

Marrok Fellwood, sitting beside his new lady friend, Eirlys, was delighted and hugged her in jubilation, then realised he might have gone too far, for this was only their second outing.

"Oh, I do beg your pardon, Eirlys; I got a bit carried away."

"No, problem, Marrok. I'm pleased they won, too."

"Now that the match has finished, would you like a cream tea in the village hall?"

"Yes, I'd like that, thank you, but I must check on Catherine and Jilly first. They're over there with their grandparents."

"Very well, and I'll need to do the same with mine. I've allowed Jinnie and Eliza to wander around on their own for the afternoon, but I left Martin and Paul playing with Sabina Carter's sons. Shall I meet you at the entrance to the hall in a few minutes? Bring your daughters with you if they want to come."

Fifteen minutes later, with Catherine and Jilly's grandparents continuing to mind them and Sabina having assured Marrok the boys were fine, the pair arrived at the door of the village hall together. Sabina, watching from a distance, smiled when she saw Marrok tentatively take Eirlys's hand and lead her inside.

CHAPTER 17

Lady Margery was delighted to welcome Robert and Annie to her luxurious London home. However, it did not take long for the astute lady to determine that all was not well between them, and when matters had not improved after a few days, she took her great-nephew aside to question him.

"Robert, whatever is troubling you and Annie? You're usually devoted to each other, yet now it seems you can hardly bear to be in the same room as one another. I don't understand."

Robert sighed and explained that his mother, Eleanor, had expressed a desire to have Danny returned to her.

"That's ridiculous. What can she be thinking, and surely, Charles has told her that it's impossible?"

"Yes, he has, and so have I, but she won't let it go. She's been spying on the boy when he comes to the Manor House garden to play with Selina, and that's annoyed Annie because it's made Danny feel uncomfortable. I think the matter has come to a head because Mama has been missing Victoria and her three children since she moved to Lynton."

"I can understand that, but Eleanor has never been particularly maternal, so why now? Surely she must understand that the boy has never known any family other than that of Sabina? It would be cruel to uproot him now."

"She does, but is adamant that she wants contact with him. She's even considering accepting Annie into the family after all this time, so she can spend time with the boy."

The old lady raised her eyebrows in surprise. "My goodness, she must be determined, for I never thought that would happen, but surely, that's a good thing, isn't it? I think you should encourage her to do that. The families would not have to meet often, but it would be wonderful to dispense with the terrible enmity that has existed since your marriage."

"I agree, and that's what I think too, for I can see no other solution, but unfortunately, Annie will not entertain the suggestion, which is why we're at loggerheads. She refuses to even consider meeting with my parents and is furious with me for suggesting it."

"Oh, I see, but why?"

Robert hesitated. "I'm afraid I can't tell you, Aunty Margery, for you would be so angry that you would be unable to keep the information to yourself. All I can tell you is that Annie will never socialise with my father, for in the past, he did her a great wrong of which even Mama is unaware. Now, please don't press me, for I will not tell you, but I will say that I respect Annie's feelings on the matter, and I should have given them more credence before I tried to persuade her otherwise. So, we're at a stalemate and I can see no way forward."

Lady Margery was more curious than ever, for as far as she was aware, it was Lady Eleanor that Annie had a problem with rather than her husband, Charles.

"Well, I respect your privacy, but despite what you may think, I can keep my mouth shut if I have to. If you change your mind and want to confide in me, I'll do my best to help, but I need to know the whole story. However, I will not press you, and you know where to find me if you want to talk. Now, about the Jubilee celebrations, if you've not made other plans, would you and Annie like to join Sam, Peter,

Christopher, and me to observe the queen and the procession?"

"That would be wonderful, thank you, but where do you plan to view it from? No doubt, the streets will be lined with crowds of people."

"Oh yes, they will. Someone was telling me the other day that miles of scaffolding have been erected around the streets of London to afford a decent view to as many people as possible. However, I have the matter in hand, for I have reserved the best grandstand seats along The Mall from where we'll have an excellent view of the queen as she leaves Buckingham Palace in her carriage and again when she returns after the service in Westminster Abbey. It should be quite a spectacle, as I understand there will be a parade of colonial troops and military regiments all dressed in their regalia. I'm looking forward to it, and especially seeing my visitors' faces. They will never have seen anything like it, but then, neither have we."

Lady Margery was puzzled after her conversation with Robert, and for the life of her, she could not understand Annie's strong feelings about Charles Fellwood. However, manners prevented her from enquiring further, so she put on as cheerful a front as possible and pretended not to notice the tension between the young couple.

The morning of the twenty-first of June dawned dry and clear, and at first light, Lady Margery and her guests were assembled in the hallway and ready to leave. They had agreed that Lady Margery, Robert and Annie would travel in the Victoria carriage, and the others would travel in her landau. In the first pale light of dawn, the gas lamps that lined the streets glowed softly, and the horses' hoofbeats rang out as they trotted over the cobblestones and joined a long line of polished black carriages heading in the same direction. At St James's Palace, the drivers drew to a halt, quickly helped their passengers to alight, and advised them that they would need to walk the rest of the way.

"Come on, my dears, we need to walk down Marlborough Road, and although it's so crowded today, it should only be a short walk of ten minutes or so to The Mall."

Lady Margery led the way through the throng of spectators, her companions easily keeping sight of her elaborate turquoise silk dress and the ostrich feather in her hat, which bobbed up and down as she hurried along. At the entrance to the grandstand on The Mall, she handed over the expensive tickets, which were printed on white cards and edged in gold, to a smartly dressed steward. He directed them to their seats, where they prepared themselves for a lengthy wait, for the Queen's carriage was not due to leave the palace until after eleven o'clock.

Fortunately, there was no shortage of refreshments available for purchase, and to pass the time, Robert and Christopher obtained a selection of savoury sandwiches and small cakes, washed down with delicious lemonade, which was refreshingly welcoming in the warm sunshine.

Later that morning, amidst gasps of delight and cheers from the crowd, Queen Victoria left Buckingham Palace in an open landau pulled by six handsome cream horses. Dressed in her customary black silk gown, she was sombrely dressed, still mourning her beloved Prince Albert. However, the outfit was enhanced by the blue sash of the Order of the Garter and an intricate white veil of Honiton lace, on which sat a tiny diamond crown.

As she proceeded down The Mall, the Queen waved at the cheering crowd, which included Lady Margery and her companions.

"I wondered if you might have been invited to Westminster Abbey, Aunty Margery? Percy and Mama, too?"

"No chance of that, my boy. We may be rich and titled, but we're not quite high enough up the social ladder for that. I understand there will be more than fifty kings and heads of the overseas colonies attending the service at the Abbey, and then at a Jubilee Luncheon in the Palace. I'm hoping that if we wait here in our seats, we'll see the queen return later, and there is talk that she may appear on the Palace balcony to acknowledge her subjects. I would like to see that, but I can't bear the thought of walking through these terrible crowds. I suggest we wait here and see her carriage pass again, and then head for home, where we could enjoy a light snack on the balcony to keep us going until the grand ball that I'm hosting tonight." She waved her hand at Sam, Peter and Christopher. "I hope you three gentlemen don't mind, but I took the liberty of choosing some appropriate clothes for you to wear, and a valet will help you to dress."

"Ah, we wanted to talk to you about that, Margery. Please don't think we're ungrateful, but would you mind if we three gave the ball a miss? We would much prefer a quiet evening to put our feet up and chat about everything we've seen today, and Peter and I are already tired. It's so kind of you to bring us to the capital and make us welcome, but we'll feel out of place among so many grand folk, and not everyone will be as forgiving as you for any errors of behaviour we might make."

"As you like, of course. You are my friends, and I don't care what people think, but I wouldn't want you to feel uncomfortable. I must confess, a night with my feet up sounds rather wonderful, but I must welcome my guests. Oh, look, the queen is returning in her carriage. Let's watch her pass by and then head for home where we can relax in comfort."

CHAPTER 18

Lady Margery and her guests returned to Montgomery House by early afternoon, allowing them time to rest before attending the grand ball to be held that evening. They had enjoyed seeing Queen Victoria in her carriage, marvelled at the costumes of the marching bands and regiments, and were impressed by all the pageantry that accompanied such occasions.

Leaving Lady Margery, Christopher, Sam, and Peter lounging on the balcony after their late lunch, Robert and Annie retired to their suite of rooms, and Robert sank thankfully into an armchair.

"I enjoyed that, but I'm glad we have time to put our feet up for a couple of hours before the ball this evening, though I don't suppose you'll have as long as me to relax by the time the maids have fussed over your hair and dress."

"I envy Peter, Christopher, and Sam spending a quiet evening together; would you mind if I did the same and gave the ball a miss?"

"I know you dislike these occasions, but it would be impolite not to attend, seeing as Aunty Margery is our hostess, and she longs to show you off to her friends, as do I. I'll be proud to walk into the room with you on my arm and hear you announced as my wife. Do say you'll come,

Annie? It would be awkward for you not to, and I'll be right there at your side."

Annie sighed reluctantly, having known it was unlikely she could avoid attending.

"Very well, but please don't leave me on my own. I never know what to say to all these rich people, and many will be waiting for me to make a mistake, knowing I was once a kitchen maid. At least I know Frank Eastleigh won't be there to embarrass me, though I'm surprised Victoria didn't decide to accompany your mother and Sarah. Do you know if they will attend the ball with Percy?"

"Yes, I thought Victoria might have come, but she's enjoying her new house in Lynton and didn't want to leave the children. I know Mama and Sarah are invited, but I haven't heard if they're coming. If so, we'll be polite and say hello and move on, though you would be fine chatting with Percy or Sarah, wouldn't you?"

"Yes, it's only your mother I want to steer clear of, and I'm sure she'll feel the same way about me."

A few hours later, Robert and Annie surveyed each other before descending the sweeping staircase and walking to the ballroom to be announced. Robert was attired in a crisp white shirt, black trousers, and a tailcoat. The trousers had a satin stripe down the outside of each leg, and he wore shiny black patent leather shoes on his feet. A white waistcoat and bowtie completed his outfit, for, not having to leave the house, he did not require his bowler hat, cape, or white gloves.

He gazed at his wife in awe, for she looked so incredibly beautiful. Annie wore her favourite colour of emerald green, which she knew enhanced the vibrant red of her hair and matched her green eyes. Her bustle dress was made of silk and sported metallic embroidery. The tight-fitting bodice was boned, and a corset emphasised her tiny waist, belying the fact that she was the mother of three children. Her long, often unruly, auburn hair was swept up and back, and the off-the-shoulder style of her dress exposed the creamy texture of her shoulders and neck. Her outfit was completed with a small tiara of seed pearls, long white gloves that extended over her elbows, and in her hand, she carried a delicate, hand-painted fan.

"My goodness, you'll turn some heads tonight. Where did you get such a stunning outfit? I haven't seen it before."

"This is all thanks to Aunty Margery and her modiste. They took care of everything, and she wouldn't even let me pay, though to be fair, I think she enjoyed the experience far more than I did. I would be so much happier at home in my comfortable day dress and my hair in braids. This corset is already killing me, and there are still hours to go. I doubt I'll be able to eat anything, the way the maid has tightened my stays."

"I'm sorry you're uncomfortable, but enjoy knowing you will be the most beautiful woman present tonight, and I am so proud of you. Come on, I can't wait to show you off."

Annie's heart was pounding, and she felt breathless as she descended the stairs on Robert's arm and entered the ballroom where their names were announced. They found themselves in pleasant surroundings: the musicians played soft background music, romantic gaslights illuminated the room, and the air was filled with the delicate perfume from the many vases of flowers. Many eyes gazed at the couple, and particularly at the young woman who, from such a humble start in life, had captivated one of the most eligible bachelors in the land a few years earlier.

As Robert escorted his wife around the room, introducing her to friends and acquaintances, he noted with relish the longing in men's eyes as they feasted their eyes on his partner. Annie felt embarrassed under such scrutiny and noted one or two snide and whispered comments from some of the ladyfolk who resented the way their menfolk admired her. From the corner of her eye, she glimpsed her mother-in-law, Lady Eleanor Fellwood, with her youngest daughter, Sarah, and nephew, Sir Percy Chichester, and was grateful when Robert carefully steered her in the opposite direction.

As they fraternised with the guests, smartly dressed waiters bearing trays of canapés and champagne circulated amongst them. When a gong sounded, the gentlemen took their partners' arms and led them to the long tables, covered with snowy white tablecloths and decorated with exotic blooms, to locate their place names. Annie knew it was unlikely she would be seated near her husband, for traditionally, couples were split up to encourage social interaction. However, she could have kissed Aunty Margery with relief when she discovered she was positioned between Geoffrey Turner, the doctor who had operated on Danny, and Percy Chichester, Robert's cousin. Both men were known to Annie and friends with whom she was comfortable. Opposite her was a young man, unknown to her, to his right, Clara Turner, the doctor's wife, and to his left, Aunty Margery herself.

Lady Margery noted the relief on her great-niece's face, smiled, and permitted herself the briefest of winks before introducing her guest to Annie and the others.

"Annie, may I introduce James McIntyre, the son of one of my oldest friends in Scotland. James, this is Anne Fellwood, the wife of my great nephew, Robert."

The young man smiled at Annie, his clear blue eyes taking in her elegant appearance as he assured her it was a pleasure to make her acquaintance, and that he hoped she would grant him a dance later in the evening. Annie nodded, then blushed and dropped her eyes to her plate, feeling slightly embarrassed by his direct and appreciative gaze. Geoffrey Turner came to the rescue by asking after her brother, Danny.

"How is the young man? I haven't seen him for a few months now, but tell me, does he still limp?"

"Barely at all, and he's delighted with all you and Doctor Brown have done for him; we all are. He's a different child from the one born with so many disabilities a few years ago."

Annie carefully avoided drinking champagne, for she knew from experience that whilst she enjoyed the drink, it went straight to her head, and she wanted to keep her wits about her. The first course was turtle soup, a popular delicacy of the time, but one which Annie was not keen on. She declined her serving, knowing there were many courses to come, and was conscious of how tight her corset felt even with an empty stomach. However, feeling extremely hungry by this time, she partook of a little of the poached salmon, served with a delicious cucumber sauce.

For the main course, there was a choice of roasted saddle of lamb with mint sauce, fillet of beef with truffle sauce, or Annie's favourite, roast duckling with orange sauce. She accepted a small portion, accompanied by asparagus, baby carrots, and duchesse potatoes.

Her new acquaintance, James McIntyre, was attentive and, noticing that she had not taken a drink, encouraged her to try the Madeira wine, which, he assured her, was excellent, and, unknown to him, was Annie's favourite. Although she had been determined not to drink any alcohol, he persuaded her to sample a small glass, and she found it helped her to relax a little.

Lady Margery knew that the most successful dinner parties were leisurely affairs, and after a pause of almost half an hour, most guests took an interest in the next course of dessert. The selection on offer did not disappoint, as for such a grand occasion, no expense was spared, and for many, their choice was difficult.

Having never heard of it before, Annie chose a portion of Nesselrode pudding, which consisted of ice cream with chestnuts and fruit, and was delicious. Lady Margery and Clara Turner favoured strawberries and cream, whilst Geoffrey and James opted for a slice of Victoria sponge, named in honour of the long-serving monarch.

By the time a selection of cheeses had been served with biscuits and fruit, accompanied by port, Madeira wine, or claret, the guests were relieved to move to the drawing room, where brandy, cognac, and coffee were available, along with cigars for the men. In the ballroom, the band began playing waltzes, polkas, and quadrilles to entice people onto the dance floor.

Annie had eaten and drunk sparingly, though she had trouble preventing the over-zealous waiters from topping up her glass of Madeira at every opportunity. However, she was as relieved as everyone else to stretch her legs and delighted when Robert once more took her arm and led her towards the ballroom where the first strains of *The Blue Danube* could be heard.

"This is your favourite tune by Strauss, I believe. Annie, would you like to dance? I know you enjoy a waltz."

Fortunately, Annie was an excellent dancer, having been taught by Victoria and Sarah, Robert's two sisters, many years earlier. Robert led her onto the dance floor, and she relaxed into his arms, beginning to think that she might even enjoy the evening a little, for surely the worst was now over. At the end of the dance, Robert whispered in her ear.

"Would you excuse me for a little while, Annie? I've spotted a couple of businessmen on the far side of the room, and I'd like to chat with them. They're influential people who have expressed an interest in our weekend breaks at Hartford. If I return you to Geoffrey and Clara, they will keep you company in my absence."

Annie was annoyed, but before she could object, James McIntyre tapped Robert on the shoulder and asked if he might have the next dance with his wife.

"Yes, of course, James; I wonder, would you be kind enough to escort my wife back to the Turners after your dance, please?"

As the young man nodded his willingness to oblige, Robert strode purposefully across the room towards his quarry.

"I believe this next dance sounds like a polka; are you comfortable with that, Anne?"

"Yes, I like the polka; it's my favourite dance, but Robert's not keen on it. No wonder he made his escape."

"Then, please, allow me; it will be a pleasure."

James was an excellent dancer, and Annie enjoyed twirling around the floor with him, though she kept hoping Robert would soon return to her side. Unfortunately, Robert's business chat took far longer than he anticipated, and try as he might, it was difficult to get away from his new acquaintances, especially when they were promising to book several hunting weekends for large parties throughout the year. He kept glancing around to make sure Annie was all right, and each time she was dancing, something which he knew she enjoyed and probably where she felt the safest.

Lady Margery was also keeping an eye on her niece and had noticed the attention James was paying to her. Having seen them dance for a second time, she decided she must intervene to protect Annie's reputation, something she knew Annie may not even consider. However, before she could do so, an old friend came to chat with her, and when she next glanced at the dance floor, she was relieved to see Annie dancing with Geoffrey Turner.

A little later in the evening, James returned to Annie's side and suggested they might seek some refreshment together. With Robert still nowhere in sight, she took his arm as he led her to the impressive banquet that Lady Margery had provided. Furious as she was with her husband for neglecting her, she allowed herself to indulge in another glass of Madeira wine, and then regretted it as she felt distinctly light-headed, a fact Robert immediately recognised when he finally returned to her side.

"I think it's time we retired for the night, Annie. You're looking rather tired."

"No, I'm not tired, Robert; I'm having a wonderful time, thanks to James, who has taken good care of me."

"I'm much obliged, James. Unfortunately, my business conversation lasted far longer than anticipated. However, I'm here now and want to spend some time with my wife. I'm sure there are many other young ladies with whom you would like to dance."

Without further ado, Robert swept Annie into another waltz and muttered under his breath.

"Have you been drinking? You seem a little glassy-eyed."

"Only a few glasses of Madeira, and I must say I feel better for them. Quite relaxed, in fact. What a kind young man your aunt's friend is. He's been so attentive and has even asked if he might call on us tomorrow. I said yes. I hope you don't mind."

"I wish you hadn't agreed to that, for I have more business meetings tomorrow."

"Oh, I didn't know, but no matter, Aunty Margery will be with me anyway, and he's an interesting man to talk to."

Robert did not deign to reply as the dance ended, and he escorted Annie from the room, bidding goodbye to a few friends as they went.

Upstairs in a quiet drawing room, Sam, Peter, and Christopher were enjoying putting the world to rights over a large glass of brandy. The three men sat with their feet up, and Sam swirled his drink around the glass, whilst Peter drank his, from necessity, with a straw.

"Isn't life strange? A short while ago, none of us could have imagined being somewhere like this, enjoying expensive cognac."

"No, it's unbelievable what's happened to us; we're so lucky, but what do you think is troubling Annie and Robert? They don't seem to be getting along, do they?"

"No, they don't, but I hope they sort it out soon, for they've always seemed so much in love. Speaking of love, I've a feeling that's an ailment that might be afflicting you, Sam Fellwood."

"What! Don't be ridiculous, Peter. People don't fall in love at my age; what are you thinking of?"

"I'm thinking that when I last saw you together, you and Florrie seemed to be getting along rather well, that's all. And why not? You could do far worse."

"I like Florrie, it's true. I enjoy her company, and we find the same things funny."

"There you are then, nothing wrong with that, and what about Marrok?"

"What do you mean, what about Marrok?"

"Well, I reckon he's taken a shine to that widow who's moved into Kerscott Farm with her parents. She's got a funny name. Eirlys, Eirlys Williams, that's it. I liked her family when I met them, although I struggled to understand their Welsh accent. It's sad that she was widowed so young, and with two children to raise; I wonder what happened to her husband."

"I chatted to her father when I showed him around the farm, and he said his son-in-law died in a riding accident, so she's lucky her parents have taken her in. I think Marrok does like her, and he planned to invite her to the Jubilee celebrations in Hartford. I'd like to see him marry again, so I hope it works out for them. Anyway, I can hear the fireworks outside. Let's watch from the balcony."

CHAPTER 19

After leaving the Jubilee Ball, Annie and Robert ascended the grand staircase. On reaching their bedroom, Annie's maid quickly helped her to undress and unpin her hair, and Annie heaved a sigh of relief as she was freed from the tight corset she had endured all evening. She knew her husband was annoyed with her for having imbibed perhaps one glass of wine too many and for dancing so many times. However, whilst dancing, she felt safe from being drawn into conversations in which she had no wish to engage.

Annie was equally annoyed with Robert for seemingly abandoning her despite having expressly asked him to stay by her side. She climbed into bed, and as soon as her head hit the pillow, she immediately fell fast asleep as the wine took its toll. Robert lay beside her, thinking how beautiful she looked in the soft lamplight. He gently pushed a tendril of her hair away and planted a loving kiss on her soft cheek before pulling the covers over her and extinguishing the lamp.

He regretted neglecting her for longer than he intended that night, particularly as the handsome young friend of his aunt had monopolised her company. However, what Annie did not know was that Robert had taken out a substantial loan and was making every effort to repay it as soon as possible to reduce the hefty interest charges. The cost of the alterations to Hartford Manor to accommodate the visitors attending the hunting weekends was considerably more than he had budgeted for, and although the venture was doing well, it was essential to generate business. The visit to London for the Jubilee celebrations presented an ideal opportunity. He knew that Annie, having lived most of her early life at subsistence level, would only worry if she knew how much money he had borrowed, and so he kept the information from her.

Although he trusted his wife implicitly, he felt unreasonably cross that James had asked if he might call at the house the next day, though, as the son of a close friend of his Aunt Margery, there was no reason why he should not. He debated whether to cancel the meetings he had arranged over the next few days and then decided that would be ridiculous, for Annie would not be left alone in the company of the young man, and Aunty Margery would ensure the correct etiquette was followed.

The next morning, Annie, suffering from a headache, was decidedly wan, but Robert did not comment, knowing it would annoy her. He accompanied her to breakfast, where they joined his aunt, Sam, Peter, and Christopher and discussed the ball's success.

"Robert, are you sure we can't persuade you to cancel your arrangements today so you can join us?"

"No, I'm sorry, Aunt, but the gentleman I've arranged to meet is only in the capital today, as he will return to Oxford later. He's an influential man, and, having attended Hartford Manor a few weeks ago, is willing to recommend our new venture to his friends. He's invited me to lunch at his club today to meet a few of them whilst they're in London, and it's far too important an opportunity to cancel the engagement."

"That's a shame. Still, we'll take care of Annie in your absence. After you had retired last night, James agreed to join us on a sightseeing excursion around London this morning. It's his first visit to the capital, and he wants to see as much of it as possible. He's staying with friends nearby and should be arriving here soon. I think it will be a dry day, so we can fold the roof down and enjoy a better view of everything. Is that all right with you, Annie?"

"That sounds delightful, thank you."

"We'll need to take the Victoria carriage and the landau again, as we are too many of us for one vehicle. Annie, perhaps you could accompany me and James in the carriage, and the rest of you can travel in the landau, as you did yesterday. I thought we'd start with a visit to Trafalgar Square, which was named after the famous naval Battle of Trafalgar in 1805, and fought by Admiral Horatio Nelson. Have any of you heard of him?"

All her guests nodded.

"Yes, I remember learning about him at school; he was a famous national hero, for he saved Britain from being invaded by Napoleon."

"That's right, Christopher; you're well informed. I'll tell you all a little more when we arrive at our destination."

Lady Margery had been planning their excursion for some time and had discussed the route with her drivers, both distinguished-looking gentlemen who had worked for the Montgomery family for many years. They were dressed in smart coats, top hats, and gloves, and assisted their passengers inside the vehicles, where they relaxed on the comfortable leather seats.

After a pleasant journey, the landau pulled to the side of the road, followed by the Victoria carriage, and the drivers climbed down to help their passengers alight. James immediately offered Annie his arm to escort her around the famous square. They were followed by Christopher and Peter, whilst Sam took his aunt's arm and she provided a few more titbits of information.

"See the huge column with a figure of Nelson on top and the four bronze lions surrounding it? It's a fitting tribute to a great man."

The area was decorated with the same bunting and flowers that were visible throughout the city, as people continued to celebrate the jubilee. The many stalls included those offering mementoes of the occasion, as well as flower sellers, shoeshine boys, matchgirls, a juggler, and an acrobat.

"Oh, what a strange creature. What is it?"

"Poor little thing; I think it's a Capuchin monkey, collecting money for the organ grinder. He's cute, but I don't like to see the collar and chain around his neck."

The small monkey was dressed in a bright red velvet waistcoat with shiny gold buttons, and his tiny green trousers were decorated with gold trim. On his head, he wore a jaunty pillbox hat, held in place by a chin strap. He danced in front of the growing crowd, holding out a cup for donations, and screeched loudly from time to time. Annie and her companions watched for several minutes, fascinated by the small animal and enjoying the tunes played by the organ grinder.

"Oh, I know this one, *Twinkle, Twinkle Little Star*, my Mum used to sing it to me. How lovely."

They listened for a while longer as the organ belted out popular songs of the time, including *London Bridge Is Falling Down* and *Pretty Polly Perkins of Paddington Green*, but although James and Lady Margery knew the tunes, none of the Devon travellers were familiar with them and after a few minutes, they boarded their carriages and continued on their way.

The drivers, as directed by their mistress earlier, drove the landau and the Victoria carriage along Pall Mall, turned into St James's Street, past some exclusive gentlemen's clubs and on through Piccadilly to Hyde Park Corner. After half a mile or so, they entered the famous park through the Apsley Gate and drove along the South Carriage Drive, which ran adjacent to Rotten Row. Having enjoyed viewing some magnificent horses and their riders, they went on to circle the Serpentine, where the drivers halted their vehicles, allowing their passengers to enjoy a short walk and admire the many mute swans and ducklings. All around, families were enjoying the day's festivities, many picnicking in the park, while ladies strolled in the sunshine in their colourful summer gowns, carrying parasols.

"This has been an interesting trip, Aunty Margery; thank you for bringing me. I've enjoyed it."

"You're welcome, Annie. Now, I suggest we return to the house and have some lunch. James, are you able to join us?"

"Yes, thank you, Lady Margery, and I'd like to hear a little about Devon, if I may. It's a place I've never visited and would like to do so at some point, for I may feature it in my next book."

"Oh, are you an author, James?"

"Yes, I've written three books, but they're all set in London, and I would like the next one to be in a rural setting."

"Perhaps you could visit us at Hartford Manor and do some research?"

The young man beamed at Annie in delight.

"I'd like that, thank you."

CHAPTER 20

Despite her differences with her husband, Annie enjoyed her trip to London, particularly the excursions with Lady Margery and the other visitors, whilst Robert kindled his business opportunities. Lady Margery was familiar with the capital and enjoyed showing it off to her friends. Being such a wealthy lady, she and her companions enjoyed every comfort and rode in style wherever they went. However, as the days went by, she became increasingly concerned about James's interest in Annie, a married woman.

Eventually, the celebrations and the holiday came to an end, and it was time for the visitors to depart. Although fond of James, it was with some relief that Lady Margery waved goodbye to him as he departed to visit other friends in the city. However, she was aware that Annie had invited him to visit Hartford Manor and decided to warn Robert of the obvious attraction the young Scotsman had developed for his wife. Taking her nephew to one side, she had a quiet word.

"Robert, I don't like to interfere, but I feel I must warn you about something. I know you and Annie are not getting along at the moment; that's easy for everyone to see, and I urge you to resolve the matter soon. It hasn't helped that Annie feels you have neglected her while in London, although you know she's uncomfortable away from her familiar surroundings, and she's understandably angry. She's become friendly with James and is enjoying his company, and I'm sure that's all it is on her part, but I'm concerned that he's showing so much interest in a married woman, and he really should know better. You need to put things right between you and Annie and spend more time with her."

"Things are strained between Annie and me, I confess, and I know I've neglected her, but not from choice. I feel guilty about it, but you see, I've taken out a substantial loan to cover the cost of the alterations to the Manor House, and I need to obtain as much business as I can to pay it back."

"Oh, Robert, why didn't you ask me if you needed money?"

"I like to be independent, and it will be fine, but I prefer to repay any money I owe as quickly as possible, if only to reduce the crippling interest charges. Once the hunting weekends become established, I'm confident they will make a handsome profit, but I must concentrate on procuring bookings for a few months."

"Does Annie know this?"

"She knows I've borrowed some money but has no idea how much. I don't usually keep anything from her, but having been so poor for most of her life, she doesn't understand how these things work, and she would be terribly worried to think we're in so much debt. I haven't told her, and I don't want you to."

"I understand your motives, but it might be best to tell her the truth. She's annoyed with you about the issue of your mother wanting to see Danny, and she doesn't understand why you seem to be neglecting her. It's not good, my boy, and she's invited James to stay with you in Hartford to research the area for his next book. I don't think you should leave them on their own too much; it's asking for trouble."

"I trust Annie completely; she would never be unfaithful to me."

"I'm sure you're right, but nevertheless, I'm not sure James understands that. I suspect he's noticed the rift between you and hopes she's falling for him. Think about it, anyway, and if possible, find a solution to the problem concerning Danny."

"I wish I could, but it seems impossible to keep everyone happy."

Robert, Sam, Peter, and Christopher were to return to Eggleston Station, where Dodger Watkins, the carriage driver from Hartford Manor, would collect them. Sam, Peter, and Christopher planned to stay a few days at the Manor House, allowing them the opportunity to visit friends and relatives in the village. Sam would then return to Sugworthy Farm, and his son, Marrok and family, and Peter and Christopher to Primrose Cottage on Lady Margery's Enderby estate, where they lived with Christopher's wife, Clarice, and baby son, Peter. In truth, Christopher would have preferred to return to his family straight away, but could not abandon his grandfather, for whom he was a carer.

Annie and Lady Margery were to depart the train at Thorverton station and travel to Grantley House in Brampford Speke. Annie had explained to Lady Margery that her Aunty Emily and Uncle Hubert were having trouble with their servants, and she was more than willing to help.

At Thorverton station, the porter assisted Lady Margery and Annie from the train and escorted them and their luggage to a waiting carriage, driven by Hubert March. In no time, they were on their way to Grantley House.

"How are Granny and Grandad, Uncle Hubert? Has Grandad recovered from his illness?"

"He's well on the mend, my dear, and there's no need to fret. He's been out of bed for a few days, and he and Betsey are hoping to return to Hartford soon."

"That's good, and how about Aunty Emily and Jonnie, and Millie and Willie, and Edward?"

"Yes, they're all well, thank you, and looking forward to seeing you, Annie."

"Have you settled into Grantley House, now, Mr March?"

"Call me Hubert, please. Well, yes and no. It's a grand house, and we want for nothing, but we miss Hilldale Farm and its cosy rooms. Grantley House is enormous, and we're not accustomed to managing household staff. Unfortunately, we have to live there to care for Jonathan, as it was stipulated in his father's will that he must reside there. It seems strange to me to make a demand like that. I mean, why does it matter where the lad lives?"

"Maybe his father wanted him to get used to living there now as a child, to fulfil his rightful place in society when he's older, but then, all the circumstances surrounding Sir Edgar's affairs were unusual. Has any more been heard of Lady Lilliana?"

"I believe she avoided jail and is living in her townhouse in London, though her lover, Sir Clive Robinson, is serving a lengthy sentence in Newgate. I wouldn't be surprised if he gets released early, though. Money often talks if you're rich enough."

"Yes, that can happen. Annie mentioned that the staff at the house are not paying you the respect you deserve; we'll have to see about that."

"It's mainly the housekeeper, Mrs Watson, and the butler, Mr Watson, we're having trouble with. They're husband and wife, and I believe they moved to the house with Lady Lilliana when she arrived as a new bride, or so she thought, and so, of course, they're loyal to her."

"Don't worry, Hubert, I'm sure we can get it sorted out; I've been dealing with staff all my life, and if they don't like their new employers, there will be plenty of folk willing to replace them. Tell me, why are you driving the carriage? Are there no drivers employed at Grantley House, or are they being difficult as well?"

"Oh, yes, there are drivers, and they're willing, but I don't have enough to do, and I love driving this carriage with these wonderful horses. I had to allow a footman to come with me, but I could have managed."

"Have you visited Grantley House before, Aunty Margery?"

"No, not that I can recall, though I believe I met Sir Edgar and Lady Lilliana once or twice at functions in London. I certainly didn't know either of them well."

"Here we are then, Grantley House. Emily has invited Millie, Willie and Edward to join us for a meal, so it will be an excellent opportunity for you all to catch up with one another."

Hubert stopped the carriage outside the front of the house, and the footman assisted the passengers to alight. They mounted the steps to where the family greeted them, and Mr Watson held the front door open, but remained silent, with a surly expression as the ladies passed through. Lady Margery, bringing up the rear of the party, stopped and surveyed the man, haughtily.

"May I ask if you are the butler, sir?"

"I am, ma'am."

"I see, and what is your name?"

"Watson, ma'am."

"Well, Watson, it's customary in my household to welcome visitors with a smile and a few words. Is that not how you are used to behaving?"

"Of course, ma'am; I beg your pardon."

"I should think so. Ensure you pay attention to such details in the future, and while we're on the subject of details, I suggest your shoes could do with a polish, and a clean shirt would not go amiss. I'm accustomed to higher standards. Do not let me see you looking slovenly again, do you understand?"

The butler, his face beetroot red from embarrassment and indignation, replied humbly, much to the amusement of a passing maid who hurried away with a smirk on her face, no doubt to divulge this titbit of gossip to the kitchen staff.

Emily led the party into the drawing room, where Ned was seated in an armchair, his feet resting on a footstool and a blanket across his legs. She closed the door, a wide grin on her face, while the others exploded with laughter.

"Oh, Margery, I am going to enjoy you staying here. I don't know how I kept a straight face."

Annie ran to Ned and embraced him. "Thank goodness, you're looking so much better, Grandad; you had me so worried. Are you feeling well enough to travel back to Hartford in a few days?"

"Yes, thank you. Betsey's potion worked its magic, and I'm fine again now. We've had a wonderful time, but we're ready to go home to our little cottage, aren't we, my dear?"

"Yes, we've loved spending time with everyone here, but there's no place like home. Perhaps you, Emily, Hubert, and Jonnie can spend a little time in Hartford when Jonnie has finished school for the summer. He doesn't have to live here all the time, does he?"

"No, he can come and go as he pleases, but he should live here most of the time."

"Did you change schools, Jonnie?"

"Yes, I did. In the morning, Grandad takes me to Newton St Cyres School on the pony and trap and then fetches me again in the afternoon, so I go to school with Albert, Rosie, and Walter. I like it much better than Brampford Speke school, and all of Walter's friends are my friends now as well. A few of them are coming here to play on Saturday; I can't wait."

"And how about you, Millie? Are you keeping well? I see you have a small bump to show you're with child."

Millie placed her hand protectively on her abdomen and smiled.

"I'm feeling a little nauseous in the mornings, but it's improving, and this little one is beginning to move, or at least I think it is; I keep feeling the tiniest flutter and then it stops."

Betsey, Emily, and Annie all smiled knowingly. "Yes, that will be the baby moving, and you're looking well, my dear."

Over the next few days, Lady Margery continued her campaign to bring the household staff under control. The younger maids, kitchen workers, and footmen were courteous and pleasant, and as Emily and Hubert had said, it was only the elderly Mr and Mrs Watson whose behaviour exhibited a marked lack of respect, though, in their prestigious positions as butler and housekeeper, they were in command of the others and should have set a good example.

On the first morning of their stay, Lady Margery was shocked at the limited choice for breakfast and dissatisfied that the cutlery was not gleaming. She said nothing, but later invited Emily and Betsey to show her and Annie around the house. In each room they entered, the elderly lady examined every detail with interest, noting the cobwebs in the corners, the lacklustre appearance of the ancient oak furniture, the absence of a cheery fire, and the musty smell in many rooms. The magnificent wooden carvings on the sweeping staircase, in particular, had not seen a duster for some time. After completing their tour, the ladies enjoyed coffee and cake on the sunny balcony with Hubert and Ned, and Lady Margery gave her verdict.

"That was an interesting tour of the house; thank you. It's a wonderful dwelling, but it's not being efficiently cared for, as I'm sure you ladies already know. It's in need of a thorough clean, and the household staff would benefit from new uniforms to smarten them up and boost their self-esteem. I think you must make a choice. Do you want the current butler and housekeeper to remain? Or, would it be better to seek new employees? Those in post are not doing their jobs properly, though whether that's because they can't, or won't, I don't know. The Watsons are of an age when they might be considering retirement, and, though they do not deserve it, the promise of a small lump sum might make them amenable to that. Alternatively, they could simply be dismissed, though I suspect their disappointing behaviour is due to misplaced loyalty to Lady Lilliana, who was, as we know, shabbily treated by her bigamous husband. Either way, I'm willing to help. Personally, I think they will find it difficult to continue in their posts, and it's time to seek new employees."

"My goodness, you don't beat about the bush, Margery. I don't know what you think, Hubert, but I'd rather have new employees. I don't think the Watsons will ever take to us, and I feel quite uncomfortable living here."

"Yes, I agree, Emily, and I think what Margery has said is true. They will never forgive what happened to Lady Lilliana, although none of it is our fault, but where would we find a new butler and housekeeper?"

"That's easy, Hubert. Emily and I can interview the existing staff to determine if any have the necessary experience, and if not, we can advertise, although that will take longer. We'll likely find suitable people already working here, as the existing butler and housekeeper have been here for many years. How about the cook? Is the food good, and has she been here for a while?"

"Yes, we can't fault the food, and I believe Mrs Thompson has been here for a long time. I've only spoken to her a few times, but she was friendly and polite."

"In that case, I suggest we have a discreet chat with Mrs Thompson as soon as possible."

CHAPTER 21

Mrs Thompson was in her mid-fifties and more than a little concerned at being called into the study by her employers. She tentatively knocked on the door and entered nervously when invited to do so. Hubert was content for Emily and Lady Margery to handle the matter, and it was agreed that Margery would do most of the talking, as she was the more confident of the two.

"Come in, Mrs Thompson. There's nothing to worry about, and please take a seat. I must congratulate you on your cooking, for I have enjoyed the food at Grantley House immensely during my visit, though I confess I was surprised there was so little choice at breakfast."

"Thank you, ma'am. I'm afraid the choice of food is the best I can provide since Mrs Watson cut my allowance for supplies."

"I see. I wondered if that was the case, and thank you for explaining. We would like your advice on a staffing matter, but it is essential that we can rely on your discretion. May we do that? If we share a confidence with you, can we trust you to keep it to yourself?"

"Oh, yes, ma'am, I know how to keep my mouth shut, if I have to."

"Exactly. In that case, if for some reason, Mr and Mrs Watson decided to retire, are there any existing members of the household staff that you think could step up to replace them? I believe you have worked here for some considerable time, and so you will know that better than anyone."

The cook was shocked, but recovered herself and considered the matter.

"Yes, I think so. Susan Smith, who has been the deputy housekeeper for several years, would be a suitable candidate for the post. She's kind and reliable and knows as much about running this house as Mrs Watson. She's never married, and this house is her life. I believe her parents worked here, and she was born on the Grantley estate."

"She didn't arrive at the house with Lady Lilliana, then?"

"No, as I say, she's been here all her life."

"How about a butler? Does anyone spring to mind?"

Yes, I would have no hesitation in recommending Jim Carpenter. He's been the head footman for over ten years and stands in for Mr Watson when he has a day off, or if he's ill."

"Good, so he didn't come here with Lady Lilliana either, then?"

"No, she moved in much longer ago, following her marriage to, er, well, to Sir Edgar."

"It's all right, Mrs Thompson. I understand the situation. You have been extremely helpful, thank you, but please keep this conversation strictly to yourself. Is that understood?"

"Yes, ma'am, of course."

As the door closed behind the cook, Lady Margery glanced at Emily and smiled.

"There, that wasn't difficult, was it? Do you know the people that Mrs Thompson has recommended, and if so, do you think they're suitable?"

"Yes, I do. They're both willing and pleasant, and I think you're right; life would be so much easier if the current housekeeper and butler were no longer here. I find them intimidating."

"Shall we proceed then? I suggest we interview Susan Smith and Jim Carpenter first to see if they would like to be promoted, and then we can move on to dealing with the Watsons. Would you be happy to pay them a small lump sum in recognition of their long service? I think it would make matters progress more smoothly."

"Yes, I wouldn't like to turn them away with no future employment, for I'm sure they gave years of faithful service to Lady Lilliana. The Grantley solicitor has provided a generous allowance for Hubert and me to use for whatever we think is necessary, but we've barely touched the money."

"Excellent. We should be able to expedite the matter within the day, then, with a bit of luck."

Susan Smith and Jim Carpenter were interviewed separately and were thrilled and surprised to be offered a promotion, which they both eagerly accepted. Lady Margery emphasised the need to make Hubert, Emily, and Jonathan feel welcome in their new home and to assist them in any way possible. She felt both employees understood what she was getting at, knowing how unhelpful the current butler and housekeeper had been to the new owners. They were told they would be starting the next day, and that in the case of Susan Smith, Lady Margery would expect to see the entire house spick and span on her next visit.

"Oh, yes, ma'am, I'll do my best to ensure it will be. I love this house, and it hasn't been kept as I would like recently. It will be a pleasure to restore it to its former glory."

"Are there enough staff to make that possible?"

"No, ma'am, and that's the problem. A few maids didn't get along with Mr and Mrs Watson, so they sought other employment, and they've never been replaced. It's put a lot of pressure on the remaining staff, which is why the house isn't looking its best. It's not that we don't all love

Grantley House, but it's a large establishment and there aren't enough hours in the day for us to keep it as we would like."

"I wondered if that was the case, for I've noticed the lack of staff. How many additional maids are required?"

"Three have left in the last few months, and before that, when Lady Lilliana was in residence, standards were much higher; she would not have tolerated things the way they are now."

"I see. In that case, may I leave you to interview three new maids and have them start as soon as possible? Do you think you'll have any difficulty in finding suitable candidates?"

"No, ma'am, there are plenty of folk looking for work, and I can think of two reliable girls straight away."

"Excellent; then please put matters in hand. In your new role, you will also be responsible for managing the accounts and the household budget, and I suspect you may find some discrepancies. It appears that the amount allocated to Mrs Thompson for food supplies was reduced some time ago, and I would like you to restore it to its original amount. I suggest you discuss this with the cook and let Mrs March know if there are any problems. Thank you, Miss Smith; you may go, and please ask Mr and Mrs Watson to join us."

The two senior members of staff were curious why some of their colleagues were being summoned to the study, and grew concerned when they refused to divulge the reason. When bidden, they entered the room together in some trepidation, for they had the measure of Lady Montgomery and knew she was not a lady to suffer fools gladly.

"Ah, Mr and Mrs Watson; thank you for coming. We won't keep you long."

Lady Margery did not offer the two employees a seat but left them standing uncomfortably before the desk.

"It has come to my notice that you have not been affording the new owners of Grantley House the service and respect they deserve, and I'm afraid your employment is to be terminated immediately."

The butler and the housekeeper gasped, and a stunned Mr Watson recovered himself first and opened his mouth to speak, but Lady Margery held up her hand.

"Let me stop you there, sir. I'm not interested in your apologies or the reasons for your behaviour, though I understand that you have worked here for a long time and suspect you are loyal to your former employer. Now, you are both approaching a time when you might be considering retirement in the not-so-distant future, and in recognition of your long service, Mr and Mrs March are willing to offer you a small lump sum to make that more comfortable. I would say it is far more than you deserve, considering how you have treated them, and I strongly suspect that you have been stealing money from the household budget since Lady Lilliana's departure. No matter; that problem should be resolved when you leave. Now, please pack your belongings, then return here to collect your pay. You are dismissed."

Without a further word, the stunned employees left the room, and Lady Margery turned to Emily with a broad smile.

A short while later, Mr and Mrs Watson were seen struggling down the driveway carrying bags and pushing a small handcart laden with their belongings. Lady Margery and Emily watched them go as they entertained Hubert, Annie, Betsey, and Ned by telling them of the priceless expressions on their former employees' faces as they were dismissed.

A few days later, Annie, Lady Margery, Betsey and Ned travelled back to Hartford together in the Grantley carriage, which Ned said he would prefer to the train. There had been a particularly dry spell of weather over the last few weeks, and with the roads in a reasonable condition, the journey was smoother than it might otherwise have been. However, the distance involved necessitated an overnight stop at The Portsmouth Arms near Umberleigh to avoid the passengers becoming too exhausted. The next day, they were on their way after breakfast and arrived back in Hartford at four o'clock.

The carriage dropped Betsey and Ned off at The Red Lion Inn, where they wanted to visit Fred and Charlotte and their family and partake of an evening meal before continuing on to Sunset Cottage. It then continued on to Hartford Manor, where Lady Margery planned to reside for a few days before returning to Enderby House.

Having ensured Lady Margery was attended to and having established that Robert was, as expected, out and about on the estate, Annie hurried to the nursery to see her children. They were delighted to see their mother, and she spent the next hour playing with them, giving them their tea, and helping Naomi, their nursemaid, to bathe them. Having tucked the twins into bed and read Selina a story, she was walking down the stairs as Robert entered the hallway.

"Oh, Annie, I'm so glad to see you! Did you have a pleasant journey?"

"Yes, not bad, thank you, and our stay at The Portsmouth Arms was comfortable enough last night. Aunty Margery has retired to her room to rest and would like to take her evening meal there. How are you? Is everything all right here?"

"Yes, all good; I've missed you so much."

Robert took Annie's hand and led her into the study, where they spent most evenings. On closing the door, he pulled her to him and kissed her, hoping their differences could be put aside. Annie returned his embrace, but moved away sooner than she would normally have done.

"I'm glad to be home, though I enjoyed sightseeing in London and seeing the Jubilee celebrations. Thankfully, Grandad is back to his usual self, and Aunty Margery has resolved the staffing difficulties that Aunty Emily and Uncle

Hubert were having at Grantley House. Any news here? Have you seen your parents since you returned?"

"I saw Papa last week, but Mama and Sarah only got back from London a day or two ago, and I haven't seen them yet. There's a letter waiting for you on the sideboard; were you expecting one?"

Annie was tempted to ask if there were any developments concerning Danny, but decided to leave that for another time.

"No, and I can't think who would be writing to me as I've only just left Aunty Emily and the rest of them. Could you pass it to me, please? Thanks. Oh, it's from James McIntyre, you know the young man we met in London."

Robert scowled. "Yes, I know. What does he want?"

"When we were in London, he mentioned that he wants to base his next book in Devon and was considering visiting the county to do some research. He's asking if he can come and stay for a week or two. That would be all right, wouldn't it? He was kind enough to look after me while you were busy with all your meetings."

"Yes, I noticed how well you both got along. I'm not keen, to be honest. We could do with some time to ourselves without more visitors around. Surely he could stay at The Red Lion Inn; that would be much better for his research."

"I'm afraid I gave him the impression he could stay here; I didn't think you'd mind."

"It might have been nice if you'd asked me."

"Well, as I barely saw you in London, that would have been difficult. Do you want me to reply and tell him he can't stay here? It would be rather rude."

"No, it's too late now, but I'm not happy about it."

CHAPTER 22

Eli Cutcliffe was finding living in the pigsty at the bottom of the garden of the Lodge House relatively comfortable, for the weather was warmer, and he no longer shivered all through the night. Helen, Stephen, and Danny ensured he had plenty to eat, and their mother frequently remarked that her children were forever hungry. The boy was lonely, though, for he spent many hours alone and was eager to find his father as soon as possible.

Stephen had pointed out the cottage where John and Noeleen lived, and that it was John's habit to return home for his lunch. Having surveyed the route between the Hartford estate where John worked and his cottage, Eli selected a quiet corner with sufficient bushes for him to wait unobserved. Having no idea of the time, and with nothing better to do, Eli was in position far too early and waited impatiently. He was hungry, for the children had not had the opportunity to take him any food that morning. He always ate everything they provided straight away for fear of attracting more rats and mice, which he knew shared his dwelling.

As he lay quietly in the long grass, a delicious aroma reached his nostrils, making him salivate and his belly rumble, and he realised that the old woman's cottage, where he had stolen a cake a few weeks earlier, was only a stone's throw away. The temptation was too great, and he decided he must risk missing John to find something to eat. After all, he could always lie in wait for his father another day.

He crept along the path to the back door, but this time it was closed, and he gently lifted the latch and pushed it open as quietly as he could. Unfortunately, it had been some years since the hinges were last oiled, and to his horror, the door creaked loudly.

"Who's there? Help! Can you help me? Please, come in; I've fallen and I can't get up."

The boy eyed the hot pasties cooling on a rack and was torn between making a quick getaway with something to fill his hungry belly and helping the old lady. He hesitated, then crept over to the table.

"Oh, please, come in. I can hear you out there. I need a hand to get back on my feet."

Deciding he couldn't abandon the old woman, Eli peered around the door into the sitting room, where he saw Nancy Brookes lying on the floor, the blood from a cut on her head running into her eyes, and her walking stick out of reach.

"Hello, my dear; don't be frightened. I'm in no position to hurt you; is it you who's been stealing my food? If so, it doesn't matter. If you help me, you can take what you like, and I promise you I won't tell the policeman. Can you give me a hand?"

Eli was not a bad boy at heart, and he knew he couldn't run off and leave this helpless old lady lying there. He went towards her, picking up her walking stick as he passed and knelt beside her.

"Thank you, son. I'm so grateful. Could you pass me that damp cloth by the sink so that I can wipe this blood out of my eyes? I must have knocked myself out, for I don't know how long I've been lying here."

"I don't think you've been there long; the pasties smell like they're not long out of the oven."

He passed her the cloth, and she mopped the cut, but could not see what she was doing.

"Shall I clean it up for you? Perhaps if I hold the cloth on the wound for a few minutes, it will stop the bleeding; that's what Ma used to do when she'd taken a beating."

Nancy nodded gratefully, thinking this poor lad had known some difficult times. After a few minutes, he gently removed the compress and was relieved to see that the bleeding had stopped.

"There, I think it's stopped. Shall I help you up?"

"Yes, please, though there's not much to you; I don't know if we'll manage it. Perhaps if you can help me onto my knees, I might be able to grab hold of the table and haul myself up."

After much wincing at the pain in her legs and a considerable effort from Eli, the boy eventually got the old woman onto her knees. She paused as the room swam before her, but then smiled weakly before grabbing the edge of the table and struggling to heave herself up. With the boy supporting her, she finally regained her feet, and he quickly pushed a chair under her.

"Oh, thank God, you came along, lad. I was worried I might lie there for days, for I never know when I'll next have a visitor. Now, if you make us a cup of tea, we'll eat a pasty together. Two, if you like."

While the boy pulled the kettle forward on the stove to boil, and, following Nancy's directions, put the tea leaves into the pink china teapot, Nancy slowly got to her feet and tried a couple of steps. Relieved that nothing was broken, she sank thankfully into her favourite armchair beside the stove and lifted her feet onto the footstool.

Eli made them both a strong cup of tea and put two pasties on plates, one for each of them, before sitting in the armchair opposite her.

"Eat up, then, lad. You've earned your pasty today. Is it you who's been stealing my food? You can tell me the truth, for I won't report you after helping me this morning."

"Yes, I'm sorry. I'm not normally a thief, but I've had to steal to eat for the last few weeks. Perhaps I could do a few jobs to make up for it?"

"Yes, maybe, but why are you in such dire straits? Where are your parents?"

"Well, Ma's dead, and the man I thought was my father turned out not to be."

"How did you find that out?"

"Ma told me as she lay dying. Jem has always treated us badly, even my brothers and sisters, who are his, but especially me, as I'm the oldest. Ma told me she was expecting me before she married Jem, and when I was born early, he guessed I wasn't his and beat the truth out of her. She reckoned if I stayed after she'd passed on, he'd treat me even worse, so she told me to leave and try to find my real father."

"Oh, so you know who he is?"

Yes, she wasn't a prostitute. She told me he's called John Cutcliffe and that he used to work on the Hartford estate."

Nancy took a sharp breath. "John Cutcliffe, you say? How old are you, and what's your name?"

"I'm called Eli and I think I'm about ten."

"So that would mean you were born in 1877, back when John was married to his first wife, Hannah."

"You know John Cutcliffe, then?"

"Aye, I know him, and I ought to for he's my son, and if what you tell me is right, then you're my grandson!"

"Oh, my goodness, I'm so glad I helped you. Can you arrange for me to meet my father? I was lying in wait for him to pass on his way home for his dinner, when I smelt your pasties. I'm hoping he might give me a home when I tell him about Ma."

"Where are you living?"

"I'd rather not say, if you don't mind. I've made friends with some children in the village, and they're letting me stay in a tumbledown old building in their garden. They've been giving me food when they get the chance, and I don't want to get them into trouble."

"Fair enough. Have you seen your father then?"

"Yes, someone pointed him out to me when I went to the cricket match at the jubilee party. I heard he's married again and lives in a cottage down the road. I thought it best to talk to him on his own first, for his wife might not be pleased to hear he has another son."

"No, she won't be; I can assure you of that. It's a good job you were born before John married Noeleen, for she's a strictly religious woman with high morals, and she would not tolerate John playing around. Mind you, I never knew he did. I thought he'd always been a faithful husband to Hannah."

"Ma didn't know much about him but said he treated her kindly, and she only saw him once. She said he'd gone to the Barnstaple Fair and was too drunk to ride home. She was having a difficult time, and after enjoying a few drinks with him, they ended up spending the night together. That's how she was sure I was his, cos she didn't marry Jem until about six weeks later and knew she was already carrying a child."

"What a strange day this has been. First, I fall and hurt myself, and then I find out I have a grandson. If what you say is true, you're John's only son, for he lost his first wife, Hannah, son Tommy, and daughter Mary in the diphtheria epidemic back in 1880. He has two other daughters, though: Daisy, who's now out at work, and Rachael, who's still in school. You might have seen her at the jubilee celebrations, for she was chosen as the Jubilee Queen. I can see a likeness between you and her, now I think about it."

"When do you think I can see my dad? I don't like living where I am, cos I'm on my own so much and I get bored. There are rats, too, and it will be too cold in the winter. I hope he'll take me in, for I have nowhere else to go. Ma did say if Dad didn't want to know me, to try to get a job or go to the workhouse, but I don't want to go there if I can help it."

"I'm not sure he'll take you in, for he won't want his wife to know about you, but I think I might have a solution. If he'd pay me for your keep, you could live here with me. What do you think? Would you like that? It would give you a roof over your head, and as you can see, I'm unsteady on my feet these days and could do with some help."

"Ooh, yes, I'd love to live with you. I promise you wouldn't regret it, and I'd be happy to look after you. I've never had a granny or a grandad, but I'd like that."

"Well, he should pay for his mistakes, so I shall expect him to stump up some money for your keep because I struggle to make ends meet as it is. Fortunately, I married for a second time, and my husband, Cecil, was not badly off and owned this cottage. Sadly, he died a few years ago, and I'm having to eke out the little bit of savings he left me and hope it will last until I meet my Maker. Come back tomorrow morning, and you can wait here to meet John. I'll send him a message to let him know I'd like to see him. He always comes if he knows I need him."

CHAPTER 23

Later that day, when she had recovered a little from the shock of her fall, Nancy called on her next-door neighbour, Esther Symons, a kindly soul who kept an eye on the old woman. Esther's husband, Sam, worked on the Hartford estate with John Cutcliffe, and Nancy asked if he could pass a message to John to call in at lunchtime the next day.

Esther was breast-feeding her baby daughter, a little girl called Susie, whilst two-year-old Tim and four-year-old Robin played with some bricks. Seeing the cut on her neighbour's head, she insisted Nancy sit down and have a cup of tea, assuring her that, of course, Sam would deliver the message in the morning.

Nancy was delighted to see that the new arrival was thriving, and the two boys were healthy, for she knew Sam and Esther had lost all five of their children in the terrible outbreak of diphtheria. The same epidemic that had taken her two grandchildren and their mother. After having a friendly chat and enjoying a piece of cake with her cup of tea, Nancy went home and spent the evening wondering how her son would take the news that he had a son.

The next day, Eli arrived at Nancy's cottage at nine o'clock in the morning, and she opened the door in surprise.

"You're early, lad. I thought you were coming around lunchtime."

"Well, I have nothing to do, so I thought maybe I could help you with a few jobs in return for the food I stole; how's your head today?"

"It throbs a bit, but I'm all right, thank you. That's kind of you, Eli, and yes, I can certainly find you something to do. Could you chop some firewood for me and fill up my basket? That would be a big help, for I'm still a bit unsteady on my pins this morning."

Nancy and her new grandson spent a pleasant morning together, and she was delighted to find that he was a hard worker. Having chopped a large pile of firewood, he stacked it near her Bodley stove, then fed the chickens, dug potatoes in the garden, and walked to the shop to fetch some shopping. Eli knew a good thing when he saw it, and his intention was to make himself indispensable. His plan was working well, and by mid-morning, Nancy was hoping John would agree to her suggestion of the lad living with her, for she could see that life would be so much easier with him around.

"It's time for a break, Eli. Sit down for a few minutes and have a mug of milk and a few biscuits. Now, when John comes later, I think it would be best if I speak to him on my own first and then introduce you; is that all right with you?"

"Aye, whatever you think's best. Where do you want me to go while you talk to him?"

"I thought you could do a bit of weeding in the garden, then I can give you a shout when I need you to come in."

Eli enjoyed working in the garden, though Nancy had to hobble outside and tell him which plants were weeds and which ones were crops. Before old age and rheumatism had set in, limiting her mobility, Nancy was a keen gardener, and it grieved her to see so many weeds between her flowers and vegetables. John kindly planted crops for her each year and tried to keep on top of the weeding, but with his own garden to attend to as well as his full-time job, he had little time to spare, and her garden was always a little neglected.

Not long after midday, John arrived and was surprised to see a young lad weeding the garden. He let himself in through the kitchen door, and when he saw the wound on his mother's head, he exclaimed in horror.

"Oh, Mum, have you had another fall? That looks sore."

"Aye, I don't know what happened, but I woke up on the floor yesterday; I'd probably still be there if it wasn't for that young lad outside."

"I saw him weeding the garden, but I didn't recognise him. What was he doing here yesterday to find you on the floor?"

"I think you'd better sit down, lad, for it's a long story, and it's why I wanted to see you. The boy is called Eli, and he's been stealing food from my kitchen and other folk in the village for a few weeks now."

"Well, he won't do it again when he's felt the back of my hand! He needs to be taught a lesson."

"No, wait until I've told you everything before you judge him, for as usual, there are two sides to every story. He was waiting outside, hoping to have a word with you as you passed on your way home to lunch yesterday, and he smelt my pasties that I'd just taken out of the oven. He let himself in the back door, intending to steal one, and I called out to him for help as I was on the floor and couldn't get up. Luckily, he came to my rescue, attended to my cut that was bleeding, and helped me up."

"What did he want with me? I don't know him."

"Do you remember going to Barnstaple Fair about ten years ago, having too much to drink and staying the night with a young girl called Louisa?"

"Aye, I do, and I'm not proud of it. I drank a lot back then, and I'd had a bit too much that day and was too drunk to ride home. I got chatting with Louisa in one of the inns. She'd had a row with her boyfriend and was a bit fed up, and we hit it off. It was never intended, but seeing how drunk I was, she allowed me to stay the night at her place, and well, one thing led to another, like it does sometimes. I'd never been unfaithful to Hannah before that, or since, and certainly not while I've been married to Noeleen, and as you know, I barely drink these days. But how do you know about Louisa, and why do you ask?"

"They say your sins will find you out, and that's what's happened here. I'm afraid there were consequences of your night with Louisa, and he's outside weeding my garden. Eli is your son, John."

"What! No, he can't be. Louisa never contacted me to tell me she was with child."

"No, she didn't because she made it up with her boyfriend and married Jem six weeks later, knowing she was already carrying your child. She didn't tell him, but when the baby arrived earlier than expected, he was suspicious and beat the truth out of her. Marrying Jem turned out to be the worst thing she ever did, for he treated her and all their children badly, but especially Eli, who he knew wasn't his."

"Oh, no, I'm sorry to hear that, for she was a warm and kind-hearted girl. Where is she now?"

"She passed away from one beating too many by the sound of it, but before she died, she told Eli the truth about you being his father and told him to find you. Eli's hoping you'll give him a home, John."

John passed a hand over his eyes and stared at his mother in disbelief.

"How can I be sure he's mine, though?"

"I think he is, John. He looks like Rachael, and if you remember this woman, then it sounds as if her story is true."

"That's all very well, but how can I explain this to Noeleen? You know what she's like. She'll fly off the handle, even if this did happen before I knew her."

"I have a suggestion, and that is that Eli lives here with me. I could do with his help around the house, and he's a friendly lad, willing and kind. It would be reassuring for me to have someone else living here as I get older, in case I fall again, but you'd have to pay for his keep. I struggle to make ends meet these days, and it's been like that since I lost Cecil. As you know, I'd have taken Daisy and Rachael in if I could after Hannah died, but it was impossible. You'll get your money back one day, though, because you're my only living child, and one day, when I'm gone, this cottage will belong to you."

"Well, if you're sure, then that sounds like the perfect solution. I'll have to work extra hours, for Noeleen will notice if I give her less money, but I'd like to do right by the lad, for I liked his mother, and if she sent him to find me, I'll not shirk my responsibilities."

"Good. You'd better call him in for some dinner then."

Eli nervously entered the kitchen and observed the large man standing before him.

"Don't worry, Eli, everything will be all right. This is your father, John."

John beamed, held out his hand, and ruffled Eli's hair, which he noted was the same colour as Louisa's unruly blond curls.

"Hello lad, my mother's right, you do look like our Rachael. It's nice to meet you, Eli. Until today, I didn't know you existed, but I was fond of your mother. She was a kind soul, although I only knew her for a few hours, and I'll do right by you. I lost my other son, Tommy, and I'm so glad you've found me."

CHAPTER 24

Eli was delighted with the way things had turned out and couldn't quite believe he would be living in such a cosy cottage with a pleasant old lady, who told him he must call her Aunty Nancy. As John did not want Noeleen to know his guilty secret, Nancy suggested passing Eli off as a distant relative of her late husband, Cecil, and that his name would be Eli Brookes. Eli was a little disappointed not to be called Eli Cutcliffe after his father, but willing to go along with the charade if it meant he had a roof over his head and food in his belly.

After John returned to work that afternoon, Nancy took the boy upstairs and, together, they made up a single bed in the spare bedroom. She asked him if he had any belongings to bring.

"No, I only have the clothes I stand up in, but I must go back to where I've been staying and tell the children who've been looking after me what's happened. I need to tell them I'm called Eli Brookes too, because I told them John Cutcliffe is my father."

"Oh dear, did you? That's a shame. Do you think they'll keep their mouths shut? Maybe you could say you were mistaken, but I've offered you a home anyway, to keep me company. You could tell them how you found me lying on the floor."

Not wanting to jeopardise his position with his granny, the boy nodded. "Yes, I'll do that."

"Have you ever been to school, Eli? Can you read and write?"

"No, I've never been. I always had to stay at home and help Ma with the little ones. Then, when I was eight, Jem got me a job as an errand boy with the local butcher, and I used to deliver the meat. I wonder what will happen to my brothers and sisters now because I can't see Jem looking after them; poor little blighters."

"That is a worry, but there's nothing you can do about it. How many children were there?"

"Another five after me. The baby, Rosie, was only six months old when Ma died. What do you think will happen to them? I didn't tell them I was going because I knew they'd be upset and want to go with me."

"Unless there are any relatives to take them in, I expect they'll be taken to the workhouse, but that may be the best thing for them. It's not a great life there, but they'd be fed, clothed, and educated and probably better cared for than where they are now. Next week, I'll talk to Mr Atkins, the headmaster at the school and find out when you can start."

"Oh, it's all right; I'm not bothered about going to school, thank you. Jem always said it was a waste of time; he couldn't read or write, and he said it had never done him any harm."

"No, I must insist that you attend school, Eli, for you need to do better in life than Jem, and for that, you need an education. I can help you, and we'll have you reading and writing in no time. Anyway, all your friends will be there, so I'm sure you'll enjoy it once you get used to it. Now, go and tell your friends that you'll be staying here tonight and then come back for your tea. I have a friend coming for a chat this afternoon, and she has a big family, so I'm going to ask her if she has any old clothes going spare because the ones you're wearing are falling off you. You can have a scrub in the bath later, too. I don't want to be rude, but you don't smell so sweet."

Eli was perturbed at Nancy's plans for him. He didn't remember ever having a bath, and he certainly had no wish to attend school. However, he decided that the benefits outweighed the negatives, and if he had to suffer such indignities, then it would be worth it for a warm bed and regular meals. By the time he reached the old pigsty, the children had finished school for the day, and before long, he was visited by Stephen, Helen, and Danny, and he told them of his stroke of luck.

"So, you're not John Cutcliffe's son, then? It's funny because you do look like his daughter, Rachael."

"Well, it seems not, so Ma must have got that wrong, but it doesn't matter. Even if I were his son, I don't suppose he'd have wanted to know me. I'm glad I found the old woman on the floor and helped her, though. She's a kind lady and said that if I do odd jobs around the house, I can stay there and she'll take care of me. It'll be a better home than I've ever known, with no Jem to knock me about. She says I'm to be known as Eli Brookes, and I have to call her Aunty Nancy. The only trouble is, she says, I have to take a bath and go to school. I don't like the sound of that. Have you ever bathed?"

"Yes, of course. We have a bath every week and change our clothes, and you are a bit smelly, Eli. I can see why Mrs Brookes wants you to wash. I reckon you'll enjoy it. School's all right as well. I expect you'll go in with the little ones until you can read and write, but you'll see us at playtime."

Nancy Brookes welcomed her friend Betsey Carter with a warm smile and a big hug, for the pair had been friends since childhood. Knowing Betsey could be trusted to keep a confidence, Nancy told her about Eli being her grandson, but how they planned to keep that quiet because John didn't want Noeleen finding out.

"Yes, I can understand that. Perhaps it's a case of least said, soonest mended. Noeleen's so strict about everything that I feel sorry for her two daughters, Ruth and Susannah. She gives them a hard time if they so much as smile at a lad, and it's only natural now they're in their teens. Clarice is so happy since she married Christopher Webber and escaped her mother's clutches. It's a shame John can't recognise the lad as his own, though. After losing Tommy, I expect he'd like to have another son to carry on his name."

"Yes, that is a pity, but you can't have everything. Now, I want to ask a favour, if I may, Betsey. I know you have a lot of grandchildren, and I wondered if they have any spare clothes they've outgrown that might fit Eli. He says he's ten, but he's small for his age, and dressed in rags; smelly rags at that. I've told him he has to take a bath later, and I'm not sure he's ever had one."

"Yes, of course. I'm calling in to see Sabina on the way home, so I'll ask her; she's bound to have something suitable. I know she keeps Willie's cast-offs for Edward, Stephen and Danny, but I'm sure she'll spare something for you. When I see Charlotte and Eveline, I'll ask them as well. I think there's a rummage sale being held in the schoolroom on Saturday, too, so you could probably pick up a few bargains there."

"Thank you, I'll take a look."

"Where is the boy now?"

"He's been living in a tumbledown building in the village, and some children have been keeping him fed, so he's gone to tell them he'll be sleeping here tonight. He wouldn't tell me where because he didn't want to get them into trouble."

"Ah, I think I might know where that is, and who the children are. Sabina mentioned the other day that Stephen, Helen, and Danny have been spending a lot of time in the old pigsty in the Lodge House garden and have made it into a den. She was complaining that they were eating like horses, too. I reckon now we know why."

Leaving Nancy, Betsey walked slowly through the village to visit her daughter-in-law, for that was how she still thought of Sabina, even though it had been seven years since her son, Tom, had passed away. In some ways, it seemed like yesterday that Sabina had broken the awful news to her and Ned about Tom's death from consumption, but in others, it was such a long time since she had set eyes on her son. She knew it wouldn't matter how long it was; she would never stop missing him and his two brothers, William and George. Some days, she felt so bitter at losing three sons, but knew it was not unusual, and she was glad that at least they had been adults and enjoyed a reasonable life.

She let herself in through the back door, calling out to Sabina as she went, and, seeing the pram parked in a corner of the kitchen, was pleased to find Annie must be there with the twins as well. The other women called out to her, and she found them in the sitting room, with David and Thomas playing on the floor with Katel. As she entered, she felt an atmosphere in the room and glanced about anxiously.

"Is everything all right? Should I come back another time if you're chatting about something?"

"No, it's fine, Gran. I was telling Mum and Liza that we're no nearer to solving the problem of Lady Eleanor wanting to see Danny. Do you remember I mentioned it to you when we were in Brampford Speke?"

"Yes, I remember, and I believe you and Robert had words over it; have you at least resolved that?"

"No, unfortunately not. He still thinks the easiest way to satisfy her need to spend time with Danny is for me to agree to accept his parents, but that's not going to happen. He thinks because his father has had a stroke and is now a disabled old man who can't harm me, I should be willing to put up with him, but I'm not, and I'm fed up with Lady Eleanor looking down her nose at me. If she did but know the truth, she might see things differently."

"Oh, well, it's a shame to let this come between you and Robert. You should never go to bed on a row. I was hoping that during your trip to London, you would have made it up."

"That's another sore point. I barely saw Robert in London; he was too busy drumming up business for his hunting weekends at the Manor to spend time with me. I particularly asked him to stay by my side at the Jubilee Ball because I'm not comfortable at such events, and he couldn't even do that. It was lucky I had the Turners and Aunty Margery for company. I also met a young man called James McIntyre, who's from Scotland and the son of one of Aunty Margery's friends, and he was kind enough to dance with me a couple of times. Now, Robert is angry with me because I invited him to come and stay at the Manor. He's an author planning to set his next book in Devon, so he's conducting research, and I thought it would be fun to show him around."

The three elder women exchanged worried glances, and Betsey tentatively commented.

"I'm not sure that's wise, my love. You're a married woman, and it's not right for a young man to take so much interest in you. I must ask, Annie, are you trying to make Robert jealous? Because if you are, you're playing a dangerous game."

If anyone else, even Sabina, had dared to suggest this to Annie, she would likely have retorted in anger. However, she had a deep respect for her beloved granny and could not risk upsetting her. Instead, she took a deep breath and chose her words carefully.

"No, Gran; I'm not trying to make him jealous, but if Robert can't be bothered to spend time with me, then he can hardly complain if I spend it with someone else. James is merely a friend, but I enjoy his company. I'm sure you'll like him too, when you meet him."

"Be careful, Annie. It's not like Robert to neglect you; he worships the ground you walk on, and just remember what our life was like before you married him. I don't think you should do anything to jeopardise that. The Fellwoods are rich and influential, and you'd not be wise to upset them."

Seeing Annie's anger bubbling beneath the surface, Betsey decided it might be an opportune moment to change the subject before someone said something they might regret.

"I'm sure Annie will sort things out and not give any of us cause for concern. Now, on a different matter, I've just visited Nancy Brookes, and she's taken pity on a ragamuffin of a lad who's turned up on her doorstep. He claims to be a distant relative of her late husband and knows enough about the family for her to believe him. Even so, I'm not sure she'd have taken him in, but he arrived to find her lying on the floor after a fall and helped her up. She thinks it will be beneficial for her to have someone living with her as she's a bit unsteady on her legs these days, and he can help around the house. I haven't seen him yet, but the lad's about ten, and small for his age, and she needs some clothes for him as he's dressed in filthy rags. I said I'd ask if you have anything suitable, Sabina, though I expect you to pass Willie's clothes down to your younger boys."

"Yes, I do, but I'm sure I can find a few things. I'll send Stephen along with them later on."

"Thank you. Nancy will be pleased. I suspect Stephen and the others already know this boy, for he told Nancy some children had let him stay in an old pigsty in their garden and have been keeping him fed. He wouldn't say who they are, but I suspect this may be why your children have been so hungry lately."

"It's nice to know they're willing to help someone worse off than themselves."

"Yes, it is. Now, did you know that Mary Ann is planning to have baby Etheline christened in a week or two? It will be a difficult day for her without George, so we must all do our best to support her. I wonder who she'll pick for godparents?"

CHAPTER 25

Breakfast time at the Manor House was not the jovial meal that it had once been, and although Annie and Robert ate together, there was a strained silence. They were polite to one another and made the effort when with the children, but the customary warmth in their relationship was missing. Matters had worsened the previous morning when Robert reluctantly told her he must return to London in the next week or so.

If Annie had but known it, he was as distraught about the situation as she was, but reluctant to trouble her with their financial burden, and equally determined to secure as many bookings as possible for his new business. However, he hated the thought of being parted from her again, considering the rift that had developed between them.

It was, therefore, a further blow when another letter was received from James McIntyre asking if he might come to stay during the next week. The letter was addressed to both Annie and Robert, and as it was handed to him with the rest of his mail, he opened it.

"Well, that's just perfect! Now, James McIntyre wants to come and stay next week, when I'll be in London. Did he know I was going?"

"How could he have known you were planning to visit London? Does it matter?"

"Well, it seems convenient that he wants to come and stay when I'll be away; does he want you all to himself?"

"Robert, how can you say that? The letter is addressed to us both, and he had no way of knowing you would be away on business. In any case, why does it matter; don't you trust me?"

"It's not you that I don't trust, but I'm not sure his motives for visiting us are strictly related to researching his book. I saw the way he looked at you in London, and monopolised your company, despite the fact that you're a married woman."

"Now you're being ridiculous. He was being polite because you were otherwise engaged, and he proved to be good company for us all, not only me. If you're that concerned about it, then write back to him and tell him he can't come. I'm not bothered one way or the other."

"I can hardly do that without appearing rude, when you've invited him, can I?"

"Does the letter say when he will arrive?"

"Yes, on Saturday."

"And when are you going to London?"

"On the following Monday."

"Good. At least you'll be here with him for a couple of days, and he might stay with Aunty Margery after that. You'll soon see that it's not me he's interested in at all, but simply the Devon countryside. His maternal great-grandparents lived in this area, and he wants to locate their gravestone and visit the village where they lived. He intends to base his next novel there in their memory."

"Do you know where they lived?"

"I believe it was Lynton, or it could have been Lynmouth, and I was telling him what a picturesque area it is and that Victoria bought a house there recently. I had thought to visit her if we accompanied him."

"Yes, all right, then. We could go on Sunday, if you like. I'll send a note to Victoria to ask if it's convenient for us to call."

"Do that, and when you get to know James better, I think you'll like him. We'll need a dry day to visit Lynton and Lynmouth; otherwise, it will be too misty to enjoy the scenery. Perhaps you should tell Victoria that we'll only come if it's fine weather.

Without further ado, Robert penned a letter to his sister, glad that he and Annie had something to do together.

James McIntyre arrived at Eggleston station early on Saturday evening and was collected by Dodger in the carriage. The weather was atrocious, with heavy rain and storm-force winds, and it was with some relief that the young man entered the hallway, where Robert and Annie greeted him. He shook Robert by the hand and leaned over and kissed that of Annie.

"Thank you so much for letting me stay, Robert. I've been meaning to come to Devon for a long time. I was particularly fond of my grandmother, and she always urged me to visit her birthplace, which she felt was the most wonderful place on earth. I wish she were still here and could accompany me. Do you know Lynton and Lynmouth well?"

"Yes, the twin towns have stunning scenery surrounding them and my sister, Victoria, bought a house there a few months ago. Annie and I thought we'd take you there for a visit tomorrow, but we'll need the weather to improve to do that, or you'll not be able to appreciate the views."

"Thank you, that's kind of you; I'll enjoy that. I'd like to stay here for a week or two, if that's all right with you, though I must spend a few days with Lady Margery at Enderby House. If the weather is no better tomorrow, perhaps we could visit Lynton next week?"

"Unfortunately, I have to travel to London on business on Monday for a week or so, so it would have to be tomorrow for me, but I'm sure Annie will accompany you. Anyway, please come in and make yourself at home. Dinner will be served in an hour, but perhaps you would like to join us for a drink?"

The evening passed pleasantly enough, and Robert had to concede that James was likeable, though he still didn't like the way the young man's eyes lingered on his wife.

Unfortunately, the weather was no better the next day, and so the visit to Lynton was cancelled. Victoria had replied to Robert's note, telling him she would not be going anywhere for the next week or two and to visit on any convenient day.

On Monday morning, Robert embraced and kissed Annie before setting off to London, and the couple clung to one another, each enjoying the reassuring close contact despite their differences. Annie watched her husband board the carriage with tears in her eyes. She hated to be parted from him, while the distance that had developed between them was still an issue. Sighing deeply, she went inside the house and forced a smile onto her face as James descended the staircase.

"Good morning, James. I hope you slept well."

"I did, thank you. Was that Robert leaving? I intended to say goodbye."

"Yes, he wants to get an early train. The weather is fine this morning, so we could visit Lynton today, unless you have other plans?"

"I'd like that, thank you."

"We'll go after breakfast, then. I thought we'd take Selina with us, for she loves to play with her cousins, and they don't see much of each other these days. Robert's younger sister, Sarah, is also going to accompany us as she'd like the opportunity to visit Victoria."

"That's fine; the more the merrier. If possible, I'd like to search the Lynton churchyard for my great-grandparents' gravestone if we can."

"Yes, I thought you'd want to do that. We'll do it en route to Victoria's house."

Annie had purposely invited Sarah along for company, as otherwise a chaperone would be necessary, and this way it would save taking a maid. She had taken heed of Betsey's advice and knew she should not be alone with the young man or her reputation would be tarnished. She thought of James as a friend of the family and was sure he understood that. She hoped so, for despite her annoyance with her husband, she loved Robert with all her heart and would never jeopardise their marriage.

The journey to Lynton was enjoyable, for as they crossed Exmoor, the sun rose in a bright blue sky and the heather was out in all its purple glory. Selina excitedly pointed out a group of Exmoor ponies and promised to show James how well she could ride the next day.

They called at Lynton church on the way to Victoria's house and spent a pleasant hour searching for the gravestones of the Churchill family. Selina was delighted when she was the one to find the gravestone in question, and the ladies left James to spend a few quiet moments at his ancestors' grave.

After a stroll around the picturesque little town, they called at The Royal Oak, an ancient thatched hostelry, for some coffee.

"If you feel like a walk, I suggest we descend the footpath to Lynmouth, for it will provide some amazing views. I'll ask Dodger to wait at the bottom with the carriage, for I assure you, you will not want to walk back up the hill; it's more like a mountain."

"Ooh, yes, let's do that, Mummy. I've never walked there before. Have you, Sarah?"

Sarah, now a pretty seventeen-year-old, smiled fondly at her niece.

"No, I haven't, Selina, and I'd like to do that too."

"That's settled then."

Leaving the inn, Annie instructed Dodger to descend the steep hill and wait for them at the bottom and then led the group to a footpath which disappeared into the woods and zigzagged down the seven hundred feet of the gorge. Selina insisted on holding Sarah's hand as they descended, and, smiling widely, James courteously offered Annie his arm, which she took gratefully. When she stumbled over some rough terrain, he caught her in his arms, and as she gazed into his deep brown eyes, she wondered if her family was right and his intentions might not be as honourable as she imagined.

By the time they reached the bottom of the slope, their legs felt like jelly, and it was with some relief that they strolled towards the West Lyn River. As they admired the boulder-strewn, fast-flowing torrent, James noticed a curious building at the water's edge.

"That's an unusual tower. Do you know what it's for?"

"Well, as it happens, I do, thanks to Aunty Margery. She told me about it one day when we visited. It's called the Rhenish Tower, after some similar towers on the River Rhine. It's a bathhouse, and you can go inside and bathe in privacy in the fresh saltwater from the sea."

"How interesting."

"Can we go inside and bathe, Mummy?"

"No, not today, Selina. I think the water would be too cold, and anyway, we're going to see Aunty Victoria, and you can play with Caroline, Joshua and Francis. I think you would rather do that?"

The little girl grinned, revealing a large gap where she had lost her two front teeth. "Yes, I would; can we go now?"

"We can, but first I'll ask Dodger to take us to The Valley of Rocks, for it is spectacular. If we can stop the carriage and glance back towards it, we can look for the shape of The White Lady in the rocks."

Dodger duly halted the carriage on the far hillside, much to the relief of the horses. One or two artists were endeavouring to capture the magnificent scenery on canvas, and along a narrow pathway ambled a long line of donkeys providing rides for the visitors. The party descended from the carriage and gazed back towards the valley, so popular with tourists.

"There, look, Selina. Do you see the shape of The White Lady in the rocks?"

"Oh yes. I think she looks like a witch."

"Some say she's the *Guardian of the Cliffs*, others, the ghost of a lost lover. Anyway, shall we continue our journey now? We're not far from Victoria's house."

James lifted Selina from the carriage and assisted Annie and Sarah down the steps. Annie noted with amusement that Sarah had fallen under his spell, as, taking his hand, she blushed most becomingly. As they approached the front of the house, Victoria waved to them from the balcony where she was enjoying the warm sunshine with the children playing alongside her. She embraced Sarah, Annie, and Selina and smiled as she was introduced to James. He bent over her hand and kissed it.

"What a gorgeous day, after such a lot of rain, but the countryside is much fresher for it. Please sit down, and I'll arrange for some drinks to be brought. I'm hoping you'll stay for lunch."

"Yes, that would be perfect, thank you. What a picturesque spot this is. I'm quite envious. Have you settled in?"

"Yes, thank you. There's still work to be done on the house and garden, and that will be ongoing for some time, but the rooms we use the most have been refurbished and are comfortable."

"Have the children taken to their new surroundings?"

"Yes, as you can see, they're thriving. Caroline is five now, and I'm trying to decide whether to send her to the local school or employ a governess. I believe you have chosen to send Selina to school, Annie?"

"Yes, Robert allowed me to decide, and I knew Selina would be happier at the school with my siblings and her cousins. However, I think when it's Thomas and David's turn, he may want to employ a governess, and then send them to boarding school when they're older; we'll see when the time comes."

"Traditionally, the Fellwoods have not attended school until they were much older, and then it would be a boarding school, but I can see the benefit of mixing with other children. Caroline would enjoy the company of some friends her age, but I don't want her to pick up bad habits. Sarah, how are Mama and Papa? Are they well?"

"Yes, fine, thank you. Mama misses you and the children, but we enjoyed our trip to London to see the jubilee celebrations. Papa's been a bit under the weather and didn't feel strong enough to take the journey."

"Did you stay with cousin Percy?"

"We did, and had a fabulous time; he has such an impressive house."

"I thought you might have been presented to Queen Victoria. You're old enough to be a debutante."

"Mama did suggest it, but I said I'd rather wait until next year, when Papa may be able to come as well."

"What about you, Annie? Did you and Robert enjoy the festivities?"

"We did, thank you. We stayed with Aunty Margery in Belgravia, and, of course, that's how we met James."

By the time the group left Lynton, Annie could see that Victoria, too, had taken to the young man and was delighted, for she would be pleased to see her sister-in-law happily married again.

CHAPTER 26

Betsey gently pushed back the thin blanket, swung her feet over the side of the bed, and reached for her soft leather slippers, a Christmas present from Annie that she treasured. She tiptoed from the room, determined not to wake Ned if she could help it, for it was early and she had heard the church clock strike six. Closing the door quietly behind her, she descended the stairs and went to the kitchen, where she pulled the kettle forward onto the stove, for her first job was always to make a cup of tea.

She glanced out of the kitchen window and saw that it would be another sunny day. Her view was that of the churchyard, an outlook she was happy with, for after all, two of her sons, a few grandchildren, and many of her friends were buried there, and she often went to chat with them. It was a habit some might find ridiculous, but it gave her comfort, and at her age, she cared little for what folk thought. Even now, in her seventies, the old woman found it impossible to lie in bed after so many years of getting up with the lark. When she and Ned had owned The Red Lion Inn, an early start was a necessity, and she still thought this was the best time of day.

Whilst the water in the kettle came to the boil, she opened the back door and wandered around the garden, which was so much smaller than the one at the inn. It was big enough for her and Ned now, and she still liked to potter about and tend to her plants, though thankfully, Arthur Webber, her daughter-in-law, Sabina's second husband, did all the hard work.

She sniffed the fragrant, deep pink Damask rose, her pride and joy, and this year, a profusion of blooms. The lavender bushes that were planted alongside the garden path released their heady perfume as she brushed against them, and she inhaled appreciatively. Pausing to admire the tall, stately spires of the pink, yellow and red hollyhocks planted against the wall, she picked off one or two deadheads and noted that a few late-flowering foxgloves would soon need cutting back.

Interspersed at random with the marigolds, pinks, and larkspur were many vegetables, and Betsey wanted to see what was ready to harvest for their dinner. Her favourites, the runner beans, had reached the top of their long sticks, and in an hour or two, the scarlet flowers would be swarming with bees. She gathered some of the tender beans and put them into her basket, then pulled a few carrots from the old soil-filled water barrel where Ned planted them to deter the pesky carrot fly. She remembered that Arthur had dug some new potatoes for her the day before, and knew there were plenty left to accompany the leg of lamb that she planned to roast.

Thinking she had picked enough, she noticed that their second row of peas was ready, and unable to resist, gathered enough for a meal and sampled several, thinking that they were far better raw. Ready now for her first cup of tea, she strolled back to the kitchen, picking some fresh mint and rosemary on her way and noting the redcurrants and blackcurrants also needed picking and thinking that Ned could sit on a stool later and do that for her; her part would be to make a crumble and some jam.

By the time she reached the kitchen, the kettle was boiling, and she brewed a pot of tea and carried a cup upstairs to Ned, for she knew he would be awake by now, and this was their routine. She liked him to take it easy in the mornings and not rush things. She opened the door quietly, in case he was still asleep, but he smiled at her and pulled himself up. She plumped up the pillows behind him, kissed him, and wished him a good morning.

"Good morning, to you, too, my love. Up with the lark as usual, I see; thanks for the tea."

"Yes, it's a lovely morning, and far too nice to lie in bed. I've picked peas, beans and carrots for dinner, so they will be delicious later with our roast lamb and mint sauce."

"Mm, my favourite, especially with new potatoes. Do you have anything planned for today?"

"I arranged to visit Mary Ann this afternoon because she wants to talk about the christening on Sunday. It's about time, for the child is nearly eighteen months old, but with losing George, I can understand why the baptism has been delayed. Will you come with me?"

"Yes, I like to see the little ones."

At half past two, having eaten a delicious dinner and washed the dishes, Betsey and Ned strolled arm in arm the short distance to the village shop. As they closed the door behind them, the shop bell rang, and their granddaughter, Harriet, smiled when she saw who her next customers were.

"Hello, Granny and Grandad, how are you both? Have you come to buy something, or to see Mary Ann?"

"Both, actually, but we'll see Mary Ann first, and I'll pick up the few bits I need on the way out. Now, did I see you walking hand in hand with Francis Rudd yesterday?"

Harriet blushed. "Yes, you did, Gran; it's early days, but we've been seeing a bit of each other lately."

"Well, you could do far worse; he has a sound business at the smithy, and it's time you were wed. I hope it works out for you, my dear. Is it all right if we go through to see Mary Ann?"

"Yes, of course; she's in the garden and you know the way."

Mary Ann was relaxing in the sunshine and watching her children play. The second wife of Betsey and Ned's son, George, she had borne him three daughters: Nellie, aged four, Sophie, going on three, and baby Etheline. George also had three children by his first wife, Alice, and although he was not keen on starting a second family, nature had taken its course, and naturally, once they were born, he loved the three little girls.

"Hello, Mary Ann, how are you?"

"I'm well, thank you, Betsey. How about you and Ned?"

"Yes, we mustn't grumble. What lovely weather we're having. I hope it stays like this for the christening at the weekend."

"I'm hoping so."

Betsey and Ned sat on a bench under the apple tree where it was shaded from the hot August sunshine, and Mary Ann asked her servant, Cissie, to bring some fresh lemonade and tea. The middle-aged woman soon returned, smiling at the visitors and bearing a tray laden with fresh scones, cream and jam.

"Hello Cissie, how are you? Those scones look delicious."

"I'm fine, thank you, Betsey. I hope you enjoy them; I only made them this morning."

When the tea and lemonade were poured and the scones laden with cream and jam, the discussion turned to the christening.

"Is everything arranged for Sunday, or do you need any help?"

"I think everything is organised, and no, I think we'll be all right, but thank you for asking. The service is scheduled for two o'clock at the church, and then everyone will proceed to The Red Lion as usual. Fred and Charlotte are providing a spread for us, and if the weather is still fine, we'll eat in the garden. If not, we'll use the big function room, because no doubt, Betsey's Kitchen will be full of visitors. They're so busy at the inn these days; the canal boats are a big draw for tourists to the area."

"Yes, I've heard the venture is doing well. Robert certainly has his head screwed on the right way, doesn't he, and I'm delighted that Fred's in partnership with him. He and Charlotte are making far better use of the meadow and garden than we ever did. It will be nice to see Robert at the christening; we haven't seen him for a while."

"No, he won't be there, Ned. Annie told me yesterday that he's had to visit London again on business; it's to do with the hunting weekends they're offering at the Manor now. Annie came to ask if she could bring a visitor who's staying with them. A young man called James McIntyre, he's a friend of Lady Margery, and Robert and Annie, met him in London."

"Oh, she's bringing him to the christening, is she? Well, I hope she knows what she's doing. I think that particular young man is far too interested in my granddaughter, given that she's a married woman."

"I don't know about that, Betsey; I haven't met him yet, but I don't think you need to worry, Robert and Annie are devoted to each other."

"Yes, that's true," Betsey spoke reassuringly, but her eyes were troubled. "What about the godparents; will it be Harriet, Theresa, and Francis?"

"Yes, if George were alive, I know he'd have wanted his three eldest children to be Etheline's godparents. Did I mention she'll be baptised Rosie Etheline? She's named Rosie after my mum, but George wanted her to be known as Etheline, so we decided to do it this way."

"No, I didn't know, but that's a pretty name."

On Sunday morning, the scorching weather continued, much to Mary Ann's delight. Etheline, being older than usual for the ceremony, was not impressed with the proceedings and screamed loudly as the vicar took her from Harriet and marked the sign of a cross on her forehead with the holy water from the font. With tears rolling down her cheeks, the toddler held out her arms to her mother and sobbed for some minutes until they left the church and she once again felt safe.

"There now, what was all that noise about? You're all right, now, Etty, stop crying."

Betsey smiled as she heard Mary Ann talking to the child, for she had thought Etheline was a bit of a mouthful, despite her son's wishes, and Etty was much better.

The family walked the short distance to the inn and congregated in the garden, where a trestle table, covered with a snowy white tablecloth, was laden with food. In the centre was a magnificent christening cake, baked by Mrs Potts, the former cook at Hartford Manor, and from whom Annie had begged a favour. The old lady was pleased to help, for she enjoyed baking, and since her change of position to housekeeper, she did not have the opportunity often. The cake was a masterpiece. As there were many guests, the cake was presented in two tiers, both covered in smooth white icing and decorated with the most delicate flowers, crafted in pink icing. Piped across the top tier were the words "Rosie Etheline", and Mrs Potts beamed with pleasure at the many compliments she received on her handiwork.

Betsey and Ned circulated and enjoyed chatting with their family and friends before sitting with their daughter, Eveline, and her husband, Charlie Chugg, at one of the picnic tables. Eveline and Charlie's four adopted children were with them: twins, Joseph and Matthew, Amelia, and Martha, now a sturdy little girl despite her difficult start in life. Whilst Betsey caught up with all the gossip from her daughter and the children, Ned chatted to Alfred Chugg, Charlie's brother and with whom Ned had gone to school.

"How are you, Alfred? Got the same aches and pains as me?"

"Aye, I expect so, Ned. Old age doesn't come alone, does it?"

"No, I'm afraid not, but at least we're still here. I haven't seen Jimmy here today. Is he not well?"

"No, he's all right, but he's a bit unpredictable these days and I can't depend on him as I once did."

"That doesn't sound like Jimmy; I've always found him to be reliable."

"Yes, he is usually, but lately he's taken to riding into Barnstaple at least once a week, and he either comes home in the early hours or not at all."

"Sounds to me like he's found himself a woman."

"Yes, it seems so, and 'tis high time now he's in his late thirties. The trouble is, I think he's fallen in with the wrong crowd, and I've even heard he's been seen in The Tucker's Arms, and you know what a reputation that place has got."

"Isn't that where Theresa was held captive for Frank Eastleigh to use as he saw fit?"

"Aye, that's it, and it's owned by Noah Berryman and his wife, Fat Meg, and a worse pair of rogues t'would be hard to imagine."

"That is a worry, Alfred. I think you need to have a word with him."

"I suppose so, but it's not so easy now he's old enough to know his own mind."

Their conversation was interrupted by Betsey, who came to tell Ned that she was going to talk to Sabina and Arthur and wondered if he wanted to join her.

"I'll be along in a minute, my dear; I'm enjoying my chat with Alfred, but I'll catch you up."

Betsey glanced across the meadow to where Sabina was sitting with Annie and the children, and the young man from Scotland to whom Betsey was determined to be introduced. Also part of the group was Sam Fellwood, his son, Marrok, and two women whom Betsey did not recognise. As she approached the party, she was greeted by Annie.

"Hello, Gran, I was going to come and chat with you soon. We're slowly making our way around to see the whole family. May I introduce James McIntyre, who is from the highlands of Scotland, and is the son of one of Aunty Margery's best friends. James, this is my granny, Betsey Carter."

Betsey surveyed the handsome young man before her. He was around thirty years of age and impeccably dressed in a traditional, dark grey, tailored suit, a crisp white shirt with a high, winged collar, and a lighter grey waistcoat featuring a herringbone design. A gold pocket watch on a chain and a stylish dark red cravat completed his outfit. His brown hair was short, and he sported a moustache, beard, and sideburns. He took Betsey's hand and put his lips to it.

"Good afternoon, ma'am. I'm delighted to meet you, for I've heard much about you."

He spoke with a charming Scottish accent, and Betsey, who had been watching him all afternoon, decided Robert was right to be concerned, given the attention he was paying to her granddaughter.

"Good afternoon, sir. How are you enjoying your visit to Devon? How does it compare with Scotland?"

"Och, well, it's no use asking a Scotsman such a question, ma'am, for I have to say there's no place like bonny Scotland. However, I must concede Devon has some stunning scenery, though not the grand mountains of my homeland."

"And how is your research coming on for your book? Will it be a work of fiction?"

"I'm satisfied with my progress so far, thank you, and yes, my book will be a work of fiction. My great-grandparents were born in Lynton, which is why I wanted to visit the county, and I was fortunate enough to find their tombstone when I visited with Sarah and Annie the other day; it was a poignant moment for me."

"And how is Robert? Have you heard from him, Annie? Poor man, I'm sure he didn't want to leave you and the children and travel all the way back to London again so soon. He's working so hard to make his new project a success; you must be proud of him."

"I am, and yes, he sent me a telegram to let me know he'd arrived safely at Percy's house. I hope he'll be back before too long. Gran, have you noticed that Sam and Marrok have brought lady friends? Isn't that a turn-up for the books? Let me introduce you." Annie steered her grandmother towards Sam and Marrok. "Hello, Uncle Sam and Marrok, my gran wanted to say hello."

"Ah, now, I can see you properly, I can see who you are, Florrie. How are you?"

"Hello, Betsey, I haven't seen you for a long time. I'm well, thank you, and enjoying looking after the Fellwoods. Sam kindly invited me to accompany him today; I hope no one minds."

"No, of course not. Now, Marrok, won't you introduce me to your young lady? I don't think we've met."

"Hello, Betsey; it's nice to see you again. This is Eirlys Williams, and she and her parents are the new tenants of Kerscott Farm, the one next to Sugworthy. Eirlys and her family are from Wales."

"I'm pleased to meet you, my dear. Have you settled in all right?"

"Yes, thank you." The young woman smiled at Marrok. "I think I'm going to like it here."

CHAPTER 27

Bored with their visit to church for the christening and having eaten their fill, four of the younger boys in the family amused themselves playing marbles in a corner of the yard behind The Red Lion Inn. Brothers Stephen and Danny faced stiff opposition from their cousins, Eddie and Bentley. Oblivious of the mud they were getting on their hands and knees, they took turns to knuckle down and take their shot. Each boy had a marble collection, which they were keen to increase, and the matter was being taken extremely seriously.

Stephen, the eldest of the group, was outraged when, with a lucky strike, his younger brother, Danny, won the game and relieved him of his favourite marble, a pretty glass specimen with a blue swirl inside, and much more attractive than the common reddish-brown ones made of clay. Triumphant at his rare victory over his brother, Danny could not resist the urge to gloat, and, grabbing his prize, he danced around singing, 'I've beaten Stephen, and I've won his favourite.'

Naturally, this added to the boy's anguish, and Stephen raced after and soon caught his younger brother, bringing him to the ground with a tackle and prising the marble from his hand. Unfortunately, for Stephen, Sabina, walking by, witnessed the event, and, grabbing her son by his arm, pulled him around to face her.

"What do you think you're doing, Stephen? Eddie, did Danny win that marble fair and square?"

"Yes, he did, Aunty Sabina."

"Then you give it back to Danny immediately, Stephen. I'm ashamed of you, and it will be an early night for you, my lad."

Stephen flung the marble onto the ground.

"Here, take the stupid marble, then, but just so you know, you're not really my brother! You're a foundling because your mum and dad didn't want you with your crooked feet and horrible mouth! And I wish our Annie had never found you."

Sabina's jaw dropped open, horrified at the words coming from her son's mouth.

"Stephen! Enough! Come with me. Danny, I'll talk to you in a little while, but take no notice of Stephen; he's a naughty boy and angry that you won his favourite marble."

Pulling her son along, Sabina guided Stephen into the dairy where she hoped they would not be disturbed.

"Stephen, what a horrible thing to say to your brother; I hope you're ashamed of yourself. How would you have liked it if you'd been born with a deformed mouth and feet? And what's all this about him being a foundling? Of course, he's your brother."

"He's not! I heard you and Annie talking about it the other day when I fell over and hurt myself. I heard you say he was a foundling and you'd looked after him since he was a few hours old."

Sabina paled as she realised the boy had overheard their conversation.

"What else did you hear, Stephen?"

"Nothing, but I've been thinking about it ever since because Danny doesn't look like any of us. He has dark hair, and all of us Carters have blond or ginger hair. Is he a foundling, Mum?"

Knowing he would accept nothing less than the truth, Sabina tried to think of the best way to handle this situation.

"Yes, it's true, Danny is a foundling, but I love him just as much as any of my own children, and I hope you do, too, Stephen. Annie found Danny in the woods outside our back door when he was only a few hours old, and, because I'd recently given birth to Helen, I had milk and could feed him. I suspect that's why he was left close to our cottage. As you pointed out so cruelly to Danny, he was deformed, and I think maybe his birth mother didn't feel able to cope with him. I was going to tell him one day, but he'll have to know now, thanks to you. I hope you're pleased with yourself."

Stephen hung his head.

"I'm sorry, Mum; I was angry because he won my favourite marble and teased me about it. I didn't mean to be so nasty."

"No, maybe not, but you can't take the words back now, so in future, think before you speak out in anger. And it's not me that you owe an apology to, but Danny, and I suggest you do that right now. And, Stephen, do not mention this to anyone else, please."

Sabina went in search of Danny, who had abandoned the game of marbles and was sitting on one of the swings, gently rocking to and fro. She could see from his tear-stained cheeks that he had been crying, and he avoided her gaze. Gently, she knelt before him and took his hands in hers.

"Danny, we need to have a little chat about what Stephen said to you, but I want you to know that I love you as much as any of your brothers and sisters. So, come with me because Stephen has something he wants to say to you."

The little boy slid from the wooden seat, and Sabina pulled him to her and hugged him. She led him towards the dairy, where Stephen was sitting on an upturned crate looking downcast.

"Well, Stephen, what do you have to say to Danny?"

"I'm sorry for what I said, Danny; I didn't mean it. I was angry that you won my marble, and your feet and mouth are fine now they're fixed. You are my brother, and I'll fight anyone who says you aren't."

"I think there's been enough fighting for one day, Stephen. Danny, do you have something to say to your brother?"

"Yeah, all right, then. I shouldn't have gloated about your marble; I know it's your favourite. You can have it back if you want."

"No, you won it fair and square. You'd better watch out, though, because I intend to win it back next time we play."

"Right, thank you, boys. You may go, Stephen, but behave yourself and no more mention of Danny being a foundling if you please. Danny, I need to talk to you."

Sabina waited until Stephen was out of earshot, sat on the only chair in the dairy, and pulled Danny onto her knee. Normally, he might have complained that he was too big for a cuddle, but today, he needed the comfort.

"I was always going to tell you that you are a foundling one day, Danny, when I felt the time was right, but unfortunately, Stephen has hastened this conversation when it could have waited until you were older.

"Annie heard a baby crying one day when she went out of our back door, and she found you in the woods, wrapped in an old piece of sacking, so she picked you up and brought you into the kitchen. You were tiny, and we could see straight away that there were problems with your mouth and feet. I was still breastfeeding Helen, so I had milk and could feed you as well, though it was difficult because I didn't eat enough to provide milk for two babies. You struggled to feed as most of the milk ran out of your mouth, and for a long time, I didn't think you would survive.

"Anyway, I persevered, and you were such a determined little chap that eventually you thrived and I've always loved you just as much as if I'd given birth to you myself."

"Why do you think my real mum dumped me? Do you know who it was?"

"I don't know how anyone could bear to part with their baby, whatever was wrong with it. Perhaps she wasn't married and couldn't support you, and thought you stood a better chance with me. We'll probably never know, but it doesn't matter. I chose to keep you, for I couldn't bear to send you to the workhouse, and now you're one of the Carter family, and always will be, so don't go worrying about it.

"Now, I have some news that I think will please you. Granny Betsey told me today that Aunty Emily and Uncle Hubert are going to visit with Edward, Willie, Millie, and Jonnie and stay a few days in Hartford. It will be wonderful to see them all, particularly Willie and Edward, for I miss them and I'm sure you do too. They're arriving tomorrow, and so you'll be able to play with Jonnie; I know you liked him, didn't you?"

"Yes, I did."

"Good, and Annie has invited us to the Manor House on Friday, so it will be quite a family gathering, and you'll have lots of children to play with. Annie has such a marvellous garden for hide and seek, doesn't she?"

Sabina thought this news would please the little boy, but he frowned and said, "I don't want to go to Annie's house, Mum; can I stay at home with Liza?"

"Well, I expect Liza will go with us, but why don't you want to go? I thought you liked going to the Manor House, and surely you want to play with all the others?"

"I do, but that lady from next door keeps looking at me through the hedge, and I don't like it. It's creepy."

"I expect she's watching all of you play because she likes to see children enjoying themselves; it's nothing to worry about."

"No, it's not that; she's always looking straight at me, and she smiles at me, but I think she's staring at my mouth and my feet, and I don't like it."

"I'll walk down the garden with you and make sure she's not around; will that be all right?"

The little boy nodded uncertainly.

CHAPTER 28

The Grantley carriage arrived at Hartford in the late afternoon and called first at The Red Lion Inn, where Emily, Hubert, and Jonathan were to stay. Rosella, Eddie, and Bentley were sitting on the mounting block outside the inn, waiting for their visitors to arrive. Their families could hardly believe the change in the relationship between Bentley and Jonathan, for when the two boys had lived under the same roof, they were sworn enemies, fighting like cats and dogs to the despair of all those around them. However, within a couple of weeks of starting school, they had learned to help each other. Bentley assisted Jonnie with his reading and writing, and Jonnie showed Bentley how to dance around the maypole, and since then, they had been inseparable.

Seeing the carriage appear around the corner, the children waved wildly, whilst Jonathan put his arm out of the window and waved back. Bentley jumped off the mounting block and ran through the inn door to where Betsey and Ned were waiting with Fred, Charlotte, and Sarah to welcome their visitors.

"They're here, Mum, Granny, and everyone, they're here!"

The carriage came to a halt, and the driver climbed down to help Emily and Hubert descend the steps.

However, the elderly couple allowed their grandson to alight before them, for they were aware of the child's impatience to see his friends.

"Gran, can I play with Bentley, Eddie, and Rosie, please?"

"Yes, of course, if that's all right with Charlotte and Sarah?"

The women nodded. "Yes, but come to the kitchen and have a drink and something to eat first, Jonnie; you must be hungry."

Emily and Hubert were greeted by their family, and Emily and Betsey hugged each other before waving goodbye to Edward, Millie, and Willie, who were to travel on to the Lodge House, where they would stay with Sabina and Arthur. The journey only took a few minutes, and their welcome was as warm as that at The Red Lion. Sabina hugged Edward, then Willie and Millie, delighted to see her sons and daughter-in-law.

"Oh, my goodness, I've missed you all so much, and what have you been feeding Edward? I swear he's grown a couple of inches."

Edward grinned as he was also hugged by Liza, and his sisters, Mary and Helen. Stephen and Danny wore broad smiles in welcome. Next, it was Willie's turn.

"Hello, Mary; I didn't expect you to be here, but it's lovely to see you."

"Yes, you too, Willie; it's my day off, so Mum invited me to tea so I could see you all. Hello, Millie, I hear congratulations are in order. When's the baby due?"

"Thanks, Mary; the doctor thinks around mid-November, so I've only got about three months to go."

Emily and Hubert spent the next few days relaxing and recovering from their taxing journey. They enjoyed spending time with Betsey and Ned, whilst the children from The Red Lion and The Lodge House met up each day and spent the entire day playing outside, arriving home only when they were hungry. After his time alone in Grantley House, Jonnie was delighted to have so many cousins to play with. They introduced him to other friends in the village, including Eli Brookes, who was now enjoying living with Nancy. Jonnie was fascinated to hear how Eli had lived in the old pigsty for weeks and how the others had kept him fed. Emily feared that when the time came to go home, Jonnie would not be keen to return to Brampford Speke.

On Friday, the family prepared itself for the visit to the Manor House to see Annie and her children. Emily and Hubert rode in the carriage and called at Sunset Cottage for Betsey and Ned, while the others walked the short distance.

Selina was beside herself with excitement and had been pestering Annie since breakfast time as to when the visitors would arrive. Maisie and Mrs Potts had prepared an extensive array of food that would be served outside under a couple of lofty chestnut trees, which provided shelter from the scorching August sunshine. Comfortable chairs were arranged for the older visitors, and ample rugs for the children to sprawl on. Annie had invited Aunty Margery, and the old lady was delighted to have the opportunity to spend time with her friend, James McIntrye, who was still a guest. When the rest of the family arrived, Annie, James, and the old lady were sitting comfortably in the shade, sipping cold lemonade whilst Selina and the twins ran around on the grass.

The greetings over, the family relaxed in the cool shade and waited for their lunch to be brought to them. Sabina and Betsey were displeased to see that James was still Annie's guest and exchanged glances as they noted his continued presence.

"Is Robert still in London, Annie? I thought he'd be back by now."

"Yes, me too, but I had a letter from him yesterday saying his business is taking rather longer than he anticipated, and so he'll have to stay a few more days."

"And how about you, James? When are you returning to London, or will it be to Scotland?"

"Neither, actually, Mrs Webber; I'm enjoying myself here in Devon and have decided to rent a property in the area to continue my research and write my book. It will give me the opportunity to spend a little more time with Lady Margery, Annie, and Robert."

"That's great news, my boy. I shall enjoy having you around, and perhaps your mother will visit; I'd like to see her again. Now, Emily and Hubert, I must ask, how are you getting on with the new staff at Grantley House? Are they more obedient than that awful housekeeper and butler that I relieved you of?"

"Oh, Margery, we're so grateful to you. The new staff are wonderful. Polite, willing, and friendly; it's made such a difference, and we're enjoying living at Grantley House now."

"Excellent, and how about Jonathan, Millie? Has he settled in at Newton St Cyres School?"

"Yes, he's so much happier now that he goes to school with Albert, Rosie and Walter. I'm so glad Aunty Betsey suggested it."

"Oh, look, here comes the food. I hope you're all hungry, for Maisie has prepared quite a spread."

Annie was not wrong, and an hour or so later, having eaten their fill, the children were allowed to run off and play, while the adults lounged around lazily.

"I'm going to stretch my legs and walk off some of that delicious lunch; would you like to come with me, Arthur?"

Leaving Annie in charge of Katel, Sabina took Arthur's hand, and the couple strolled down the garden.

"We should do this more often, my dear."

"Yes, we should, but there is a reason for this today. I want to walk along this hedge that borders the west wing garden and see if we can spot Lady Eleanor spying on us."

"And if you do, what will you do about it? Please don't tell me you will challenge her?"

"No, don't panic, Arthur. Oh, look, there she is, just like Danny said, hiding in the trees. How pathetic."

"Don't you feel a bit sorry for her, wanting her son back?"

"No, not in the slightest. She shouldn't have parted with him in the first place. She had the money to care for him or hire a nanny, so she has only herself to blame. She's upsetting Danny with this spying, and it must stop. It won't lead anywhere because Annie's adamant she wants nothing to do with her or Lord Fellwood. How could it possibly work for them to see Danny and ignore the rest of the family? He's already upset about discovering he's a foundling; I don't want him to guess who his parents are. Think how he'd feel knowing his own mother chose to send him away."

"But what can you do about it?"

"I'm going to ask Lady Margery to have a word with Lady Eleanor and tell her to forget about Danny; he's content where he is, and she must accept that."

Returning to the family, Arthur sat next to Willie, and the two men chatted about gardening and farming matters.

"Are you enjoying your job as a gardener, Arthur?"

"Yes, I am, and working with Dudley is such a pleasure. We're so lucky to work together as father and son, and the walled garden at Hartford Manor is a joy to care for. How about you? Do you like it at Brampford Speke?"

"I wasn't sure at first, but things are improving. Since Millie and Jonnie inherited their father's estate, I'm in the fortunate position of not needing to work, but I need something to do. I enjoyed working at Sugworthy Farm for Mr Houle, and even more so when Marrok Fellwood took over, and I shall visit the farm before I return home. It was difficult at Brampford Speke when I first moved there, as I was a newcomer, and some of the staff resented my position as farm manager. However, now that they're getting to know me and can see that I have sound farming knowledge, they're beginning to accept me. I think they like the fact that I don't only give orders, but roll up my sleeves and do a day's work like the rest of them."

"Is the land fertile?"

"Aye, some of it's hilly, and we keep the sheep there, but we cultivate the flatter land, and an adequate supply of fresh water runs through the valley. Perhaps you and Sabina could come and stay some time?"

"I'd like that, thanks; I could leave Dudley in charge. Yes, we'll take you up on that."

Out of the corner of his eye, Arthur saw his wife approach Lady Margery and whisper in her ear, and he hoped she knew what she was doing. However, Sabina was a determined woman, and he knew better than to argue with her.

Lady Margery was surprised at Sabina's request for a chat, but accompanied the younger woman inside the house, where Sabina led the way to the cool library.

"Is something troubling you, my dear?"

"It is, yes, and I think you're the only one who may be able to help."

"Then please unburden yourself, and if I can assist you, then I will."

"Thank you, there are two matters that are concerning me, and I've always been one to speak plainly, so I'm just going to come out with it."

"I'm of the same ilk; so please go ahead."

"I understand from Annie that you're aware of Danny's parentage and know that I took him in at birth when his mother rejected him?"

Lady Margery took a sharp breath. "My goodness, that is a delicate matter; but yes, I guessed some time ago, and Robert confirmed it. You see, the child is so much like Robert and David, and my brother, George, had the same deformity to his mouth as Danny; perhaps it's hereditary. Unfortunately, poor George was also mentally retarded, and he died young, but please go on. What leads you to discuss this with me today?"

"Since Victoria left Hartford Manor with her three children and went to live in Lynton, her mother has missed them and has told Robert she would like Danny back, or at least be able to spend time with him."

"Yes, I know. Robert told me, but it's ridiculous. There can be no turning the clock back."

"Exactly my thoughts, particularly given the fact that she and Lord Charles will not accept Annie as their daughter-in-law because she was once a servant. How could it possibly work? Now, unfortunately, my son, Stephen, recently blurted out that Danny is a foundling when the pair quarrelled over a marble. Danny is terribly upset but doesn't know who his parents are. I told him we don't know. I don't normally lie to my children, but it seemed the best thing to do."

"Oh, dear, poor lamb."

"Indeed, and to make matters worse, Eleanor has taken to spying on Danny through the hedge when she hears him and the other children playing in this garden. Danny has noticed and is upset by it, particularly as he knows Lady Eleanor has always shunned his family. Arthur and I walked down the garden earlier, and I spotted her lurking in the bushes. I would like you to ask her to stop this nonsense. Danny is content and cared for, and she should take comfort from that and leave the boy alone."

"I see, well, that will be a difficult conversation, but I agree with you, and I'm not one to shirk my duties. I will do as you say, but you mentioned there are two matters worrying you? I'm almost afraid to ask, but what is the other?"

"You may have noticed a rift between Robert and Annie recently?"

"Yes, it's difficult not to, and it's such a shame for they're usually inseparable."

"Lady Eleanor is so desperate to spend time with Danny that she's considering accepting Annie into the family, for she can see there is no way it could work otherwise."

"Yes, Robert mentioned that as well, and I thought it would be a good thing, for it might be one way Eleanor could get to know the boy a little, without upsetting anyone."

"That's what Robert thinks, too, but Annie is unwilling to spend time with Lord and Lady Fellwood, and she's furious with Robert for not considering her feelings in the matter. He seems to think she should be grateful that they are, at last, willing to acknowledge her as his wife."

"Why is Annie so against it? She would not need to see them often, but it could be a solution to a difficult problem and make life less complicated; it's generally easier if everyone gets along."

Sabina hesitated. "That, I can't tell you, for it's not my place to share the information, but if you knew the reason, you would agree with Annie and respect her feelings."

"Robert refused to confide this to me as well, and though I respect his and your privacy, it's difficult for me to help without knowing the full story, but no matter, what is it you want me to do?"

"I'm concerned that your friend's son, James McIntyre, is taking far too much interest in my daughter. She's a married woman with a family, and though I think she's only being friendly to him and enjoying his company, I suspect the young man is hoping it's more than that. He's taking advantage of the rift between her and Robert and of his continued absence whilst he's in London. I trust Annie and have warned her not to be alone with James, or her reputation will be compromised, but it would be better if he were not here at all. I want James to leave Hartford Manor today, if possible; perhaps you could invite him to Enderby?"

Lady Margery thought for a few moments and then patted the other woman's hand.

"Leave it to me, my dear, and I'll see what I can do."

CHAPTER 29

Never one to procrastinate once she had reached a decision, Lady Margery decided to visit Charles and Eleanor immediately and resolve the matter. Within ten minutes of leaving Sabina, she was admitted to the drawing room of the west wing, where she found the patio doors wide open and her nephew and his wife sitting on the terrace.

"Aunty Margery, what a lovely surprise. We were not expecting you today."

"No, my dears, I realise that; I hope I'm not imposing?"

"Of course not. May we offer you some refreshment?"

"No, I'm fine, thank you. I've had lunch with Annie and her family, and I thought, being so close, I would call and see you as well. How are you both?" After a few pleasantries, Lady Margery decided to speak plainly. "I must be honest and tell you the real reason for my visit today."

"Please do."

"Mrs Webber took me to one side earlier and told me some rather distressing news. Apparently, her son, Stephen, recently overheard a conversation in which the fact that Danny is a foundling was mentioned. Unfortunately, when he and Danny later had a minor disagreement over a game, Stephen blurted out the truth. Danny now knows he was not born into the Carter family and is most upset."

"Does he know we're his parents?"

"Fortunately, not, Charles. Sabina consoled him and lied when he asked that question, thinking it was for the best."

"I'm not sure that's the case. I'd rather the truth came out. I regret parting with my son now, and I would like him back."

"Eleanor, surely you can see that's impossible?"

"No, I don't see that at all."

"What plausible excuse could you give the boy for abandoning him in the first place? He'd hate you for it and would never forgive you."

"Well, maybe it would be best if he doesn't know of our relationship, then, but I can see no harm in us spending time with him and getting to know him. He's so much like David; it breaks my heart to see him when he visits next door, or we pass him on the driveway. If he had been adopted miles away, it might have been different, for I would never have set eyes on him again, but it's so distressing to keep seeing him."

"And that's the main reason I'm here. Danny has noticed you spying on him when he plays in the Manor House garden, and it's upsetting him. He doesn't understand your interest in him and thinks you're staring at his mouth and feet, which, although now corrected, he's still conscious of. Mrs Webber has asked me to request that you stop."

"Eleanor, my dear, I think that's a reasonable request and one which echoes my own sentiments. Surely, you have no wish to upset the boy, and how can you expect him to understand your interest in him? You should stop this spying."

"Yes, so you keep telling me, Charles, but I feel strongly about this. If I could spend time with the child, I would not need to spy on him. I'm hoping that when Robert returns from London, he will arrange something."

"But what about the rest of the Carter family? You've always made it clear what you think of them; how can you receive Danny and not his adoptive mother or siblings, especially Annie and your grandchildren?"

"I realise I may have to compromise on that, but if that's what it takes, then so be it."

"I'm afraid it may not be quite as simple as you believe."

"What do you mean? Surely they would be honoured to be accepted into our family?"

Lady Margery's mouth twitched in amusement at Eleanor's pomposity, but being the well-bred individual she was, she refrained from voicing her opinion.

"Well, I don't know why, but according to Mrs Webber, Robert has already suggested that to Annie, and she has flatly refused to even consider spending time in yours and Charles's company, so it would appear the animosity is reflected on both sides."

Lady Margery noticed an alarmed expression on Charles's face and realised that he, if not his wife, knew the reason for their daughter-in-law's strong feelings. She was intrigued, but continued.

"Furthermore, it has created an unpleasant rift between Robert and Annie, which is distressing for all concerned, and I sincerely hope they can resolve the matter on his return."

"Oh, I don't know; if Robert came to his senses and divorced her, it would be better all round."

"Eleanor, that's a terrible thing to say, and though they're having a few problems, it's obvious they're deeply in love with one another. Annie is a kind, warm-hearted girl, devoted to her children, and you're wrong not to accept her. However, I've had my say, and I hope you will consider what I have told you. Danny is loved and wants for nothing, and I think you should be satisfied with that. His future could have been far less certain."

Returning to the luncheon party next door, Lady Margery briefly nodded to Sabina to indicate she had done her best, though privately she doubted that her intervention would make any difference. She remained puzzled as to how Charles could know the reason for Annie's strong aversion to spending time with him and his wife, whilst she, and presumably Eleanor, did not. She decided to discuss the matter further with Robert when she had the opportunity.

The guests were still sitting beneath the chestnut trees, and she chose a seat close to Annie and James, thinking to deal with Sabina's other request.

"James, I've seen little of you since you came to Devon, and I wondered if you would like to stay at Enderby House for a while? You could even return with me later in my carriage, if you like."

"I'd like that, thank you, but not for a few days. As I mentioned earlier, I'm hoping to rent a house in the area and spend the next few months writing my latest book. Annie has offered to accompany me to Buzzacott House tomorrow to view the property; she says it's on the edge of Exmoor and it sounds perfect."

"You are welcome to stay at Enderby for as long as you want, my boy, and save your rent money. In any case, I don't think Buzzacott House is suitable at all; it once held a terrible secret."

"That's kind of you, but I write best when I'm alone, and I believe Buzzacott House is in an isolated spot. Annie has told me of its shocking past, and indeed, that's probably why it hasn't been snapped up, but I'm not worried about any of that; it's just bricks and mortar."

Willie was aware of his mother's worries concerning James's interest in his sister, as well as her direct gaze as she tried to convey her thoughts to him.

"That's a shame, Annie. I'm planning to ride to Sugworthy Farm tomorrow with Edward, and I hoped you might accompany us. We hardly see anything of each other these days, and a ride over the moors together would be most enjoyable. Could you visit the house with James another day?"

"Oh, I'd love that, Willie. I haven't been to Sugworthy since Marrok and Sam moved in, but unfortunately, James has arranged with the agent to view the house tomorrow, and I promised to offer a second opinion; could we visit Sugworthy another day?"

"Marrok is expecting us tomorrow, but never mind. Perhaps another time."

Arthur, aware of Sabina's fingernails digging into his forearm, suddenly spoke up.

"I'm owed a day off, which I could take tomorrow. If I view Buzzacott House with you, James, that would leave Annie free to spend time with her brothers. It's not often she has the opportunity."

"That's so kind of you, Arthur, and after you've viewed the house, James, can I expect you for a few days at Enderby?"

Unable to think of any more excuses, the young man nodded, glancing ruefully at Annie.

"Yes, thank you, I'd like that."

"Wonderful, I can introduce you to my friend, Peter, who is Arthur's father and an incredibly talented artist. What is most remarkable about him is that he paints by holding his paintbrush in his teeth, for he has no hands. If I take the luggage you will need with me today, you can ride on to Enderby after you have viewed Buzzacott House, for it's in the same direction."

Sabina smiled gratefully at Lady Margery, delighted to have removed James from the Manor House before Robert's return from London.

Leaving the children in Naomi's capable hands, Annie was excited at the prospect of a day out with her brothers. She ate her breakfast with James, and they walked to the stables, chatting about the day ahead, for they planned to ride to the Lodge House together with the agent who was due to arrive shortly. Their horses were saddled and ready, and James instructed Dodger to lead them out to the yard and wait there. As Annie began to follow the stable boy, James took her hand and pulled her towards him.

"Just a minute, Annie. I was hoping to stay here for a few more days, and I was looking forward to our excursion today."

"Never mind; Arthur will accompany you to Buzzacott House and be far more knowledgeable about the property than I would have been, and I know Aunty Margery was hoping you would visit her for a few days."

"Maybe, but I enjoy your company so much, Annie." He gently tucked a stray curl behind her ear, pulled her towards him and put her fingers to his lips. "I more than like you; I'm falling in love with you."

Annie snatched her hand away and stepped back.

"Oh no! You mustn't say that, James. I'm a married woman."

"I know that, but Robert is neglecting you; more fool him. I would never do that, Annie. If you were mine, I could never bear to leave your side. Do you deny you have feelings for me, too?"

Realising she must have been giving the young man the wrong signals, fed by her annoyance with her husband, Annie was horrified. She stepped back, snatching her hand away.

"I'm fond of you, James, as a friend, but I love my husband, and despite the recent distance between us, I would never jeopardise my marriage. I'm sorry if you have misinterpreted my feelings. Now, please, enough of this."

"If you ever change your mind, Annie, I'll be waiting for you."

"No, you must abandon these notions, James. I enjoy your company, but it will never be more than that, so please do not waste your time on me. Come, we need to go."

Annie marched briskly to the yard, where Dodger eyed her anxiously. The friendship between the pair had not gone unnoticed, and though she was unaware of it, the servants were beginning to talk. Mrs Potts had confided in Maisie that the sooner Master Robert returned home, the better.

CHAPTER 30

James was dismayed at Annie's reaction to his declaration of love, but she allowed him no opportunity to discuss the matter further. Leaving him to welcome Mr Crosby, the land agent who had arrived in the yard, she swiftly mounted her horse and trotted to the Lodge House, where Arthur was waiting for James, and Willie and Edward for her.

Sabina was delighted with Arthur's offer to accompany the young man to Buzzacott House, and she promised to explain his absence from work to Jack Bater, whom she was sure would understand. Arthur was looking forward to his day on horseback, for he seldom rode these days, and he suspected he would suffer a few aches and pains the following day.

James gazed longingly at Annie, willing her to give him some sign of encouragement, but she neither smiled nor said goodbye, and he realised he must accept that his advances had been rejected. He was puzzled and disappointed, for he had been sure she was falling for him and wondered how he had got it so wrong. Annie felt guilty, wondering if she had unwittingly led the young man on when she had no intention of allowing a relationship to develop. Too late, she realised that her mother and granny may have been right.

Arthur, James, and Mr Crosby said little to each other on the ride to Buzzacott House, and on arrival, they dismounted and tethered their horses. Having shown them around, the agent left the two men to wander where they liked on their own, and they strolled around the garden, looking at the house from every angle.

"It's in good repair, and larger than I expected."

"Yes, I think it was done up ready to be sold, but there were no offers. The terrible things that happened here have put folk off."

"What exactly did happen here, Arthur? I heard some babies' bodies were found, but I haven't heard the details."

"The house was rented by a woman called Lizzie Dymond and her daughter, Thurza, and they took in unwanted babies, mostly from unmarried women who couldn't keep them. They charged the women for taking the children off their hands and promised they would be rehomed with couples who wanted children. I understand they actually did that in the past, but then they got lazy and doped the babies, didn't feed them properly, and let them die from neglect. The police found several bodies buried in the grounds and three babies that were close to death, but they all recovered.

"One of them belonged to Charlotte Carter, who lives at The Red Lion Inn and is now married to Sabina's brother-in-law, Fred. It was a child from a previous relationship that Charlotte had before meeting Fred, and her parents forced her to give up the little girl. Fortunately, mother and baby were reunited, and little Doris is now doing well. Sabina's sister-in-law, Eveline Chugg, who lives at Hollyford Farm with her husband, Charlie, adopted another baby, and they called her Martha. The other child was reunited with its mother."

"How awful. What happened to the culprits?"

"Lizzie, the mother, was hanged, but her daughter, Thurza, was slow-witted and she didn't understand what was going on, so she was sent to an asylum, which many think is worse than the death sentence, poor girl. Ah, here comes the agent now."

Having explored the newly refurbished dwelling and fallen in love with its seclusion, James was keen to rent the property. However, knowing how difficult the owner was finding it to locate a tenant, he drove a hard bargain, eventually agreeing to a six-month rental with immediate possession. He and Mr Crosby shook hands on the deal, and he was promised the key as soon as he had paid a deposit and the first month's rent.

They watched as the land agent mounted his horse for the ride back to his office, and James offered his hand to Arthur, thanking him for his company and advice.

"You're welcome, lad. I've enjoyed doing something different this morning, and I hope you'll like living here. Now, I believe you're travelling on to see Lady Margery at Enderby House, is that right?"

"Yes, she's a close friend of the family, so I'll spend a few days with her and then move in here. Fortunately, the house is furnished, so I only need to bring a few belongings, and then I can get started on writing my book."

"I hope it goes well for you. Now, if you follow this road for a few miles, you'll come to Enderby House; you can't miss it."

"Thanks again, and goodbye, Arthur."

Annie and Willie were delighted to see a wide smile appear on Edward's face when he realised where they were headed. Annie couldn't remember ever riding with her two brothers before and knew this would be a memory they would treasure for a long time to come.

It was a sunny day in August, and the light breeze ruffled their hair as they trotted along the country lanes before taking a shortcut across the open moorland. As Sugworthy Farm came into view, Willie exclaimed in delight at seeing several fields of wheat and corn. The golden yellow of the ripened crops was interspersed with bright red poppies and blue cornflowers, and Annie felt she could look at the wonderful scene forever.

They cantered into the farmyard where Marrok and Sam were sharpening scythes, ready to begin the harvest. The two younger children, Martin and Paul, had erected a small tower of stones on top of the pigsty wall and were throwing more stones to knock it down.

Marrok stood up to ease his back and see who his visitors were, and smiled in delight.

"Willie and Edward, how lovely to see you. You, too, of course, Annie."

"Ah, duckstone, eh! I was a dab hand at that as a boy."

Willie ruffled the hair of the two boys, then took a stone from them and aimed at the tower of bricks. However, he was disappointed when he narrowly missed. He passed Edward a couple of stones, indicating he should have a go.

"Seems I've lost my touch. Go on, Edward; show us how it's done."

The boy took careful aim and, with his first throw, struck the tower, which toppled over and fell into the pigsty. Edward grinned in delight and helped Martin and Paul to retrieve the stones for another go.

"How are you, Sam? I haven't seen you for a while."

"I'm fine, thank you, Annie. I've never forgotten your kindness when I was a poor old beggar and your nasty uncle was chasing me to get back the boots I'd stolen from his shop."

"It was a pleasure, Sam, and he didn't guess your hiding place, did he?"

"No, I was safe like you said I would be. Now, come in and see Florrie; she'll enjoy your company today."

In the kitchen, the housekeeper, Jinnie, and Eliza were busily baking, and all three smiled at the sight of their visitors.

"Annie, what a nice surprise. Let me clean this dough off my hands, and I'll make you a cup of tea."

"Don't worry, Florrie; you finish what you're doing and I'll put the kettle on the stove."

It was early evening by the time Annie and her two brothers set off for Hartford. It had been a wonderful day for all concerned, and Annie was looking forward to telling Sabina and Betsey all the gossip, particularly of the growing fondness between Sam and Florrie, and the budding relationship of Marrok and Eirlys Williams.

Robert concluded his business in London a few days earlier than anticipated and decided to surprise Annie with his return rather than write. Travel was so much easier nowadays on the train, without the endless days of being jolted around in a carriage, and he knew he could arrive home as quickly as a letter. As Dodger was not expecting him, there was no one to meet him at Eggleston station, so he left his luggage to be collected another day and hired a horse to ride back to Hartford Manor. He had missed his family and couldn't wait to hold Annie in his arms and cuddle his children. He hoped his absence might have resolved the distance that had developed between him and his wife.

Leaving his horse with Dodger to attend to, he went into the house, and, not seeing Annie around, hurried to the nursery where she was often to be found. The children were delighted to see him and overjoyed with the small presents he had brought them. Annie had not told Naomi of her change of plans for the day, and when Robert asked the nursemaid where her mistress was, she said she had taken Mr McIntyre to view Buzzacott House, a property she understood he was considering renting for a few months to write his next book. It was obvious from how the girl spoke of the author that she was in awe of him.

Furious to discover his wife had abandoned his children for the day to spend time with the handsome young man, Robert stormed down the stairs and went to the kitchen for a cup of tea with Mrs Potts and Maisie, something he had done so often in the past when upset or worried. Neither of the servants was aware of Annie's whereabouts, but Mrs Potts tactfully tried to pour oil on troubled waters by saying it was a nice change for Annie to have a day out, for she seldom went anywhere without her children.

However, Robert was in no mood to share confidences, and it was not long before he returned to his study where he brooded anxiously, wondering where his wife had got to. As dusk began to fall, he heard Annie's footsteps in the hallway and her exclamation when she saw the lamplight shining from under the door. She found him drinking a glass of brandy, an unusual occurrence.

"Robert, you're home! You should have let me know, and I'd have come home earlier."

"Well, I wouldn't have wanted to spoil your fun with your young man."

Annie's green eyes flashed angrily. "What do you mean? My young man? I don't have a young man. I've been to Sugworthy Farm with Willie and Edward, and until now, I'd had a wonderful day."

"So, where is your Mr McIntyre? I never see you these days, but what he's trailing along in your wake, hoping for a little attention like some pathetic puppy dog."

"Don't be ridiculous. He's not my Mr McIntyre. If you must know, he's staying with Aunty Margery for a few days, but if all you can do is accuse me of being unfaithful, then it's a pity you came home at all."

Robert hesitated. "You haven't been to Buzzacott House with James, then? That's where Naomi thought you were."

"No, I had planned to do that, though we would have been accompanied by the land agent, but then I had the opportunity to spend the day with Willie and Edward, so Arthur went with him instead, and James rode on to Enderby House afterwards. I forgot to tell Naomi of my change of plans."

There was a silence for a few moments, then Robert begrudgingly apologised, though he was only slightly mollified after learning it was her original intention to spend the day with the Scotsman, accompanied or not.

Annie, too, was less than satisfied with his stilted apology, but decided to accept it and change the subject. She told him how Danny had discovered he was a foundling.

"Oh, dear, poor Danny; was he terribly upset?"

"Yes, according to Mum, he was, and naturally, he asked if she knew who his real parents were; I'm afraid she lied and said no, but she thought it was for the best."

"Yes, I agree. I'm surprised at Stephen, he's usually a kind lad."

"I know, but he blurted out the words in anger, and then regretted it; something we've all done from time to time."

With neither of them wanting to explore the topic of Lady Eleanor wanting to have her son back, they dropped the subject and went to bed, where Annie snuggled up to Robert, hoping to put their differences to one side. She had some exciting news to share with her husband, which she thought would thrill him and bring them closer.

"How did your trip to London go?"

"Better than I thought, actually; and that's why I stayed a few more days. I socialised with various friends of Aunty Margery, Percy, and my parents, and it proved successful as I was able to tell them all about our new venture with the hunting weekends and several booked to come later in the year. As you know, I'm not a great one for such gatherings, but Aunty Margery thought it would be worth doing and, as usual, she was right."

"I'm glad it went well. I have some wonderful news to share with you, too."

"Oh, what's that?"

"It's early days, but I'm with child, and I know you've always said you'd like a big family. I wonder if it will be a boy or a girl." To Annie's surprise, there followed a difficult silence. "Aren't you pleased? I thought you would be?"

"Is it mine?"

"What! Of course, it's yours; whose do you think it is?"

"Well, your young friend James has seen rather more of you in the last couple of months than I have, so I think it's a reasonable question."

"How dare you! How dare you judge my fidelity when I have never questioned yours on your long business trips away? How do I know you haven't slept with half of the ladies in London during your absence?"

"Now you're being ridiculous."

"I don't think so. Well, I'm not even going to answer your question, so you can think what you like."

Annie pulled away from her husband's warm body and turned her back on him.

CHAPTER 31

The atmosphere in the Manor House remained tense for the next few days, and even six-year-old Selina noticed the animosity between her parents. Having read her daughter a bedtime story, Annie tucked the little girl in cosily and bent to kiss her goodnight.

"Night, night, sweetheart; sleep tight."

"Mummy, is something wrong?"

"No, nothing's wrong; what do you mean?"

"You and Papa don't seem happy anymore."

"Oh, we're just busy, and Papa's tired after his trip to London. Everything is fine and there's nothing for you to worry about. Now, you go to sleep and perhaps tomorrow we'll visit Granny Betsey and Grandad Ned; would you like that?"

"Yes, that would be nice. Night, Mummy."

Annie was dismayed that even the child had noticed the tension between her and Robert, and since the night when she informed him of her pregnancy, the pair had barely spoken, for both were strong-willed and remained angry with one another.

On the Friday of that week, Robert travelled to Barnstaple with Dodger to attend the cattle market as he was keen to buy some breeding ewes for autumn tupping. Normally, he would have left such a task to Jack Bater, his farm manager, but Jack was still laid up with an injured back and could barely move.

It was a warm sunny day, and Robert was grateful for the excuse to get out of the house and avoid any further confrontation with Annie. However, his mind was not on his work as he walked around the many pens surveying the various breeds of sheep on offer. He kept going over the conversation with his wife and regretted the harsh words he had used. However, he was convinced that she and James were more than friends, and whilst he still felt far from wanting to apologise, she had seemed so hurt that he wondered if he had overreacted. He could not forget the pain in her eyes when he accused her of being unfaithful, something he would have found inconceivable only a short while ago.

He leant on the side of a sheep pen, gazing at but not seeing the animals inside, when he was disturbed from his thoughts by his Uncle Sam and Marrok.

"Hello, Robert; you seem mighty interested in them sheep, and I hope you're not planning to bid for them, for we have our eye on a dozen of them."

Robert, brought out of his ruminations, smiled at his relatives.

"Oh, hello; yes, I do want to buy some, but don't worry, I won't bid against you; that would hardly make sense, would it, and I think there are more pens a bit further on. I've never bought Exmoor Horns before; do you know much about them?"

"Aye, they're a small and hardy breed, and suited to moorlands, nice looking too with their white wool and curved horns. They're kept more for their meat than wool quality, though; is that what you want them for?"

"Yes, we've got other breeds that are best for wool, but Jack thought we should get a flock of sheep for meat, so it sounds as if these would fit the bill; I'm going to bid for twenty, then we can breed from them, and build up a decent flock."

"How will you get them home?"

"I've brought Dodger with me, and he'll drive them home later. We brought our collie dog, Lady, with us in the pony and trap, and she'll make sure they behave themselves. Would you like to meet in The Golden Fleece later for some dinner?"

"Aye, we're going there anyway. We saw Charlie and Eveline earlier and arranged to meet them there, so it would be nice if you could join us."

It was nearly one o'clock by the time Robert concluded his business of purchasing a small flock of sheep and had seen Dodger safely on his way home, ably assisted by Lady. He hurried to The Golden Fleece, and as usual on market day, it was crowded and noisy. He glanced around the room, hoping to see his family already seated and smiled when he noticed Sam, Marrok, Eveline, and Charlie in one corner. He waved at them, and his Aunty Eveline shifted up to make room for him on the bench.

"Hello, Robert, Sam said you might join us. Did you purchase the sheep you wanted?"

"Yes, thanks, Charlie; how about you? Have you had a successful morning?"

"Yes, though I didn't need any livestock, just provisions today, but we found everything we wanted."

"How are Annie and the children? I thought Annie seemed a bit under the weather when I saw her last week."

"They're fine, thanks, Aunty Eveline, but Annie gets tired looking after the children. Thomas and David are into everything now they're two, and Annie could leave far more to our nursemaid, but prefers to look after them as much as she can herself."

"A mother's love and attention are always best, and it's the way Annie was brought up."

"Where are your children today?"

"We left them at home with Maria; they won't give her any trouble. Joseph, Matthew and Amelia spend most of their time outdoors in the summer, and Martha is a placid little girl. It's fortunate we've seen you today, because I wanted to invite you and Annie to bring the children and visit us. You could come for Sunday lunch, if you like, and bring Mum and Dad with you."

Robert paused momentarily, wondering if, given the current climate between him and his wife, this was advisable, but then smiled his thanks.

"Yes, thank you. I'll check with Betsey and Ned on the way home; what time would you like us to come?"

"Come when you like, but I'll cook the dinner to be ready at one o'clock. The children like playing together, and Alfred always enjoys putting the world to rights with Dad."

After a tasty meal, Robert collected his pony and trap and drove slowly through the crowded streets. The sun was hot on his back as his journey took him past The Tucker's Arms, a disreputable inn on the outskirts of the town. Robert had once got into a fight there, whilst searching for Annie's cousin Theresa, who had been abducted. He spotted the landlord, Noah Berryman, standing in the doorway, sunning himself, and Robert grimaced, noting that the unpleasant man was still as fat and dirty as when he last saw him. Suddenly, Robert stiffened as he recognised a man leaving the inn; a man who appeared to be much the worse for wear from drink.

Robert reined in his horse and stopped near the doorway, where Noah sneered at him.

"You can bugger off, too; your sort aren't welcome around here, and I bet you're not so brave without your pals to protect you."

Ignoring the jibes, Robert called out to the staggering man.

"Jimmy, do you want a lift home?"

Alfred Chugg's youngest son shielded his eyes from the glare of the sun to see who was talking to him.

"Ah, you won't want to travel with me in this state, sir, and in any case, I have a horse tethered somewhere."

Robert was not convinced the young man would be able to stay on a horse in his current state and spoke reassuringly.

"I don't mind, Jimmy; I could do with the company. We can lead your horse home, and you'll be more comfortable in the pony and trap."

"Aye, well, if you're sure, thank you."

Having located Jimmy's horse, Robert tethered it to the back of the trap, and they were soon on their way.

"It seems you've had more than usual to drink today, Jimmy, and that's not like you."

"No, well, it's a means to an end as they say, but between you and me, it's not working out too well."

"What do you mean? What are you trying to achieve?"

"I'd rather not say, if you don't mind, but thanks for the lift."

Before Robert could ask any more questions, his fellow traveller's head began to loll, and Jimmy fell fast asleep on his shoulder, where he remained all the way back to Hartford.

CHAPTER 32

Eli had settled into his new life with Nancy Brookes, and she was enjoying his company. Despite his serious misgivings, he enjoyed his first bath and certainly smelled sweeter for it. Not wanting to embarrass the lad, Nancy had left him to undress and get into the water and, having instructed him to scrub himself from top to bottom with the soap, had taken his clothes away to see if anything was worth salvaging. Unfortunately, the pile of rags was way beyond repair, and Nancy committed them to her Bodley stove, where she knew any unwelcome visitors living in them would also perish. However, Sabina and Eveline had come up trumps, and the boy now had a couple of decent changes of clothes.

Not one to waste time, Nancy began giving her new grandson lessons, and despite his initial reluctance, Eli proved to be a quick learner, who soon not only knew his alphabet but could count up to fifty. He found writing more of a challenge, but Nancy was satisfied that he could at least write his name before he started school.

John Cutcliffe found it difficult to see as much of his son as he would have liked, without arousing his wife's suspicions, for Noeleen was an astute woman. However, he felt he could legitimately visit his mother once a week, as it was understandable that at her age, he would want to keep an eye on her, and of this, his wife approved. Over the summer, John had fallen into the routine of calling on Nancy every Saturday afternoon for a couple of hours, and he and the boy had quickly struck up a friendship. Nancy suggested bringing Noeleen and his two daughters to meet the boy, but so far, this had not happened.

On his first day at school, Eli was understandably nervous, and Mr Atkins, the headteacher, was aware that the boy had never attended school before. Nancy had advised him that the boy was bright, knew his alphabet, and could count; and so the teacher decided to put him in the class with children of his own age, for he knew he would be teased if he were put in with the younger children.

"Is there anyone in the room that you already know, Eli?"

Eli surveyed the many curious faces until, with relief, he spotted Stephen Carter.

"Yes, sir, I know Stephen."

"Very well, then you may stand beside Stephen. I'll call the register now, which is something I do every morning, and when I call your name, you must answer 'Yes, Sir' and sit down."

Eli obliged and was one of the first to sit down, which enabled him to watch all the other children and learn their names. He was interested in hearing the name of Rachael Cutcliffe called out, and watched as an eleven-year-old girl sat down, and he realised she was his half-sister.

The children had no opportunity to talk in class, as this was something Mr Atkins would not tolerate. However, at break time, all the Carter children who had fed Eli for weeks were keen to hear if he was enjoying living with Nancy.

"Yes, it's good; she's a kind lady who feeds me well, and I like doing jobs for her. She's been teaching me to read and write, and I love the stories she reads to me."

Rachael Cutcliffe, standing nearby, was intrigued by the boy.

"Did you say you're living with Nancy Brookes?"

"Yes, that's right; I found her on the floor after she'd fallen a few weeks ago, and I helped her up. I had nowhere to live, and she offered me a home in return for doing jobs around the house."

"I'm surprised at that. Nancy's my granny, and I didn't think she had two ha'pennies to rub together. She's always moaning about how short of money she is; it's a wonder she can afford to feed you. I expect you've met my dad, John Cutcliffe? He's taken to visiting Gran every Saturday afternoon lately."

"Yes, I've met him. I think he was worried about her because she cut her head the last time she fell."

Helen was looking at Rachael and Eli with a puzzled frown.

"When we first met you, Eli, you said you were looking for your father, John Cutcliffe, and then, when you'd spoken to Nancy, you said you'd made a mistake. Well, I wonder if you did, because you and Rachael look so much alike."

Eli was horrified at these words, and Rachael scrutinised him with renewed interest.

"You do look a bit like me, Eli, but how could my dad be your father?"

"No, he isn't. Someone had told me I was related to your gran, so I thought he must be my father, but when I talked to Aunty Nancy, we worked out that I was a distant relative of her second husband, Cecil. That's why she gave me a home and told me to call her Aunty Nancy."

"I see, it's strange we look alike, though, because Cecil was no relation to me."

Luckily for Eli, the bell rang to indicate the break was over, and with much relief, he returned to the classroom, thinking he must discuss this with Nancy when he got home to make sure they got their stories straight.

On the Friday of that week, when Robert and Dodger were visiting Barnstaple, Annie escorted Selina to school and spent a few minutes chatting with the other mothers at the gate. At any other time, her husband would have invited her along for the trip, and she would have enjoyed shopping while he attended to his business, usually meeting him later for lunch. However, as they were barely speaking, neither wanted to spend time together.

With time on her hands, Annie visited the shop, now owned by her Aunty Mary Ann, since George Carter's untimely death. The shop was busy, with a short queue stretching outside the door, and Annie patiently joined it, chatting to Esther Symons, who was carrying Susie, while the toddlers, Tim and Robin, ran around and played.

"Hello, Esther, how are you? This must be Susie?"

"I'm well, thank you, ma'am, and yes, she's six weeks old now."

"No need to call me ma'am, Esther. I've known you long enough to always be Annie to you. Why, Sam even gave me away when I married Harry Rudd. How is Sam?"

"Yes, he's fine, too, thank you."

"That's good. Oh look, the queue's moving."

Annie was aware of the terrible tragedy that had struck the Symons family when they lost all five of their children in the diphtheria outbreak some seven years earlier. How could she ever forget when she had lost her little brother, Johnny, and sister, Emma?

Her two cousins, Harriet and Theresa, dealt with the queue of people efficiently, and it was not long before it was Annie's turn to be served, and there was no one else waiting.

"Good morning, Annie; how are you?"

"I'm fine, thank you, Harriet. I have a list of things we need, and I was wondering if you could have them delivered to the Manor House, please? I'd like a walk before I return home."

"Yes, of course; leave it with me and I'll see to it."

"Thank you. Now, I need to catch up on all the gossip. I hear you're walking out with Francis Rudd?"

"Yes, that's right. It's strange, isn't it? We've lived near each other all our lives, and never took much interest in one another, and now we've become close."

"I'm glad to hear it. I think Francis has been so busy rebuilding the business at the smithy since his dad and Harry died in the fire that he's had no time for courtship until now. He's a kind and considerate man, though, and you could do far worse. As you know, I was married to his brother, Harry, for a short time before his death, and his mother, Matilda, is still like a mother to me."

"Yes, they're a friendly family, and Matilda has made me welcome."

"And how about you, Theresa? Have you settled into Bluebell Cottage and are keeping well now that you are with child?"

"Yes, thank you, Annie, though I'm suffering from morning sickness, which people tell me will pass. Louis and I love living at Bluebell Cottage, and although it's small, it's convenient for Louis living next door to The Red Lion where he works, and only a short walk to the shop for me."

"I'm glad the cottage is a happy place now, for Gran had a terrible childhood there."

"I know she did, and even now she doesn't like to visit; she always prefers me to see her and Grandad at Sunset Cottage."

"When's the baby due?"

"Sometime in early February, I can't wait to be a mum."

"Will you carry on working in the shop after the birth?"

"Probably not; Louis earns enough for us to manage, and it would be difficult with the baby, though Cissie has offered to mind it."

"The shop will need a new assistant then?"

"Yes, it will, but I'm sure there will be plenty of people keen to take the job."

Annie left the shop, delighted to think that her two cousins had finally found love, as both were in their twenties. She smiled as she thought about Theresa, for it seemed strange to see her boyish figure with a bump, while still being so slimly built. Inevitably, her thoughts turned to the precious child she too carried, and how she would have loved to share her news with Harriet and Theresa. However, given the way her husband had received her announcement, she was in no mood to celebrate her condition.

CHAPTER 33

It had been a long, hot summer, and the fine weather showed no signs of breaking. Gardeners and farmers alike grumbled that their crops and vegetables were desperate for rain, but most folk were enjoying the warmth, knowing there would be a cold winter ahead of them. With Selina safely at school and the twins being cared for by Naomi, Annie fancied a few hours to herself to think about her problems. She knew Robert only wanted to do the right thing by his mother, Danny, and her. Like most men, he wanted a quiet life, and she hated the distance that had developed between them. She loved him with all her heart and was desperately sad to think he had even considered the child she carried might not be his. However, a small part of her also felt guilty, for she wondered if she had subconsciously given off the wrong signals to James. It certainly seemed so, given his shocking declaration of love.

She hoped a long walk in the fresh air might clear her head and help her to think of a way to break the ice between herself and her husband. As she had time on her hands, she decided to walk over the cliffs towards Hangman's Hill, and then turn back and stroll over the moors to return. It would be a long and circuitous route, but she was in no hurry, and Hangman's Hill was a favourite spot for her and Robert when they ventured out for a picnic. Something they usually did on horseback, for it was several miles.

Annie was soon red in the face from the exertion, as the route led her steeply uphill. She stopped once or twice to catch her breath and relieve a stitch in her side. The gorse, a bright yellow, stood out against the rich purple-pink of the plentiful heather and white sea scabious. She had always taken a keen interest in flowers and wildlife and was delighted to see a kestrel hovering high above the cliff top as it scanned the countryside for its next meal, whilst many herring gulls screamed at each other, as they circled and wheeled in the light breeze.

She tried to think of an amicable solution to Lady Eleanor's request that her son, Danny, be returned to her, but the whole thing seemed impossible. How could the woman think he would want to see her, knowing she had abandoned him at birth? It was a ridiculous notion, and what would Lord and Lady Fellwood's precious aristocratic friends think? Had the stupid woman even thought of that? However, being a mother herself, she could think of nothing worse than seeing one of her children every day but being unable to spend time with them. But then, she consoled herself, she would never have given up one of her children in the first place, no matter what was wrong with them.

These thoughts led Annie on to consider Robert's suggestion that if Charles and Eleanor agreed to welcome her into their family, eventually the invitations could be widened to include her relations, and especially Danny. The matter angered her, for up until now, her in-laws had shunned her, whilst all along it was Lord Fellwood who was at fault for raping her seven years ago, and not, as Lady Eleanor believed, that she was an unmarried mother and a woman of loose morals. What annoyed her the most was that Robert had assumed she would be grateful to be accepted at last, with no thought of whether she would be willing to spend time with the man who attacked her.

Deep in thought and blinded by tears, she sat near the cliff edge and gazed out to sea. A fishing boat was visible on the horizon, and far below her, basking in the sun was a family of seals. Suddenly, she thought she heard a cry from somewhere, but seeing no one, she assumed it must have been one of the seagulls squawking. She lay back and gazed at the cloudless blue sky and allowed her wet eyes to close, thinking that after a disturbed night with the twins, she could do with forty winks. After only a few moments, she heard the cry again, and this time realised it was, without doubt, someone shouting for help.

Rising to her feet, she glanced around and was puzzled to see no one. When the plea came again, she suspected it was coming from over the cliff edge and, not having much of a head for heights, inched forward on her stomach to peer down. To her horror, she saw a woman lying awkwardly in a cleft in the rocks.

"Hello? Hello, it's all right, I can see you. Are you hurt?"

The woman turned to face her, and Annie gasped in shock, for it was the last person she expected, or wanted, to see. The expression on Lady Eleanor's face mirrored that on her own, and it would have been difficult for a spectator to know which of the pair was the most upset at the circumstances they found themselves in.

"Lady Eleanor, what's happened?"

"My horse reared when an eagle flew overhead, and threw me, the stupid animal. I landed on the cliff edge, and as I tried to scramble up, the ground crumbled and I fell. I think I've broken my ankle and now I can't climb back up; can you help me?"

"Yes, of course. If I reach down as far as I can, and you reach up, maybe I can take your hand and help you back up."

With some difficulty, the woman rose to her feet and, standing on one leg, reached up as far as she could while

Annie, lying on the ground, reached down, but was still a couple of inches away from the outstretched hand.

"It's no good, you're too far away. Can you scramble up a bit?"

Lady Eleanor rose unsteadily, but could not bear to put any weight on her injured foot. She searched for anything to use as a handhold, but there was nothing suitable, and Annie was horrified to see how unstable the ground around her was.

"I think it's too dangerous; you'll have to wait there while I fetch help. What happened to your horse? Did it bolt?"

"Yes, it galloped off as soon as it had thrown me; it probably knew I would teach it a lesson when I had the chance. Are you on horseback?"

"No, I've walked, but I'll search for your horse because it would be much quicker for me to ride back."

"He took off at quite a speed, and he's a nervous creature; I suspect he'll make his way home. Perhaps if you scrambled down the cliff a little, you could help me up? I don't want to stay here for hours on my own."

Annie observed the loose ground and was not keen on doing any such thing. However, she spotted a route that looked reasonably safe and agreed to try it. Cautiously, she lowered herself over the cliff and tested the ground nervously. It seemed sound, and so, holding on to clumps of heather, she began to descend towards the injured woman. When she was almost within reach, she wrapped one hand around a stunted bush and reached down towards her mother-in-law with the other.

As their fingertips touched, and both dared to hope a rescue was possible, the bush became uprooted from the shallow soil, and Annie began to slither down the slope! Eleanor grabbed her hand and, with the other holding on to a small tree, arrested Annie's descent. Both women were terrified of falling over the cliff edge, but, white-faced,

Annie desperately sought purchase in the loose rocks for her boots, and slowly, Eleanor pulled her up.

They lay side by side for a few moments, both so shocked and relieved to still be alive that they had no words.

At Hartford School, it was Helen Carter's turn to ring the bell that week, a task which taught the pupils to tell the time accurately. She kept glancing nervously at the clock on the wall, waiting for the big hand to reach the six, as school ended at half past three. If she were a minute early or late, it would result in staying behind to write lines. However, Helen was a clever little girl, and so far she had never made a mistake. Rising from her seat, she walked towards the headmaster's desk, raised the large handbell and rang it loudly three times.

The children rose to their feet, and Mr Atkins instructed them to put their chairs on their desks so the room could be swept. One row at a time, they left the room in an orderly fashion, but once outside, they ran around laughing, delighted that school was over for the day. Most children made their way home alone, some walking several miles in all weathers, but Annie always fetched Selina. Not all parents could afford this luxury; for most had to work or stay at home looking after younger children, but Annie enjoyed her walk to collect Selina each day and hear about what she had done at school.

Selina exited the classroom and walked to the school gate, where she expected to see her mother. However, seeing no one in sight, she wondered what to do. She knew the way home and could easily walk most of the way with Stephen, Helen, and Danny, but she was puzzled why her mother was not there, for she had never been missing before. Helen noticed Selina standing by the gate and approached her.

"What's wrong, Selina? Where's Annie?"

"I don't know; she said she'd collect me today, and I don't know whether to walk home or wait for her."

"I think you should walk home with me to the Lodge House; you'll only have to walk up the drive to the Manor House on your own then. Perhaps she forgot the time, though it's not like her to do that."

"Yes, all right, I'll do that, thanks."

It didn't take long for the two girls to walk the short distance through the village to the Lodge House at the entrance to the Manor House drive. Only a few months separated them in age, and a spectator could have been forgiven for assuming they were sisters, but, in fact, Helen was Selina's aunt.

"You'd better come in and see if Annie's chatting to Mum and Liza; she might have forgotten the time."

They entered through the back door into the kitchen, where Stephen and Danny were already sitting at the large table and tucking into a piece of Liza's jam sponge. Sabina glanced up as the girls entered the room.

"Hello, Selina; I didn't expect to see you today. Where's your mum?"

"She didn't collect me from school, so I walked home with Helen; I thought Mum might be here."

"No, I haven't seen her today; how strange. Annie would never forget to collect you from school. Did she say she might be late?"

"No, she said, see you later, like she always does. It's all right, I'll walk up the drive on my own; perhaps she forgot."

"She would never forget; I'll come with you. I want to make sure she's all right."

CHAPTER 34

Delighted with his purchase of the new flock of sheep and having enjoyed his dinner at The Golden Fleece with his family, Robert was in high spirits as he drove the pony and trap home. Having given the matter of his differences with Annie a great deal of thought, he had decided that perhaps he owed her an apology. On the way, he passed Dodger driving the sheep and stopped for a few words. The only thing that marred his enjoyment of the journey was Jimmy Chugg's head lolling on his shoulder and the strong smell of alcohol emanating from him.

Instead of driving the pony and trap straight to the Manor House, he turned left on the road to Hollyford Farm to deliver Jimmy safely home, where he suspected the young man would probably receive a reprimand from his father, for all he was in his thirties and old enough to do as he liked.

Alfred Chugg was walking across the yard as Robert arrived, and he shielded his eyes from the sunshine to see who it was, fully expecting it to be Charlie and Eveline returning from the market.

"Hello, Robert, I didn't expect to see you today, and what's wrong with Jimmy? Oh, I can see what's wrong; he's drunk again."

"I'm afraid so, Alfred. I saw him staggering out of The Tucker's Arms and thought I'd better make sure he got home all right."

"I'm much obliged to you. Jimmy, Jimmy, wake up! You should be ashamed of yourself for bringing Mr Fellwood out of his way like this. Whatever are you thinking of these days?"

Jimmy opened a bleary eye and glanced around him, then smiled at his father.

"Hello, Dad; sorry, Robert, I must have fallen asleep."

"No wonder, the state you're in. Why do you keep getting so drunk, Jimmy, when all your life you've barely touched the drink?"

"I'm enjoying myself, Dad, and about time too, some would say. Thanks for bringing me home, Robert. I appreciate it."

Jimmy wobbled dangerously as he climbed down from the pony and trap, and with a sigh, Alfred slung his son's arm around his neck and helped him into the house.

"Would you like to come in for a drink or something to eat, Robert? You're welcome."

"No, it's all right, thanks, Alfred. I'd better get home. Take care, Jimmy, no good ever came of going to The Tucker's Arms; it has a terrible reputation. I'd find somewhere else to enjoy myself if I were you."

Robert hastened home and called in to see Jack Bater and tell him about the sheep he had purchased. As they were talking, Dodger arrived, and all three men admired the new flock.

"How are you, Jack? Is your back any better?"

"Yes, a bit, thank you. I think I'll be able to return to work tomorrow if I'm careful for a day or two. Thank you for being so understanding, not many would be."

"Good, I'll see you tomorrow then; Dodger, get one of the farmhands to help you put the sheep in the barn for the night, and we'll take them out to the pasture tomorrow."

Leaving the pony and trap for other farmhands to attend to, Robert entered the Manor House through the kitchen as was his custom. Inside, he found Mrs Potts and Maisie enjoying a cup of tea, and they urged him to join them and sample a slice of the carrot cake that Maisie had made earlier. He was about to refuse, saying he needed to speak to Annie, when Mrs Potts said there was something she wanted to talk to him about. He noticed that the old lady appeared to be anxious about something, and could not refuse her request. When he was settled with a strong cup of tea and a generous slice of cake, he asked the housekeeper how he could help.

"Well, sir, I've been meaning to have a word with you about this for a long time. Arthur and I are on the wrong side of seventy now, and we get tired these days. We think it's time we retired, and we wondered if you would consider renting John Cutcliffe's cottage to us? It's stood empty since he married Noeleen Gubb and moved into her house, and it would suit us. I know you'll need our rooms here in the house for a new housekeeper if I leave."

"Yes, of course, you can have the cottage, Mrs Potts. You should have asked sooner if the work was getting too much for you. No need to pay rent, though. You and Arthur have worked here for donkey's years, and you can live there for free for the rest of your lives."

"Oh, sir, that's so kind of you. We were worried about how long our savings would last once we stopped working, but we can pay something."

"No, I insist, it's the least I can do to thank you for all your years of service. You've been like a mother to me, Ethel, and I don't know what I would have done without you. Will you and Arthur be all right to carry on for a few weeks until we find replacements for you both?"

"Yes, sir, we'd never leave you in the lurch. Now, I think Maisie has something to tell you as well."

Maisie confided that she was with child and would also need to leave in a few months.

"That's wonderful, Maisie; I'm delighted for you and Martin. When do you want to leave?"

"The baby's not due until February, so I thought perhaps I'd leave at Christmas if that's all right?"

"That's fine, and I hope everything goes well. I'll discuss all this with Annie, and then we can start looking for some new staff; you'll be a hard act to follow, though, and we'll miss you both."

Leaving the cook and the housekeeper much relieved for getting their requests off their chests, Robert sped up the stairs to the nursery, where he expected to find Annie. However, he was surprised to see Sabina there and looking anxious.

"Hello, Sabina; is everything all right? Where's Annie?"

"Oh, my goodness. I hoped she was with you. We don't know where she is. She didn't collect Selina from school, and she would never forget to do that."

Robert paled as his first thought was that his wife had left him and absconded with her young man. Then he reprimanded himself, for he knew she would never leave her children, even if she wanted to end their relationship.

"I've not seen her since first thing this morning at breakfast, then I went to the Barnstaple market with Dodger to buy some sheep. I'm a bit late home as I gave Jimmy Chugg a lift back to Hollyford Farm, and then I had a chat with Mrs Potts and Maisie. Selina, did Mummy say she'd collect you from school today?"

"Yes, she kissed me and said, 'See you later', like she always does. Where's Mummy, Papa?"

"I don't know, my love, but don't worry, I'm sure there's a simple explanation. Naomi, do you know where your mistress could be?"

"No, sir. She said she'd be leaving the twins with me today as she intended to call in at the shop after she had taken Selina to school, and then she was going for a walk, but I've not seen her since."

"Do you know where she intended to go?"

"No, she didn't say. I know she often favours the moors or walking through the mazzard greens, but I expected her back hours ago. It's not like her to leave the twins for so long."

Robert forced a smile on his face for the sake of Selina and Sabina and spoke cheerfully.

"Not to worry; I'm sure she's been held up somewhere and will be home at any moment. In the meantime, I'll see if I can find her. Sabina, if you want to get back to your family, I'll come and see you later after I've found Annie."

Robert hurried from the house and instructed a stable boy to saddle a fresh horse as quickly as possible. Within minutes, he was trotting down the driveway, passing Sabina on the way, and went straight to the village shop, where Theresa was putting up the closed sign. He hammered on the door and she opened it straight away.

"My goodness, Robert, what is it you need so urgently?"

"Have you seen Annie today?"

"Yes, she called in after she dropped Selina at school this morning and ordered a few things which I've had delivered to the Manor House kitchen; was there something wrong with the order?"

"No, nothing like that, but Annie hasn't returned home; do you know where she was going?"

"Yes, she said she had a quiet day to herself and felt like a long walk; I felt quite envious."

"Did she say where she was going?"

"No, I'm afraid not, but she often walks over the moors, and with the heather in bloom, I expect she'd go that way. She should have been back long before now, though. I hope everything is all right."

"Yes, she's probably forgotten the time, or called in on someone for a cup of tea, but I'll ride that way and look for her."

Truly puzzled and extremely concerned, Robert left the shop, mounted his horse and cantered through the village, taking the footpath that led to a series of mazzard greens and orchards. It was a track that he was familiar with, for it was where he and Annie had often met when they were courting. He trotted through the first mazzard green and into the second, where the trees were older, and glanced wistfully beneath the largest one, where he and Annie had first kissed, and he knew that he loved her. Knowing how troubled she was at present, he would not have been surprised to find her sitting there, but in his heart, he knew she would not stay away from her children this long if she could return.

He continued through several fields and orchards until the path took him onto open moorland, where he searched until the daylight was fading and he was forced to return home. As he rode through the village, he called at Sunset Cottage in case Annie was with her granny and grandad. He was reluctant to do so, for he knew it was unlikely she was there, and he didn't want to worry the elderly couple. However, he felt he must do so, in case they knew where she had gone. He still had a nagging worry that she might have left him, and if she confided in anyone, it would be her granny.

He knocked on the door, and before many minutes passed, it was opened by Betsey, who was surprised to see him.

"Master Robert, it's nice to see you, but what brings you here at this time of day? Is everything all right?"

For once, Robert did not reprimand the old lady for not calling him by his first name, something she still struggled with, and he forced a smile onto his face.

"I wondered if you had seen Annie today, Betsey?"

"No, not today. She called in yesterday and seemed a bit under the weather, but not today, no. Don't you know where she is?"

"No, I've been to the Barnstaple market today and I haven't seen her since breakfast. She dropped Selina off at school and then visited the shop, where she told Theresa she was going for a walk, but she hasn't come home, and I must admit I am worried now that it's getting dark. She would never not collect Selina from school if she said she would."

"Oh, dear, that is a worry, and no, she would never neglect Selina. I hope you don't mind me asking, but is everything all right between the two of you now?"

"No, we've had our differences over a couple of things recently, but even so, I'm sure she'd never leave the children."

"No, she wouldn't, and you must know she worships the ground you walk on. I don't know where she can be, but it won't be by choice, so you're right to be worried. Have you been searching for her?"

"Yes, I've ridden through the mazzard greens and orchards and onto the moors, but it's too dark to continue, much as I'd like to."

"No, you must give up now, and return home, or you, too, could have an accident, which will help no one. Maybe by the time you reach home, she will be there with a perfectly reasonable explanation; I hope so anyway. Do let me know when you find her, won't you, for me and Ned won't rest until we know she's safe."

Realising that Betsey was right, and sorry he had worried her, Robert rode back to the Lodge House, where he called in to see Sabina. She opened the door as soon as she heard his horse, and looked at him expectantly, but he shook his head and continued to the Manor House, where he hoped with all his heart he would find his wife.

As he galloped into the stables, Dodger came forward to take his horse, and Robert noticed the worried expression on his face.

"Has Annie arrived home, Dodger? Is she all right?"

"As far as I know, sir, she's still not home, but I'm afraid I have more worrying news, for your mother is also missing, and her horse returned without her not five minutes ago."

CHAPTER 35

For some minutes, Annie and Eleanor lay quietly side by side, too shocked and relieved that they hadn't fallen over the cliff together to say anything. They were trapped in a deep, narrow cleft in the rock, and looking up, Annie could see that it would be impossible to climb up safely without help. She was angry at herself for trying to rescue her mother-in-law, for even now she could have been hurrying home to fetch help. It was the fact that Eleanor's outstretched hand was only an inch or two from her own that had persuaded her to attempt the climb and resolve the matter.

She became aware of pain in her hand and down her back and eased herself carefully into a sitting position to investigate. She noticed a large rock in front of them that seemed securely embedded into the cliff face, and she carefully shifted backwards so that her feet were behind it. Eleanor's position was even more precarious than her own, and she patted the woman gently on the shoulder.

"Eleanor, shuffle back here towards me where it's safer. This rock seems solid, and I think we'd be better sitting behind it rather than on the loose scree. Give me your hand."

The older woman held out her hand and, with Annie's help, eased herself back to a more secure position.

"What are we going to do? Did you tell anyone where you were going?"

"No, did you?"

"No, look, your hand is bleeding."

Annie observed the large gash on her hand and forearm, reached under her skirt for her petticoat, and, using her teeth, tried to rip a piece of the material off to use as a bandage. It took some effort, and she reflected ruefully that in the past, her clothing would have torn easily when it was threadbare. Eventually, a strip became free, and again using her teeth, she tried to bind the wound.

"Let me do it for you."

Silently, Annie passed the makeshift bandage to Eleanor and allowed her to bind the wound. Her back felt like it was on fire, but she knew there was little to be done. However, when her hand and arm were dressed, she leant over and asked her companion to see if her back was bleeding much.

"It is bleeding but not a great deal; do you want me to apply a dressing?"

"No, thank you, I expect it's only a graze. How's your foot?"

"It's throbbing."

"Let me see."

Eleanor winced and cried out in pain as she lifted her skirt and moved her foot into view, and Annie could see that it was swelling rapidly.

"You must take off your boot before it swells even more."

"No, I can't, it hurts too much."

"It will hurt more if you don't. I'll do it for you."

Annie unlaced the strong leather boot and, as gently as possible, eased it off Eleanor's foot, which was lying at an impossible angle.

"No wonder you couldn't stand on it; it's definitely broken. If there were something here to use as a splint, I'd bind it up, but I can't see anything suitable. Are you hurt anywhere else?"

"I banged my head as I fell, and it's tender on this side, but it's not bleeding. How long do you think it will be before they find us?"

"I don't know. I should be collecting Selina from school this afternoon, but no one will miss me until then; how about you?"

"No, Charles may wonder where I am, but he knows I enjoy some time to myself, so I don't think he'll worry. Hopefully, my horse will wander home, and then people will realise there's something wrong and come looking for me."

A long silence followed their stilted conversation, and Annie thought she must be being punished for something to be forced to spend time alone with Robert's mother. Her companion was thinking along the same lines, and for some hours, not a word was spoken. As the sun disappeared behind the cliff face and dusk began to fall, the temperature dropped sharply, and both women were cold, for neither had a jacket or a shawl.

"Eleanor, we must huddle together for warmth if we are not to take a chill. I know it's not what either of us wants, but we must put our differences aside until we're rescued. If you lie on your side, I'll cuddle into your back, and later we'll change position."

Lady Eleanor, who had never experienced such discomfort in her life, nodded and silently allowed her estranged daughter-in-law to put her arm around her.

With the help of his nursemaid, Charles Fellwood was preparing for bed. He was puzzled that his wife had not visited him all day, for as far as he knew, he had not said or done anything to upset her. He quizzed the maid about his wife's whereabouts, but knowing Eleanor was missing, Tess thought it kinder not to worry the frail man. As she made him comfortable, there was a sharp knock on the door, and she went to answer it, puzzled as to who it could be at that hour, for Eleanor would have entered.

"I must speak with my father; is he asleep yet?"

"No, sir, though he has retired; please come in."

Charles was surprised to see his son, for Robert seldom visited him.

"Robert, is something wrong?"

"Yes, I'm afraid there is. Do you know where Mama is?"

"No, I've not seen her since first thing this morning, and it's unlike her. She usually pops in several times a day, and we often sit together in the evenings. I've been wondering if she's unwell?"

"She's not been seen since she went riding this morning, and an hour ago, her horse returned without her. Do you know where she was going?"

"Oh no! Oh, my goodness, you must send out a search party immediately. No, I don't know where she was going. I'm always telling her to let the stable lads know where she's going, which she insists Sarah does, but neglects to do so herself. Was the horse injured?"

"No, it was distressed, but unharmed."

"Does Sarah know where she might be?"

"Sarah is staying with Aunty Margery for a few days, and she left early this morning."

"Oh, yes, of course she did. I forgot."

"The strange thing is that Annie is missing as well. She took Selina to school this morning and promised to collect her at the end of the day, but failed to do so. She would never let Selina down, so there must be a reason she was unable to."

Charles was puzzled. "It's unlikely the two women are together, isn't it? They never speak to one another as far as I know, and even if they did, it would not explain why they have not come home."

"Do you think Mama might have tackled Annie about having Danny back?"

"It's possible, I suppose. She's set her heart on spending time with him, but even if she did discuss the matter with Anne, it still doesn't explain where they are. Have you organised a search party?"

"Since I discovered Annie was missing, I've ridden for miles around the village and across the moors looking for her until dusk fell, and then I had to return home. I didn't know until then that Mama was also unaccounted for. I'm afraid it's too dark to search now, but I'll send the men out at first light. I'm sorry to have burdened you with this, at this late hour, Papa, but I had to know if you could throw any light on the matter. I'll let you know as soon as there are any developments; try not to worry too much, though I appreciate that's easier said than done."

Robert poured himself a stiff drink and sat in the library before a roaring fire. The nights were already turning colder, and he hoped with all his heart that his wife and mother were somewhere warm and safe. Eventually, exhausted, he headed for his bedroom, but on the way, he stopped to check on the twins and found they were fast asleep. However, when he quietly opened Selina's bedroom door, the little girl sat up.

"Is that you, Mummy?"

"No, I'm sorry, sweetheart, it's me, Papa. Are you all right?"

"No, I want my mummy."

"I know, and I'm worried too, but I expect there's a simple explanation, and tomorrow we'll all laugh about this. Now, let's dry your tears and get you settled."

"Can I sleep in with you tonight, Papa?"

"Yes, of course, you can; come on."

Within ten minutes, Selina, now exhausted, was fast asleep, and Robert lay listening to her deep breathing. However, for him, sleep was elusive, and he heard the hall clock strike all the hours right up to four o'clock when he finally lost consciousness.

CHAPTER 36

A stiff breeze arose, chilling the two women to the bone, and they spent a mostly sleepless night shivering uncontrollably. By morning, tired and hungry, they watched the sun rise and longed for the warmth it would bring later in the day.

"How's your foot this morning?"

Eleanor lifted her long skirt to reveal her swollen ankle, which was already turning black and blue.

"Painful, as you can see. How about your injuries?"

"Not too bad, thanks. They're sore, but the bleeding has stopped. At least our families will know by this time we're missing and will be looking for us, though I'm sure they'll never guess we're together."

Eleanor raised a wry smile. "No, they will never imagine that, but I hope they find us soon."

"They will. Robert won't rest until we're both found safe and well."

"You really do love my son, don't you?"

"Of course, and if you believe nothing else about me, you can be assured of that. I've loved him from the day I met him."

"How did you meet him? Was it when you were working as a maid at the manor? I've often wondered."

"No, it was before that, and this will shock you, but Robert spotted me from the nursery window when I was stealing vegetables from the Manor House garden. He was spending time in the nursery with Sarah because she had broken her ankle. It's not something I'm proud of, for I was brought up not to steal, but my father had died of consumption, and my family was starving."

Annie noted a snooty expression on her mother-in-law's face, and she grinned.

"See, I knew you'd judge me, but I'm the eldest in our family, and my five brothers and sisters had nothing to eat, and Mum was carrying another child. There was no food in the house, and we expected to be evicted any day because with Dad dying, we knew we'd have to leave the tied cottage for a new worker. I wonder what you would have done if your children had nothing to eat?"

The question made the older woman pause for thought, as it was something she had never considered.

"Were there no relatives that could help you?"

"No, none that were willing or any better off than us. The neighbours gave us food from time to time, but they had little enough themselves. With hindsight, I think Mum should have asked for more help from my granny and grandad, who kept The Red Lion Inn, but they were my dad's parents, and she hadn't always seen eye to eye with them, and she was proud and stubborn."

"Even if Robert saw you from the nursery window, how did he meet you?"

"He was intrigued because it was pouring with rain and I was crawling along the path, dragging a sack of stolen vegetables behind me and hoping no one would see me over the low hedges. I never gave a thought to someone looking out of an upstairs window."

"Didn't you get dirty?"

"Yes, I was covered in mud and scraped my elbows and knees, but that wasn't important as long as I found us something to make a rabbit stew go a bit further. That was my other job back then; I walked miles over the moors every day, trying to shoot rabbits. My dad had taught me to shoot, and I became quite good at it."

"So did Robert catch you?"

"Yes, he was curious and lay in wait for me, and after a few mornings, he saw me creep through the hedge that backs onto the woodland." Annie grinned as she remembered the incident. "I was wearing my dad's trousers and a cap to hide my hair, and he thought I was a boy. He jumped out from behind a bush and frightened me half to death. I expected to be jailed or hanged for stealing, but we got chatting and he didn't report me. We liked each other from then on, and I took him fishing at Shebworthy Pond. After that, he used to work on the farms with me, giving me the money he earned. He was kind to us."

"I remember something about this. Yes, Harry Rudd, the blacksmith's son, came to shoe a horse, and he told Jack Bater that Robert had saved him from drowning in the pond. Jack told my husband because he knew Robert was forbidden to mix with the local youngsters, and we sent him back to boarding school early to put a stop to it all."

"Ah, so it was Harry who told tales then; we always thought it was. Harry was jealous of my friendship with Robert and wanted to split us up, even though Robert had saved his life. Robert and I were in love by then, and he'd already asked me to marry him. I always told him it was impossible, but he said we'd find a way when he left school. His father was angry when he found out Robert was mixing with the locals, and he was told to leave early the next morning to return to boarding school, but then you gave birth to Danny, and Robert brought him to our cottage to ask Mum to raise him."

Eleanor shifted uncomfortably in embarrassment.

"Yes, that's right, but it was a mistake and I regret parting with the child now; I want him back!"

The cock crowing at half past five disturbed Robert, and quietly he left the little girl sleeping, and having quickly dressed, knocked on Naomi's door. The nanny appeared, her hair in disarray and a gown pulled around her.

"I'm sorry to disturb you, Naomi, but Selina slept in my bed last night as she was upset. She's still asleep, so can you listen out for her? I don't want her to wake up alone, for she's already upset about Annie being missing. You can lie beside her, if you like."

"Yes, sir; I'll do that, thank you, and I'll hear the twins from there when they wake. I do hope you find the mistress soon, sir."

"Thank you, Naomi, so do I."

Robert sped down the stairs and entered the kitchen, where Maisie and a few of the kitchen maids were already busy.

"Good morning, Maisie. Could you prepare a cooked breakfast for me, please? I don't feel hungry, but I didn't have an evening meal last night, so I'd better have something before I venture out. I'm going to raise a search party, and then I'll come back to eat before I join them."

"Of course, sir, I get on with it straight away."

Robert hastened to the farmyard where the men were getting ready to start their day's work. Jack Bater, now mostly recovered from his bad back, was issuing instructions.

"Morning, Jack; can you get as many men together as possible to form a search party to look for Annie and my mother, please? Only keep enough men back to do the essential tasks, like the milking. I want everyone else on horseback and scouring the countryside; we must find them as soon as possible. I can't imagine they're together, but wherever they are, they must be injured to prevent them from coming home. Can you ask the men if either of the women told them where they were going yesterday? I'm going to get something to eat, and then I plan to visit Hollyford Farm and Sugworthy Farm in case Annie has gone to see Marrok and Sam, or Eveline and Charlie, though it's unlikely she would do that without telling someone."

"Aye, sir. I'm already on it. The lads are saddling every horse we have, and we'll be out looking within a few minutes."

"Excellent, thank you."

Having eaten his breakfast, Robert mounted Prince and cantered down the driveway. Knowing Sabina would be awake, he called at the Lodge House to tell her what was happening, and she was amazed to hear that his mother was missing as well. He decided not to disturb Betsey and Ned until later in the day, but instead called at The Red Lion Inn and spoke with Fred and Charlotte. Neither was able to help, but Fred, Louis, and Llewellyn insisted on helping with the search and went to saddle their horses. Robert suggested they join Jack's search party to ensure every area was covered.

He hesitated by the village shop, but then knocked in case Annie was there. Mary Ann's maid, Cissie, came to the door, surprised at such an early visitor, and assured him that she had not seen either of the missing women.

Spurring his horse on, Robert galloped to Hollyford Farm. At any other time, he would have delighted in an early morning ride, for there was a bit of a nip in the air, and it was going to be a fine day. The heavy dew glistened on the many cobwebs stretching across the bushes, and the melodic dawn chorus greeted his ears, but he spared no time to admire nature's best. As he cantered into the farmyard, he spotted Charlie carrying a pitchfork of hay on his shoulder, and reined in his horse.

"Good morning, Charlie; I'm sorry to bother you so early in the day, but have you seen Annie or my mother since yesterday morning?"

"No, I'm afraid not. Why? Are they missing?"

"Yes, neither has been seen since early yesterday, and I have a search party out looking for them."

Charlie was puzzled. "Do you think they're together?"

"I don't know what to think, but it's unlikely. Annie left on foot for a walk, and my mother's horse returned without her last evening. I have no idea where they are."

"Would you like to come in for something to eat?"

"No, thanks, I've eaten and I must carry on searching. I'm going to ride to Sugworthy Farm now to see if Marrok or Sam have seen Annie. Thanks, anyway, Charlie."

"I'll tell Alfred what's happened, and he can take over here for the day. Jimmy and I will saddle up and join the search party; don't worry; we'll find them."

CHAPTER 37

Annie stared at her mother-in-law in amazement.

"I can't believe you have the cheek to ask to have Danny back. The child is seven years old, and you've barely spared him a thought in all that time. The only life he's ever known is with my mother, and she's gone without food herself to make sure he's never wanted for anything. How could you possibly explain the matter to him? If you told him the truth, he'd hate you for abandoning him. And what about Victoria and Sarah? How would you explain the matter to them?"

"That's not true. I've never forgotten him, and now that he visits you and I see him, I think of him all the time. He's so like my first-born son, David, that it breaks my heart."

"I know you lost David, and I am sorry for that, for I can think of nothing worse than losing a child, but you chose to give Danny up, and you even had the money to ensure he was cared for. My mother has scrimped and saved and gone hungry to make sure he never did, and now you think you can ask for him back. You're being ridiculous."

"It wasn't an easy decision to give him up, but I thought it was for the best at the time. It wasn't even that I didn't love him, for all mothers love their children, but I couldn't bear the thought of watching him suffer in the way my late brother did. Poor Sydney looked like Danny when he was born, but he had no intelligence and couldn't do anything for himself. He had a nursemaid with him night and day, but even so, my mother had little time for me or her other children, and she was heartbroken when he died. I don't think it's going too far to say that having Sydney destroyed her health and her marriage, and I didn't want that to happen to us."

"I didn't know that, and it's sad, but I would still never give up my child, and now, Danny would be miserable to leave the only family that he's ever known. Surely, you can see that? He's healthy, clever, and has had all his disabilities corrected as far as is possible. The surgeons in London did an amazing job. Be happy for him that he's content."

"I am glad he's had surgery, and I suppose it would be difficult to uproot him, but I would like to get to know him; he needn't know the truth or that I'm his mother."

"Again, how is that possible? You despise me and my family and sneer at us because we're lower class. We're only having this conversation because fate has thrown us together; otherwise, you wouldn't give me the time of day. You've not even met your grandchildren, though Robert says how much you miss Victoria's family now they have moved to Lynton."

"I do miss them, that's true, but I don't think you understand what a disgrace it is for our son to have married you, a former kitchen maid. It's not about you personally; I would feel the same if he had married any servant. Many of our friends no longer want to know us, and socially, it's so difficult for Sarah. I hope she can find a suitable husband when she has her coming-out season next year."

"If your so-called friends are that shallow, then I think you're better off without them. Sarah is an attractive and desirable young lady, and I'm sure she'll find a suitable match, though I'd rather she marry for love than financial benefit. I don't suppose you were aware, but Victoria and Sarah accepted me as soon as Robert told them we were getting engaged. They were so kind, and they showed me the correct etiquette at the table, how to dress, and even taught me to dance because I didn't want to embarrass Robert. I turned down his proposal several times because I knew it would be difficult, but he would not take no for an answer."

Eleanor was surprised. "I didn't realise they had spent so much time with you, and I will say they did an excellent job; for you do carry off being a lady well, from what I have seen."

"Well, I'll take that as a compliment, and if Frank Eastleigh could have resisted the urge to embarrass Robert and me at our engagement party, then we were hoping most folk would have been unaware of my origins. He couldn't resist causing trouble, could he? I'm sorry to speak ill of the dead, but he was a despicable man."

"I have to agree that he had his faults; he was certainly unfaithful to Victoria, though I think he loved her in his own way."

"Maybe, but he had a strange way of showing it. Even when he was engaged to her, he was trying to bed me. He even attacked me once in the barn, and if it weren't for Dodger Watkins, he would have forced himself on me. Dodger fetched Robert, and he and Frank came to blows over it. They were never friends again, although they became brothers-in-law."

"Oh dear, I always wondered why they didn't get along, for they were friends as children. I wish Robert had told Charles and me of his behaviour, Victoria too, for she might have had second thoughts."

"I think Robert hoped that Frank would honour his marriage vows, following the wedding, but unfortunately, he didn't change his ways. He even had my cousin, Theresa, captured and kept a prisoner at The Tucker's Arms for his pleasure when he next visited from London. Luckily, she was rescued before that could happen."

"That's terrible. Frank has a lot to answer for, and it makes it hard on his mother. She's a friend of mine, and naturally, she grieves for her son, despite his faults. Charles and I had no clue that he was so depraved."

"No, and I think there are a lot of things that you're unaware of, but anyway, going back to Danny, how could you possibly explain your wanting to see him to Victoria and Sarah? They would never understand. And then there's Danny himself. What would he think of you wanting to get to know him? He's already unsettled by your interest in him when he plays in the Manor House garden. If you ever told him the truth, he'd despise you for abandoning him as a baby. I'm afraid I don't see any way of letting you be part of his life, even if Mum and the rest of us were willing. As my gran would say, you've made your bed, now you must lie on it."

Eleanor was silent for a few minutes, but then spoke quietly.

"What if Charles and I accepted you as Robert's wife and got to know your children, especially the twins, for they are legitimately our grandchildren. Do you think we could see Danny then?"

Annie's green eyes flashed with anger, and she struggled to keep her hands to herself as she muttered.

"I want to make this crystal clear. There is no way I will ever spend time in your company, or that of your husband. It seems that, like Robert, you think it is only up to you whether we socialise or not. I can tell you now that I have no wish to be accepted into your family. In my eyes, you're not worthy of mixing with me and my family, not the other way around. I enjoy spending time with Victoria and Sarah, for they have always been kind to me, but that's where I draw the line. And even now, when you're begging a favour, you draw a distinction between my daughter, Selina, and the twins. You don't learn, do you?"

Eleanor gaped at her daughter-in-law in surprise, for she found it hard to believe that Annie and her family would be unwilling to socialise with her and Charles.

"I suppose we could accept Selina too, for I know Robert is her father, although she was illegitimate. I'm surprised he had such low morals; he was not much better than Frank when you think about it."

"What makes you think Selina is Robert's child?"

"I saw her undress once in the garden when the children were going swimming in the lake, and I saw the birthmark on her shoulder; it runs in our family. Victoria has one that is almost identical. What's always puzzled me is why you married Harry Rudd? I'm sure if Robert had known you were with child, he would have done the right thing by you; he's like that."

"She's not …" Annie stopped, horrified that she had almost blurted out the truth about Selina's father. She continued hastily. "Robert had returned to boarding school, and I had no way of contacting him to tell him I was pregnant. Miss Wetherby sacked me as soon as she realised my condition, and Harry had been asking me to marry him for a long time."

"I suppose you let him think the child was his to gain respectability?"

Annie became even more furious and was tempted to tell the bitter woman the truth, but she knew Robert would hate his mother knowing what his father had done, and, once said, there could be no taking it back. With an enormous effort, she held her tongue.

"No, I did not let him think the child was his. You always assume the worst about me, don't you? I would never have done that to Harry; he was such a kind man, and it was so sad he died in the fire like he did."

"What were you going to say about Selina? You started to say, she's not … she's not, what? If she's not Harry Rudd's child and not Robert's, then who is her father?"

Annie pursed her lips and refused to answer.

CHAPTER 38

Robert was glad that Charlie and Jimmy were joining the search for the missing women, for the more people involved, the better. He spurred his horse into a gallop and raced towards Sugworthy Farm. He hadn't visited in a while and was delighted to see the pale-yellow thatch of the new roof gleaming in the strengthening sunshine. As he drew nearer to the ancient farmhouse, he noted the new windows and smart front door and thought what a huge improvement Marrok had made since moving in a few months earlier. He slowed his horse and cantered into the farmyard where a milkmaid was carrying a pail of milk to the dairy, and Sam was cleaning out the shippens. Marrok's twin daughters, Jinnie and Eliza, were feeding the many hens that roamed freely.

"Hello, Sam; I see you're busy this morning. I wouldn't have thought you needed to do such heavy work at your age. Surely some of the younger farmhands could do it."

"Aye, they could, but I'm doing it from choice. There's always a lot to do on a farm, and I like to keep my joints moving; they stiffen up when you get old, like me. What brings you here so early?"

"I'm looking for Annie and my mother; they've been missing since yesterday morning, and I'm so worried. I've been to Hollyford Farm to see if Annie is there, but she isn't, and so I wondered if you had seen her? I'm checking everywhere I can think of, though I don't hold out much hope because I know she wouldn't leave the children for so long."

"Nay, lad, I'm sorry, but I haven't seen her, and there's no reason your mother would come here. Do you think they're together? I thought they didn't get along?"

"They don't, and I can't imagine they're together; but it doesn't make sense that they're both missing."

"Well, come inside and have a word with Marrok; he may be able to spare some men to help you search."

Sam led the way into the kitchen, and despite his worries, Robert looked around him in amazement. When Marrok and Sam moved to Sugworthy, the farmhouse was a dilapidated and tumbledown dwelling with a leaky roof, rotten windows and doors. The dingy kitchen had not been decorated for many years, but now the room was bright and cheery, with larger windows letting in lots of light and sunshine. The walls were freshly limewashed, and there were new rugs on the freshly scrubbed flagstones.

"My goodness, what a change you've made since you moved in, Marrok; it's unbelievable."

"Thank you, Robert; yes, we're getting there. It's been hard work, but so rewarding to see the old place restored to its former glory. We're slowly working our way through the whole house, and there's still a lot to do; outside, too, for a lot of the fences and gates were in a sorry state. Brambles and thistles have overtaken some areas, and we're gradually clearing them. I've taken on a couple of new farmhands, and Dad's been amazing, paying for everything and now working hard every day, although I tell him there's no need at his age."

"Ah, I'm enjoying myself. Besides, if I clean out the shippens and stables, it leaves the younger men free to do other jobs. I take my time, and it doesn't matter if it takes me all day, and then I look forward to a tasty meal cooked by this lovely lady. What more reward could a man want?"

The old man placed his arm around Florrie and kissed her on the cheek. The housekeeper was cooking a fried breakfast, and she pushed him away good-naturedly.

"Get away with you, you old fool, can't you see I'm busy? Sit yourself down and have your breakfast."

"See how she bullies me, Robert. Come and join us for breakfast and tell us what you can about these missing women."

Robert was delighted to witness the growing romance between his great-uncle and the housekeeper, and despite his worries, he smiled at them.

"Thank you, but I've already had my breakfast, though I would appreciate a cup of tea, please, Florrie. I can't stay long because I must keep searching. The women must have already spent a night out in the open, and although the days are still warm the nights are chilly."

"It seems strange for Annie and your mother to be missing at the same time; did they go out together?"

"No, Annie dropped Selina off at school and went for a walk and then failed to collect her at the end of the day, and she would never do that. My mother went for a ride, and her horse came back without her. They probably aren't together, but it's odd they've both gone missing at the same time. Annie and I have had a few differences lately, but I know she would never leave her children, so I can only think that for some reason she's unable to come home."

"Would you like us to help with the search?"

"I'd appreciate that, Marrok, if you can spare the time."

"Yes, of course, Dad can keep an eye on things here. As soon as I've eaten this, I'll saddle up a horse and bring one of the farmhands with me; everything else can wait until we've found them. Where do you want me to look?"

"If you ride to the Manor, Jack is coordinating the search. We don't know if Annie walked along the coast or went inland over Exmoor, so there's a big area to search, though she can't have gone that far on foot. It's the same with my mother, but she was on horseback, so she could have travelled several miles. She always insisted that as children, we tell the grooms where we were going in case of something like this. If only she followed her own rules."

"Shall we ride back to the Manor with you?"

"No, I'm going to Lynton to check with my sister, Victoria, that neither Annie nor my mother is there. It's unlikely, but I need to rule it out. Thanks for the tea, Florrie. I'll see you later, Marrok."

Robert galloped off in the direction of Lynton, trying to quell his mounting fear that something terrible had happened. He could not imagine any scenario that would necessitate his wife and mother spending time together and not returning home. He cantered up the driveway of the impressive house that his sister had recently purchased and noticed that, like at Sugworthy Farm, Victoria had made considerable improvements since his last visit.

Before she bought the house, it had lain empty for over a year, and an atmosphere of neglect surrounded it. However, the lawns were now freshly mown, the beds full of herbaceous flowers, and the once-broken fountain restored to its former glory. He trotted to the stables and left Prince with a lad, instructing him to rub the horse down and feed and water him, for he knew the beast would need to rest before going any further.

He entered the house by the kitchen door, and a maid showed him into the sitting room, where he was surprised and less than thrilled to find James McIntyre sitting on a sofa beside his sister.

"Robert, what a nice surprise." Victoria rose to her feet and hugged her twin. "You know James, don't you?"

"Yes, of course; how are you, James? Have you settled into Buzzacott House?"

"I'm well, thank you, and yes, the house is perfect for my needs. It's in a desolate spot with few distractions apart from the amazing views, so I have no excuse not to get on with writing my book. I rented the house for a reasonable price, too. Given its grisly history, the owner was having difficulty finding a tenant."

"What brings you here today, Robert? Is everything all right? You look a little jaded."

Her brother explained the reason for his visit, and Victoria listened with growing concern.

"That's ridiculous; Annie and Mama can't be together, surely? They can barely bring themselves to look at one another normally."

"I know, and I honestly can't think why they're both missing. I must return to join the search as soon as possible, but my horse needs a rest, so if you don't mind, I'll have a bite to eat before I go, and then I won't need to stop again."

"Of course, it's lunchtime anyway. I'll ring for some refreshments and then change into more suitable clothing and join you in the search."

"Thank you, I'd enjoy your company."

"I'll get my horse saddled too, and help in the search, Robert."

"No, thank you, James; it's kind of you, but I think we have enough people searching now, and I wouldn't want to keep you from working on your book."

CHAPTER 39

Eleanor Fellwood glared at her daughter-in-law. "I insist you tell me the truth. When I asked you if Robert was Selina's father, you started to say, 'She's not.' She's not what? Not Robert's? She must be because I've seen the family birthmark on her shoulder. What's the point of lying about it now? You can't change it, though I'm disappointed in my son for sleeping with a kitchen maid."

"Fine. So will you just leave it, for goodness' sake; trust me, these matters are best left in the past."

After a few minutes' silence, Eleanor gasped and put her hand to her mouth.

"Oh no! Did you seduce my husband so you could blackmail him for money? Is that it? If Robert isn't the child's father, it can only be Charles, for David had left home by then. Oh, my God! That's it, isn't it? That's why he let you marry Robert; you were blackmailing him. I could never understand why he agreed to the marriage so readily. I bet you threw yourself at Charles until he couldn't resist. Thinking back, it was not long after I'd given birth to the deformed baby, and I wouldn't let him in my bed, for fear of another pregnancy. I bet you flaunted yourself at him until he couldn't refuse; we all know how weak-willed men are."

"How dare you! No, I did not throw myself at your husband. If you must know, he raped me! There. Are you satisfied now? You're married to a rapist and a woman beater, and if you wouldn't let him into your bed, perhaps some of the blame lies with you."

Eleanor's already pale face blanched. "No, he wouldn't do such a thing; he's a gentleman."

"Huh, that's what you think. It was after the New Year's Eve party. I was clearing up the glasses in the hall and carrying them to the kitchen to be washed. He lay in wait for me in the corridor and snuffed out all the lamps. I was trying to find my way by the light shining from the kitchen door when I was grabbed from behind. A hand was held across my mouth to stop me screaming, and I was carried to the west wing cellars. It was bitterly cold, and he threw me onto an old mattress. He didn't only rape me, he hit me when I screamed and told me that if I did it again, he would kill me. I was terrified, and I thought he'd kill me anyway."

"I can't believe it! Charles is not a violent man; he's never raised his hand to me in all our years of marriage."

"I think he'd had too much to drink and got carried away, though that's no excuse. I honestly thought he'd kill me to shut me up, but when he'd finished with me, he left me lying there in the dark. I didn't know where I was, but eventually I pulled my clothes on and felt my way up the stairs and along the corridors until I recognised where I was."

"Are you sure it wasn't Robert?"

"It wasn't Robert, for he was at boarding school, and he would never do such a thing anyway. I didn't know who it was for a long time, though, and at first I thought it was probably Frank Eastleigh because he had attacked me before. The man didn't speak out loud but hissed in whispers, and it was too dark to see who it was; the only thing I was certain of was the way he smelled. He wore a distinctive cologne or used a fancy perfumed soap. I didn't know who it was until I was at my mother's house one day, bathing Selina, and Robert called to discuss making repairs to the cottage. He saw the birthmark on her shoulder and worked it out."

"There must be another explanation. Perhaps one of our guests was a relative, and the birthmark was passed down from them. I must find the guest list; I expect I have it somewhere. Yes, that must be it. Charles would never be unfaithful to me."

"No, I'm sorry, but he's definitely Selina's father. When we wanted to marry, Robert insisted I bring Selina to visit Lord Fellwood, and we showed him her birthmark. He still used the soap I remembered, and he admitted attacking me, though he tried to make out it was my fault for putting temptation in his way. I mean, how ridiculous is that? And you wonder why I don't want to spend time with you and your husband. Well, now you know. He's not fit to wipe my feet on."

"Why didn't you tell anyone?"

"What could I say? Me, a kitchen maid, the lowest of the low. If I'd said I was attacked and raped, who would have believed that one of your rich and distinguished guests could act in such a way? After all, they're all gentlemen, aren't they? The only person I told was Maisie because she saw what a state I was in when I finally returned to our bedroom. Oh, and then Miss Wetherby, of course. As soon as she guessed why I was being sick every morning, she dismissed me without any wages. I told her the truth, but she was having none of it and said I must have been asking for it."

"I can't believe Harry Rudd would want to marry you in such a disgraceful condition. I mean, he was a man with excellent prospects. His family had a sound business in the smithy."

"No, I don't suppose you can understand it, but some people are just kind. He had loved me for a long time and wanted to court me, but I loved Robert and I didn't want to mislead Harry, even if nothing could come of my friendship with Robert. Harry found me crying on the moors one day, because I didn't know what to do. I couldn't tell Robert, because he was at school, and although Mum welcomed me home, I didn't want to be a burden to her and bring home another mouth to feed when we were so short of food. I was at my wits' end, and Harry persuaded me to tell him all my troubles. I expected him to walk away, but instead he said he'd marry me anyway, even if in name only."

"And was it? In name only?"

"No, it wasn't. I didn't think that was fair, and I intended to be a loyal and obedient wife to him, so I tried to make the best of it. A lot of folk realised I was already with child, but it happens, and they knew Harry had been keen on me for a long time. We were happy enough in our own way, but I knew Harry was aware that I didn't love him. Maybe I would have in time; we'll never know because sadly he died in the smithy fire."

"Did you set the fire to get rid of him?"

Annie gasped in amazement that the woman could accuse her of such a terrible thing, and she struggled not to slap the sneering woman's face!

"How dare you ask if I set the fire? Of course, I didn't. It was a terrible tragedy, and Harry only died because, after rescuing his mother and brother, he went back looking for his father. I saw him fall to his death, and it's a sight I'll never forget to the end of my days."

"How did the fire start, then?"

"We think his father probably let his pipe fall. Ben's mind was going, and he'd taken to wandering around the house at all hours and doing strange things. He died in the fire as well. It was terrible for Matilda to lose her husband and son in one night."

"When did Robert find out about the baby?"

"I kept out of his way when he came home from school at Easter because Mrs Potts told him I'd married Harry, and I knew he wouldn't understand why, for we at least had an understanding. In his eyes, anyway; I'd always told him it was impossible for us to have a future together, but he was adamant he'd find a way. I couldn't bear to see him, and I didn't want him to know what had happened. He found out, though, because he lay in wait for me in the churchyard when I visited our family graves, and insisted on knowing why I married Harry. I still wasn't going to tell him, but he saw my swollen belly and guessed I must have been pregnant before the wedding. When I told him what had happened, he said he would have married me, but it was too late because I'd already married Harry. At that stage, we still didn't know who the father was."

"That is a sad tale, but I still find it hard to believe Charles would act in such a way. We've been married for twenty-six years, and I've never had reason to doubt his fidelity. I'll have to talk to him about it when we're rescued, but I don't know how we can continue our relationship. That is, if we're ever rescued. Will they never come for us? I'm so hungry; I've not eaten since breakfast yesterday morning, and I have a terrible headache."

"Yes, I'm hungry too, but I've been much hungrier in the past. Sometimes, after my father died, I barely ate for days, and I know my mother didn't, despite the fact that she was carrying a child. We always gave the younger children in the family the food we had. You have no idea what it's like to have little children crying because they're so hungry and have nothing to give them. It's unbearable. Maybe this experience will teach you a lesson and you won't be so quick to judge the poor in future."

Eleanor hung her head and said nothing.

CHAPTER 40

Betsey Carter couldn't settle to do anything; she was so worried about Annie. The young woman was her eldest grandchild, and they were close to each other. Ned tried to comfort her, but he, too, could not understand where Annie could be. They dismissed the notion that she could have run away with James McIntyre, for while they had noticed his attraction to her, they knew Annie would never leave her children.

"For two pins, I'd borrow a horse and find her myself."

"Well, you can put that thought right out of your head, Ned Carter. The last thing I need is for you to have another funny turn with your weak heart. Half of the village is already out looking, and they'll find her, but for the life of me, I can't imagine any reason for her to be with Eleanor Fellwood. They hate each other."

"No, me neither. It's a mystery. Why don't you visit Nancy and have a chat? It will take your mind off things for a while. If I hear any news, I promise I'll send for you straight away."

"I could, I suppose. As long as you're not getting rid of me so you can join the search?"

"No, I'd love to, but I'm not strong enough and I know my limitations."

"Good, I'm glad to hear it. All right then, I will call on her for an hour or so; she always appreciates some company, although she has that lad living with her now."

Kissing her husband on the cheek and promising not to be long, Betsey ambled through the village. It was quiet, and one or two folk stopped and asked if Annie had been found, and she sadly shook her head. She heard the school bell ring, and within seconds, the children poured out from the schoolroom, delighted that their learning was over for the day. She saw Stephen and Danny racing down the lane and waved to them. They ran over to her and hugged her, as she reached into her bag for one of the toffees that were kept for such occasions. Within seconds, they were followed by Helen, Selina, and Bentley, and once more she delved into her bag.

"Granny Betsey, do you know if Mummy has come home yet?"

Selina gazed at the old lady hopefully with wide eyes. The child looked tired and wan, and Betsey's heart went out to her.

"No, my lovely, I'm afraid not, but I'm sure she'll be home soon. One thing I do know is that she won't stay away from you a minute longer than she needs to. Are you walking home with Helen today?"

"Yes, and Aunty Liza is looking after me until Papa gets home; he's been riding everywhere searching for Mummy."

"That's good. Well, I'll see you all again soon."

Betsey continued along the main street and turned into the narrow lane that led to Nancy's cottage. As she turned the corner, she spotted Eli up ahead and called out to him.

"Hello, Eli, how are you getting on at school? Do you like it?"

"Hello, Mrs Carter; yes, I do. I didn't want to go, but Aunty Nancy insisted, and I'm glad now because I'm making lots of new friends and I'm getting better at reading and writing. Aunty Nancy showed me my letters before I even went to school, so I didn't look quite so silly on my first day. Are you coming in?"

"Yes, Nancy's not expecting me, but if she's not too busy, I'd like a chat."

"I'm sure she'll be glad to see you. Come in." Eli unlatched the kitchen door and called out. "Aunty Nancy, it's me, Eli, and Mrs Carter is here to see you."

"Come in, then, both of you; how nice to see you, Betsey. Eli, there's a glass of milk and a piece of cake on the table for you, and when you've eaten that, you can go out to play while I chat to Betsey."

"Coo, thanks, Aunty."

The boy climbed onto the bench and made short work of the milk and cake as Nancy led Betsey into her sitting room.

"How are you, Betsey? Has Annie been found?"

"I'm well, thanks, but no, she's still missing. I was concerned a few weeks ago that a young man from Scotland was showing far too much interest in her, but I know she would never be unfaithful to Robert or leave her children. It's so odd that Lady Eleanor is also unaccounted for, but I can't believe there's any connection. Robert and half the village are out searching for them. Liza is looking after Katel and the other children, because even Sabina has gone out on horseback with Arthur to lend a hand. The poor woman will be so stiff and sore tomorrow, for I suspect it's years since she's ridden a horse, though I expect she'll feel better for doing something positive, rather than sitting at home worrying."

"Yes, it's always better to keep busy at times like this. I do hope she's found safe and sound."

"Thank you; Eli is a friendly lad, and he says he's enjoying school."

"Yes, I think he's bright for all he's had no education. He picked up his letters and numbers in no time. I'm pleased for John because, having lost poor little Tommy to diphtheria, he now has another son, and he's been coming here on Saturdays to get to know him."

"Has Noeleen seen Eli yet?"

"No, but she's coming with John this Saturday, and bringing Daisy and Rachael. I'm dreading it because Eli and Rachael are so alike it's uncanny, and I'm sure Noeleen will notice."

"Well, if she does, it might be for the best, then John can be open about it and claim Eli as his son. And after all, it happened long before he was married to Noeleen. We all have a past and have made mistakes; she might surprise you and take it all in her stride."

"I hope so because it's not the boy's fault, and as you say, John would like to recognise him as his son. I'm glad he found us, for he's a likeable lad, and nothing is too much trouble for him. He takes care of me and I'd like him to carry on living here, whatever happens."

At the Manor House, Jack Bater took off his flat cap and scratched his balding head as Jimmy Chugg trotted into the yard. Jack knew Exmoor and the surrounding countryside like the back of his hand, and as the many volunteers arrived to take part in the search, he meticulously sent them out to different areas. Many were on horseback to cover the ground more quickly, but he impressed upon them that Annie was on foot and could not have wandered far. However, there were many hills, valleys, glades and forests to search, and along the coast, secluded little coves, any one of which she might have enjoyed exploring.

"No luck, Jimmy?"

"Nope, I've not seen hide nor hair of Annie or her Ladyship. Where would you like me to search next?"

"I honestly don't know where else to look. The only thing I wondered is, if it's not too late, could you ride to Barnstaple and ask Annie's cousin, Francis, if he's seen her. I know she couldn't have walked there, but she could have caught a stagecoach or got a lift on a cart to go shopping. It's unlikely, but I'm running out of ideas."

"Of course, I will. It's long days now, and I can easily be there and back before dark. Do you have a different horse I could use, though? This one has already galloped for miles."

"Yes, you can take mine. It's the only one that hasn't been ridden so far today, and I was keeping it in case I needed to go out myself, but I've been too busy here coordinating the search."

"Fine; I'll grab a quick drink, and I'll be off. See you later."

Within ten minutes, Jimmy was cantering down the lanes leading towards Barnstaple. Jack's horse was a far superior beast to his own, and he felt guilty enjoying the ride when his mission was so desperate. He didn't hold out much hope of finding Annie in the town, for he thought it was unlikely she would have travelled so far on her own without telling anyone. However, he was willing to check it out, and taking a shortcut across the countryside, he let the horse have its head as he enjoyed the late afternoon sunshine on his back. He reached the town in record time and walked his horse across the town square and past the Albert Clock towards the shop run by Francis Carter.

He tethered his horse outside the shop and entered the establishment, squinting a little as his eyes became accustomed to the gloomy interior after the bright sunshine outside. Francis came towards him.

"Hello, Jimmy, it's not often we see you in the town at this time of day; how can I help you?"

"Hello, Francis, I'm not here to buy anything, but to ask if you've seen Annie in the last few days?"

"No, I haven't seen her for a couple of weeks since she came shopping with Aunt Eveline; why do you ask?"

"I'm afraid she's been missing since she went for a walk yesterday morning, and Robert is beside himself with worry. Most of the villagers have been out searching all day without success. The strange thing is that Lady Eleanor is also missing, though she was on horseback, and her horse came back without her."

"I can't believe they'll be together; they don't get on, do they?"

"No, that's what everyone says. Jack Bater has been organising the search, but he's running out of places to look. A few folk are suspicious because apparently there's been a bit of a rift between Annie and Robert lately, and a young man who's been staying at the Manor House has been taking far too much interest in her while Robert's been in London. Folk are wondering if she's run away with him."

"I can't believe that. She and Robert were made for each other, and even if there were trouble between them, Annie would never abandon her children; she dotes on them."

"Yes, that's what I think, too. Is there anywhere else in Barnstaple that you think she might go?"

"Not that I can think of, and she usually calls in to see me if she's in town, so I wouldn't think she is. What are you going to do? Ride back to Hartford again?"

"Yes, I'll walk the horse back through the High Street in case I can see her, but then I'll head back; I'd like to get home before dark. Thanks, Francis, I'll see you again soon."

"Yes, well, let me know what happens, won't you? I'm fond of Annie, and she must be in trouble to leave her children for this long."

Having assured Francis that he would keep him informed, Jimmy led his horse slowly across the town square just as the Albert Clock struck six o'clock. The High Street was still busy with folk looking for a bargain at the end of the day before the shops shut their doors. He spotted one or two people he knew and passed the time of day, asking them if they had seen Annie, but to no avail. As he passed the end of the Pannier Market, he was delighted when he spotted Nell, and he called out to her. She glanced around and smiled.

"Nell, this is a stroke of luck; I didn't expect to see you out and about this late in the day. Are you all right? You look pale and tired."

"Oh, Jimmy, can you spare a minute?"

"Nothing would please me more. I expect Winnie in The Three Tuns will let us use her parlour again for a few minutes. I need a drink and something to eat before I head back to Hartford."

Winnie welcomed them, and, within minutes, had brought Jimmy a hot pasty and a tankard of ale, though Nell declined the offer.

"I wish you'd have something to eat, Nell, for I think you've lost weight since I last saw you. Are you all right?"

"Yes, I'm fine, thanks, Jimmy, but I'm exhausted nursing Aunt Meg for it's such hard work. She hasn't long left, and knows it. I think she's worried about her sins now that she's about to meet her Maker, for she's done some terrible things in her time. She's had no qualms about capturing young girls to be used as prostitutes against their will and has covered up many of the crimes committed by Noah and her sons. She was respectable once, though, and close to my mother, and she seems determined to protect me, because she knows that once she's gone, Noah and Abe will put me to work as a prostitute, and it won't be many years before my girls face the same fate. There's something I need to give you for safekeeping, Jimmy. Will you look after this for me?"

Nell handed him a sealed envelope.

"Yes, of course; what is it?"

"I'm not sure, but Aunt Meg says it's proof of a serious crime Noah once committed, and that if I have it, he'll have no power over me or my girls, and will have to let me go. She insisted it must not be opened until after her death, but she was confident it would keep me safe and hinted it could bring me a lot of money if I used the information wisely. I have no idea what she means, and it might be the laudanum talking, for she needs ever higher doses to combat the pain.

She told me to give it to someone I trust, and that's you, Jimmy. You're the only friend I have, and I'm so relieved to have seen you today, for I've carried that envelope next to my breast for two weeks to keep it safe. It's a weight off my mind to hand it over to you. Will you keep it safe for me?"

Jimmy tucked the envelope into his inside pocket.

"It will be safe with me for as long as you want it to be."

CHAPTER 41

After consuming a light lunch with Victoria and James, Robert insisted it was time for him to resume his search for Annie and his mother. His sister left the two men alone while she went to change into more appropriate clothing for riding, and for a few minutes, there was an uncomfortable silence, eventually broken by James.

"I don't understand, Robert. Have I offended you in some way? You can hardly have too many people searching for Annie and your mother."

"I'm sorry to be so blunt, James, but I think you've seen rather too much of my wife recently as it is, and I'm not sure your intentions are entirely honourable."

The young man's face reddened with embarrassment.

"I can assure you, sir, that you have nothing to worry about. You have a beautiful wife, and I admit I enjoy her company. However, she has made it clear that she has no interest in me and has kept me firmly in my place. She's devoted to you, and you're a lucky man. I apologise if my friendship with Annie has been a matter of concern to you. Your fears are unfounded."

James's words evoked a tumultuous mix of emotions in Robert. He was so relieved to learn Annie was faithful to him, but devastated that he had doubted her and caused her so much pain. He longed to find her and take her in his arms, hoping she still loved him.

"It's important you believe me, Robert. Annie is loyal to you and showed no interest whatsoever when I made advances to her. I'm ashamed to admit that I did, but she's such an attractive woman, and I wrongly thought she was unhappy with you. I hope you'll accept my apology."

The young man held out his hand, and Robert, somewhat begrudgingly, shook it.

"Very well. I will accept your apology, and I deeply regret ever doubting my wife. You are correct in that there has been some friction between us recently over a difficult problem that we have yet to resolve. We think the world of each other, but I will concede that the issue has put pressure on our relationship."

"In that case, please allow me to help with the search; it sounds as if you need as many men as possible."

"Thank you, we do."

Victoria was relieved to find that the atmosphere between the two men had thawed somewhat in her absence. Without further ado, the three headed for the stables and were soon galloping across the countryside towards Hartford. Jack Bater met them in the yard and pre-empted Robert's question by shaking his head.

"No, sir, I'm sorry, but there's no sign of either of the women. I've sent Jimmy to Barnstaple to ask Francis if he's seen Annie, though I know it's unlikely. I've had all the areas I can think of searched, and the men and the animals are bone-tired, but they don't want to give up and risk the women spending another night out in the open. What do you want to do?"

"As the men return, I suggest you send the older ones home to get some rest and ask the younger ones to continue searching for another couple of hours. After that, the horses and the men will have to call it a day, for the light will be fading and they're already exhausted. James, could you ride to Enderby to Aunty Margery's house to check that Mama isn't there, please? I don't know why I didn't think of it before. It's possible she had an accident on the way, so please search along the route, though you would think someone would have found her by now. I'm sure if she arrived there injured, or was expected and didn't arrive, Aunty Margery would have sent word to us. Still, we need to rule it out. Victoria, you and I will check along the coast path again, for that's one of Annie's favourite walks. We'll see you later, Jack."

At any other time, the Fellwood twins would have revelled in a ride together at sunset. Each had their own commitments and responsibilities these days, and could not remember the last time they had ventured out on horseback together. They trotted through the village, shaking their heads as many of the villagers asked if the women had been found, and then cantered up the steep track to the top of the cliffs.

"It's such a long time since I rode up here, and I'd forgotten how beautiful it is. It's so nice to be out with you, Robert, though I wish it were under different circumstances. When the women are found safe and sound, we should do this more often."

"Yes, we must. It's good to spend some time with you, too, though, as you say, not for this reason. We all lead such busy lives these days that we forget to take the time to enjoy the simple pleasures in life. Do you know James McIntyre well?"

"No, but I like him. Why have you taken against him? He seems a pleasant young man, and Aunty Margery is fond of him."

"I know, but he's been spending too much time with Annie, and he's misinterpreted her friendship for deeper emotions, and he, wrongly, it seems, thought she'd leave me for him. Even Betsey and Sabina noticed his infatuation with her and were concerned."

"Oh no! I've always thought you and Annie were devoted to one another; that's why I thought you should marry her, for all she was a kitchen maid."

"We are, but this matter of Mama wanting Danny back has put so much pressure on us both."

"Hang on a minute? What did you say? Mama wants Danny back? Why would Mama want Danny back? He's got nothing to do with her?"

Robert immediately realised his mistake, for he was exhausted and worried, and had forgotten that Victoria didn't know Danny was her brother.

"Oh, ignore me. She saw him playing in our garden and said she'd like to get to know him, and Annie and Sabina are not keen on the idea."

For a moment, his sister looked puzzled, but then reached across and grabbed his reins, bringing both horses to a halt.

"That is so unlikely it can't be true, and I always know when you're lying. What are you not telling me? Come on, I want to know what you meant."

"Oh, dear, I've tried so hard to keep this from you, Vic, and now I've stupidly blurted it out. You remember Mama had a baby boy that died?" Victoria nodded. "Well, he didn't die. He survived, but was badly deformed, and the doctor thought he was brain-damaged as well. Mama rejected the child because she was worried he would be like her younger brother, who was also handicapped and died young. She insisted the boy must be adopted."

"Oh my God! That's terrible; her own son."

"Yes, I know, but she was adamant about it."

"How come you knew this and I didn't?"

"I went to say goodbye to her because I was being sent back to school early. Papa was annoyed with me because I'd been spending time with Annie and working on the local farms with her, and so he'd arranged for me to return to Westford the next morning. I entered the room before they could stop me, and I saw the baby. I begged Mama not to give him away, but she wouldn't listen, and then I had an idea. Mama wanted him sent far away where she would never see him again, but that was difficult to arrange, and he needed to be fed. Annie's mum, Sabina, had recently given birth to Helen, the baby she was carrying after her husband died of consumption, and she had breast milk. I suggested to Papa that we could give the baby to her to raise and pay her; the family were in dire straits and desperate for money, and Sabina loves children, so I thought it could work."

"Is that what happened?"

"Yes, we kept it from Mama, and I met Annie in the woods and handed the baby over, and she pretended it was a foundling. Mama only found out when Sabina and her family moved into the Lodge House after my marriage, and she saw Danny when she passed in the carriage and guessed he was her son."

"Does anyone else know?"

"Yes, Aunty Margery guessed a while ago. She noticed that Danny resembles me and David, and he stands out with his dark hair, as all the Carter family are blonds or redheads. She was disgusted, and you know what she's like, she tackled Mama about it."

"Does Sarah know?"

"No, of course, not."

"So, what are you saying now? That she wants him back?"

"Yes, she says he reminds her of David, and it's upsetting her when she sees him playing in our garden, and, of course, she's missing you and your children since you moved to Lynton."

"That's ridiculous. She must realise it's impossible? The boy would hate her for abandoning him, and she ignores all of Annie's family."

"Yes, I know, and Papa agrees. I think she realises that now, but says she wants to get to know him. I suggested that if she and Papa would receive Annie and her family, then that would be one way that she could feasibly spend some time with the boy."

"I'd be surprised if she agreed to that; she has such strong feelings about the unsuitability of your marriage."

"I know, but a mother's love for her child is strong, and she's desperate to see the boy. I think she's considering that option."

"Well, that's good then, isn't it? It would surely be better if everyone got along."

"That's what I thought, too, but Annie was furious with me for thinking it was only up to Mama and Papa to agree to such a thing. She felt I disregarded her strong feelings for not wanting to socialise with them."

"But why? It's the obvious solution, and it's not like Annie to be difficult."

"I can't tell you, but she has her reasons for hating them, and I should have respected her feelings; it seemed like the only solution to me."

"No, that's not good enough. It seems there's a lot I don't know about this family. Come on, Robert, we've always been honest with each other; you can't say something like that and not tell me. I insist."

"If I tell you, you'll wish I hadn't. I'm protecting you from something you're better off not knowing. Please leave it, Vic."

"No, it must be something important for Annie to feel that way, for she gets along with everyone. I'd rather know, however unpalatable the truth."

"Very well, but you'll wish you'd not asked. Do you remember when Miss Wetherby gave Annie the sack because she was with child and unmarried?"

"Yes, of course, but what has that to do with anything? She was carrying Harry Rudd's child, and he married her, so it turned out all right in the end, though it was so sad when he died in the smithy fire. I liked Harry, and he was a skilled farrier."

"He did marry her, and it was a noble gesture to give Annie respectability, but the child wasn't his."

"Oh, you mean Selina is your child? Oh, Robert."

Despite the seriousness of the conversation, he grinned. "No, she's not mine. Selina is our half-sister. Papa is Selina's father!"

"No! He can't be! What makes you think that?"

"I guessed when I saw Annie changing Selina's clothes one day at her mother's cottage. She was visiting, and I'd called in to assess the repairs that were required. She undressed her, and I noticed a birthmark on her shoulder; it's almost the same as yours, and as you know, it runs in our family. I put two and two together and realised she could only be Papa's child. I was away at school, and David had left home to join the army. Papa was the only male Fellwood around when the child was conceived."

"I can't believe it. Does Mama know?"

"Of course not. Do you think she'd still be with Papa if she did?"

"So, Annie had an affair with Papa when she worked at the Manor?"

"No, it's far worse than that. She was clearing up after a New Year's Eve party, and he attacked her. He'd been drinking heavily, and Mama wouldn't let him in her bed and risk another pregnancy after giving birth to the deformed baby, though that's no excuse. He dragged Annie to the cellars in the west wing, and he beat her and raped her! I know it's hard to believe, but he did."

"I can't believe it; are you sure?"

"Yes, Annie didn't know who her attacker was for a long time because it was too dark to see and he only spoke in whispers, but when I saw Selina's birthmark, I realised it had to be him. There was nothing I could do about it at the time, as Annie was married to Harry and would always abide by her vows. She would never have left him even if she didn't love him, but then he died so awfully in the fire, and eventually I told her I knew who had attacked her."

"Oh, my goodness; it's so out of character for Papa to do something like that. Is he aware that you know?"

"Yes, I took Annie and Selina to see him and showed him Selina's birthmark, and he admitted it. It's why he gave his permission for me to marry Annie."

"You blackmailed him?"

"Yes, I told him if he didn't consent to our marriage, I would tell Mama everything, and under the circumstances, I'd do the same thing again; he deserved it. We waited a respectable time after Harry's death, and until Papa had signed the estate over to me, and then we tackled him about it. He was furious but could do nothing about it."

"I can see why Annie refuses to socialise with Papa, and who can blame her? It was naïve of you to expect that she would."

"Yes, I realise that now, but he's an old man, and confined to a wheelchair since his stroke. He's no threat to Annie or anyone else anymore, and I thought with all the time that's passed, she might be able to put it behind her. It will be seven years, this New Year's Eve, since the attack happened."

"She'll never forgive him, Robert; I wouldn't. Hang on a minute, did I hear a cry then, or was it a seagull?"

CHAPTER 42

If she were honest with herself, Annie had enjoyed telling Eleanor a few home truths, for the indignation of how she had been treated had festered for years. However, following her revelation about Charles Fellwood raping her, her mother-in-law had not spoken and, at times, seemed barely conscious. At first, Annie thought she was brooding on the awful information she had received, but then she began to wonder if there was more wrong with the woman than a broken ankle.

"Eleanor, are you all right?"

She shook her mother-in-law's shoulder gently, but Eleanor's eyes remained closed, and she received no response. Suddenly, Annie listened carefully, for she thought she had heard the sound of horses' hooves, which had come to a halt. This had already happened a couple of times during the day, and although the women had called out as loudly as possible, the riders had not heard them over the stiff breeze and the cries of the many screaming seabirds. Frustratingly, the horses had galloped on as the riders tried to search as wide an area as possible. Annie stood up gingerly and shouted as loudly as she could.

"Help! Help! Please help us!"

Robert and Victoria dismounted and listened carefully.

"It is a cry for help, but where's it coming from?"

"I think it's over the edge of the cliff."

The twins lay flat on their stomachs, gazing down.

"Oh, Annie, thank God! Are you all right? Are you injured?"

"And Mama, is she, is she dead?"

"Oh, thank goodness you've found us. I'm all right; just a few cuts and bruises, but I don't know what's wrong with your mother. She's broken her ankle, but for the last few hours, she's been unconscious. I think it may be because she struck her head when she fell."

"Annie, stay still, and I'll ride for help; we're going to need a rope and a few more men to pull you up safely."

"No, Robert, you stay here with Annie, and I'll gallop back to the Manor. I'll be back before you know it."

"Thanks, Vic; mind how you go."

Robert watched his sister gallop off and then feasted his eyes on his beloved wife, the wife he thought he had lost forever.

"Oh, Annie, I'm so sorry I doubted you; can you ever forgive me?"

"Yes, of course; we've both been at fault lately, but we've had a lot to deal with. I love you so much, Robert; I couldn't bear it when you doubted that my child is yours."

Robert hung his head in shame.

"I know, and I love you too. I wish I could turn back the clock and not speak those words. I've been beside myself with worry, and saying all day that you couldn't be with Mama, yet here you are."

"We thought you'd be surprised to find us together. We've been here for so long, I'm afraid a few home truths have been spoken and secrets revealed, but maybe it will be for the best in the long run. I'll tell you about it later. Are the children all right?"

"Yes, the twins aren't even aware that you're missing, but Selina has been terribly upset; she'll be overjoyed to see you. Your mother and Betsey, too. We've all been so worried, and most of the villagers have been looking for you. Oh, I think I hear horses."

Charlie Chugg was the first to reach Robert, and he skilfully leapt from his horse, brandishing a thick rope. Annie's Uncle Fred, Arthur Webber, and Victoria were behind him, and all four wore wide smiles.

They all lay on their stomachs and peered over the cliff top.

"I'll climb down and put a rope around Annie so that the rest of you can pull her up. We'll get that done first and then think about the best way to rescue Lady Eleanor."

"It's all right, Charlie; I'll go."

"No, I'm used to climbing from my days as a sailor, Robert. It was nothing for me to climb up to the crow's nest to scout for land. I'll be down to the ladies in no time."

Giving Robert no further opportunity to object, Charlie tied two ropes around his waist and instructed Fred and Arthur to hold on to them. He abseiled down the cliffside and was beside Annie in seconds.

"Right then, Annie, let me tie this rope around you, and then you can climb up. You can't fall, for the men will be holding the rope. Can you do that?"

Annie nodded, and with Charlie hoisting her up as far as he could, she scrambled up the stony cliffside and fell into her husband's arms.

"Oh, Annie, my darling, I can't believe we've found you at last." Robert held his wife tightly, kissing her face and hair as tears flowed down his cheeks. "But you're injured. Why didn't you say? Where has all this blood come from?"

"I've cut my hand and arm and grazed my back, but it looks worse than it is. I'm all right, and it stopped bleeding ages ago. I'm worried about your mother, though. She seemed uninjured apart from her ankle, but then she fell asleep a few hours ago, and I can't wake her."

Robert untied the rope from around Annie's waist and threw it down to Charlie.

"How are we going to do this, Charlie?"

"As your mother is unconscious, I think I'd better hold her in my arms, and you'll have to pull us up together. We can't risk knocking her against the cliffside and making her injuries worse. If you tie the ropes to the horses' saddles and lead them away slowly, they can pull us up."

The men did as Charlie suggested, and it wasn't long until his face appeared over the cliff top and he laid the woman gently on the ground. Victoria had realised they would need to transport her mother on a horse and cart, and Arthur's son, Dudley, was ready and waiting. He had thrown soft hay onto the cart for her to lie on and grabbed a couple of pillows and blankets from his bed. They laid Eleanor on the cart and made her as comfortable as possible, but she didn't stir, and her face was pale.

"Well done, Charlie. You certainly haven't lost your climbing skills; thank you for doing that. I must confess I don't like heights, though I would have done it."

"My pleasure, Robert. Now, if you and Annie ride on the cart on either side of your mother, I'll lead your horse home."

"Thank you, yes, we'll do that. Did you send for the doctor, Vic?"

Yes, Doctor Luckett should be at the Manor by the time we return, and I've sent a messenger to Cullompton to ask Doctor Turner to get here as soon as he can. Geoffrey's retired from his practice in London now, and I'm sure he'll help if he can. I don't think Doctor Luckett will mind; they've worked together a few times now."

Robert lifted Annie onto the cart and wrapped one of the blankets around her, for she was shaking with the cold and shock. He climbed up on the other side of his mother and gazed at her anxiously. He stroked her forehead and spoke to her, but there was no response.

"Dudley, please take your time and avoid as many ruts as possible. We mustn't jar Mama around more than need be."

"Of course, sir."

Travelling slowly, it took a while before they reached the Manor House, and Doctor Luckett was waiting for them. He observed the unconscious woman anxiously and supervised her being carried carefully to her bed.

"Annie, do you need me to attend to your wounds, or can a maid deal with them? I think it's crucial I examine Lady Eleanor as soon as possible."

"I'm fine, Andrew. I can see my mother walking up the drive and waving to me, so she'll sort me out, as she has done so many times before. I do hope you can help Lady Eleanor."

Sabina ran the last few hundred yards and hugged Annie tightly.

"Are you all right, my love? I've been so worried."

"I'm fine, Mum; you know me, I always bounce back, and it was worth falling over a cliff to bring Robert and me close again."

"Well, I'm relieved to hear that; I've wanted to bang your heads together for being so stupid. Let's get you undressed, and I'll bathe your wounds; it won't be the first time. Then I must tell Betsey and Ned you're safe and put their minds at ease."

"Yes, please do that, but first I must see Selina and the twins."

Although she was exhausted, Annie raced up the stairs two at a time, with Robert hurrying behind her, telling her to be careful. Selina heard the commotion and came running out of her bedroom.

"Mummy, Mummy, you're home! Are you hurt?"

"No, my love, I'm fine, and I'm so sorry to have worried you. Are you all right?"

"I am now, but please don't go missing ever again."

CHAPTER 43

Doctor Luckett became increasingly worried as he examined Lady Eleanor. Apart from her broken ankle, which would mend, there was barely a mark on her. However, having lifted each of her eyelids, he had established that her pupils were unequal, and he knew that probably indicated a compression of the brain, most likely due to a haemorrhage. Annie told him Eleanor said she had hit the left side of her head as she fell and had become confused, complaining of a severe headache before losing consciousness. He stepped outside the room to where Robert, Victoria and Sarah were waiting anxiously.

"Will Mama be all right?"

"Her condition is worrying, I'm afraid, but before I explain, could we go to Charles's room, for he needs to hear this about his wife as well."

Charles Fellwood was already in bed, and his nurse sought his permission to admit the doctor and his children. Anxious for news of his wife, he readily agreed to receive them. The pleasantries over, and with everyone seated, the doctor explained.

"Lady Eleanor has a broken ankle, which is not serious. However, she has sustained a head injury which, I suspect, has led to a bleed on her brain. I have to tell you that this condition is life-threatening, for the blood is likely compressing her brain and will, at the least, lead to mental and physical impairment. I'm sorry to tell you that if left untreated, it is likely she will die."

"Oh no! How can you be sure?"

"The pupils of her eyes are uneven, and that's a sure sign of a brain injury. Annie told me that Eleanor said she had banged her head as she fell, though she was unsure whether she had lost consciousness or not. She also complained of a severe headache before she fell asleep. Those are all symptoms that concern me."

"You said if left untreated, she could die. So, presumably, you can treat these injuries."

"There is a procedure called trephination, which I have seen performed once, though I have not had experience myself."

"What does it involve?"

"It means we carefully drill one or more holes into her skull to release the blood and ease the pressure on her brain."

Shock registered on the faces of all those present, and Victoria was the first to recover sufficiently to ask questions.

"You mentioned you've seen this procedure carried out before. May I ask, did the patient live, and was he impaired?"

"I'm afraid the poor young man died, though not from the operation itself, which was a remarkable success. Sadly, as in so many cases, he died a few days later of blood poisoning, although every measure possible was taken to prevent such an outcome. However, unpalatable as this decision is, I doubt Lady Eleanor will recover consciousness if the procedure is not carried out immediately; it may already be too late to prevent brain damage. I have no way of knowing. I'm sorry it's such devastating news, but I must urge you to decide with some urgency whether you would like me to try to help her."

Charles glanced around the room at his children, who were waiting for him to comment.

"From what you've told us, we have little choice in the matter. Victoria has sent for Geoffrey Turner, and he may have more experience of treating this condition; can you wait for him to arrive?"

"No, I think not. He's unlikely to travel here until daylight tomorrow, and it will be later in the day before he arrives; I'm certain that will be too late, but I'll wait if you so wish. As you say, he might have more experience than I."

"No, in that case, please attend to her immediately, Doctor, and tell us of anything you require."

"I'll need some assistance." He glanced at the young nurse who was waiting patiently by the door. "Young lady, are you squeamish?"

"No, sir."

"Have you assisted in an operation before?"

"No, sir, but I've dressed many wounds and am willing to do my best if you explain what you want me to do."

"Very well. In that case, I'll prepare the patient for surgery and proceed. Fortunately, when I heard the lady was unconscious, I suspected a head injury and brought with me all that I would require. Please come with me, nurse."

A little over an hour later, Doctor Luckett emerged from the bedroom and smiled at the waiting family.

"The procedure went well, though we won't know how successful it was until Lady Eleanor awakens, and that might not be for some hours. Although she was unconscious, I administered chloroform to ensure she did not awaken and experience any discomfort."

"Was there a bleed as you expected?"

"Yes, and a significant one, but I would imagine it was a slow bleed, or she would already no longer be with us. I shaved a section of her head and removed a small disc of bone from her skull. As expected, I discovered a large blood clot, which I removed, cleaned the wound thoroughly, replaced the bone, and stitched the scalp back into place. Throughout the procedure, I used phenol as advocated by

Joseph Lister, which should greatly reduce the risk of infection. Times have moved on since I last watched this procedure carried out, and I am hopeful of the outcome, but only time will tell. Her colour has already improved, and her pulse is steady. Those are encouraging signs.

"Now, if you will excuse me, I'll check on Annie, for she, too, was injured in her fall, though less seriously. Nevertheless, I would like to assure myself that she's not in any danger. I'll return shortly and, if you are agreeable, will sit here in the chair next to my patient for the rest of the night. I would like to be here when Lady Eleanor wakes."

"Yes, of course, and thank you, Doctor. I'm keen to return to my wife, but she insisted I wait here for news."

Doctor Luckett examined Annie and was pleased to see that the cuts on her hand and arm and the grazes on her back had been cleaned and dressed.

"Are you sure you didn't knock your head, Annie?"

"No, mostly I slithered down on my back, which is why it's grazed. I should never have been so stupid as to try to rescue Lady Eleanor on my own, but her outstretched hand was only an inch or so from mine, and I thought I could do it. She didn't want me to leave her, and I think if she hadn't broken her ankle, I could have helped her back up. How is she?"

The doctor explained what had transpired, and Annie was shocked to hear what he had done.

"Do you think she'll be all right, Doctor?"

"I don't know, Annie, but she has a chance. Now, I know you are with child. Have you had any stomach cramps or passed any blood?"

"No, I think I'm all right, thank you. Do you think the baby will have been harmed by this accident?"

"I don't think so. Your pulse is normal, and you have no symptoms to suggest a miscarriage. I suggest that if you take it easy for a few days, you and the baby will be fine. Now, I must return to my patient, for the next few hours are critical, and I plan to sit by Lady Eleanor's bedside until she awakens."

With the doctor gone, Robert and Annie thankfully climbed into bed. He put his arm around her and drew her close, and she contentedly nestled her head on his chest.

"Oh, how I have longed to be here over the last couple of days. It was so cold and uncomfortable on the clifftop, and your mother and I even had to huddle together for warmth; something neither of us was keen on."

"I wonder who was the most horrified at the situation: you or Mama."

"I don't think there was much in it, to be honest, but I'm afraid she knows everything now. We were there for so many hours that inevitably the conversation led to Danny and her wanting to see him. From there, she kept asking so many questions that eventually I had to tell her about Charles attacking me and that Selina is your father's child."

Robert gasped. "Oh, no; I hoped she would never learn about that."

"I'm sorry, but it couldn't be helped. She was relentless with her questions, and in the end, she goaded me into telling her."

"Never mind; it's done now, and perhaps it's for the best. They do say the truth will out, and this is proof of it, but I don't know what will happen between my parents when they are next together. I don't think Mama will ever forgive Papa for being unfaithful. On that note, I'm so sorry I ever doubted you, Annie. It was clear that James was attracted to you, which was frustrating because I kept having to leave you with him. I honestly thought you were falling for him, and I knew you were annoyed with me."

"Oh, Robert, no, I wasn't interested in him in that way. I enjoyed his company, and he was kind and attentive and, yes, I was angry with you for repeatedly abandoning me, particularly at the ball where I felt like a fish out of water. I had no idea that he thought our friendship might develop into something more, and when he did make his feelings clear, I was horrified. If he had known me better, he would have realised that I would never leave you or my children."

"As we're being so honest with each other, there is something I need to tell you that might help you to understand why I've been away so much. I didn't want to tell you this because I knew you'd worry, but I've taken out a massive loan from the bank to pay for all the alterations to the Manor House. It cost far more than I expected, but it's best to do it once and do it properly, and Mr Billery is in full agreement. By installing bathrooms and every luxury now, the guests will enjoy staying here, hopefully tell all their friends, and return often. However, this means it will take some time before we can repay the money and see a profit. The reason I left you longer than I would have liked at the ball was that there were so many of Aunty Margery's rich and influential friends there, and she introduced me to them. You know what an astute businesswoman she is, and she saw a wonderful opportunity for me to get to know her friends and tell them about Hartford Manor and our hunting breaks. It worked, too, because the bookings have been pouring in since. She did say that I should have explained everything to you, and as usual, she was right."

"I wish you had told me, though I hate the thought of us owing money. I was brought up that if you couldn't afford something, then you didn't have it; even if it was food for the table."

"I know, but this is a good business venture, and Mr Billery knows it. If he didn't agree, he certainly wouldn't have loaned me the money. This is a different situation from that of your father because, luckily, we have many assets we could sell if we ever got into financial difficulty. We have plenty of land, farm animals and stock, and even precious antiques, paintings, and jewellery that would sell for far more than I have borrowed, so don't worry about any of it. We're doing well and will leave Hartford Manor in a sound financial state for our children."

"That's good to hear, especially as there is another one on the way. Are you pleased? I thought you would be."

"I'm delighted, and I'm so sorry for the way I received such wonderful news; if I could take those words back, I'd do it in a heartbeat. My only defence is that I love you so much, I was heartbroken to think you might have an affair with James. Do you think the baby will be all right after your ordeal?"

"I think so. I feel fine, and Doctor Luckett could find nothing wrong with me. It wasn't a bad fall for me; I just sort of slithered down the rocks, and that's why my back and arm are so sore and grazed. Mind you, if your mother hadn't grabbed me, I would have fallen over the cliff!"

"Don't! It doesn't bear thinking about. It's no good saying it now, but you should never have attempted to rescue her; you should have gone for help."

"Yes, I know, but she didn't want me to leave her, and she wasn't far out of reach. I wonder if she will recover? It was a pretty desperate measure to drill into her skull, wasn't it?"

"Yes, it was, but the doctor didn't think there was any choice, so we'll just have to pray for the best. I hope she makes a full recovery, but if and when she does, there are so many issues that need to be resolved. Her desire to see Danny, his discovery that he's a foundling, and Papa being Selina's father. At least she'll see you in a different light from now on and understand your feelings."

"Maybe. She was so shocked. Anyway, I'm far too tired to think about it all tonight."

"Sorry! You must be exhausted, and I'm keeping you talking when you should rest. I don't know the solution to any of those matters, but as long as we're all right again, the rest of it will have to sort itself out. We are all right, aren't we?"

"Yes, we're very all right; now kiss me, please, and hold me tight."

"My pleasure; we'll worry about everything else tomorrow."

TO BE CONTINUED …

AUTHOR'S NOTE

I hope you enjoyed reading this book as much as I enjoyed writing it. If so, I would really appreciate it if you could leave a short review on Amazon or Goodreads.

An honest review is the highest compliment you can pay to any author, and it would mean so much to me.

If you would like to find out more about me and my books, and keep up to date with new releases, please visit https://marciaclayton.co.uk/ and join my mailing list.

Thank you.

Marcia

About The Author

Marcia Clayton writes historical fiction with a sprinkling of romance and mystery in a heartwarming family saga that spans the Regency period through Victorian times.

When she was a child, Marcia's favourite pastimes were writing stories and reading, and she adored the Enid Blyton books, particularly The Famous Five and The Adventure Series. These books established her love of literature, which has remained with her to this day.

A farmer's daughter, Marcia, was born in North Devon and is proud to be a Devon Maid. Over the years, she has been employed in various occupations, mainly to work around raising her three sons, Stuart, Paul, and David. She has worked in banking and nursing and, for many years, was the School Transport Manager for the local authority. Now retired, Marcia spends a lot of her time writing historical fiction but also enjoys gardening, researching her family history, and walking in the lovely Devon countryside with Bryan, her husband of fifty-two years.

Marcia has written seven books in the historical family saga, *The Hartford Manor Series*. You can also read her free short story, *Amelia*, a spin-off tale from the first book, *The Mazzard Tree*. Amelia, a little orphan girl of 4, is abandoned in Victorian London with her brothers, Joseph and Matthew. To find out what happens to her, download the story here: https://marciaclayton.co.uk/amelia-free-download/ In addition to writing books, Marcia writes blogs about a variety of subjects and a monthly newsletter, which she shares with her readers. If you would like to join Marcia's mailing list, subscribe here to her website, *The Devon Maid Book Corner*. https://marciaclayton.co.uk/

If you enjoyed reading *Annie's Secret*, you might enjoy the other books in the series:

Betsey

The Prequel to the Hartford Manor Series

1820 North Devon, England

Betsey, a sadly neglected child, is shouldering responsibilities far beyond her years. As she does her best to care for her little brother, Norman, she is befriended by Gypsy Freda, an old woman whose family is camped nearby. Freda's granddaughter, Jane, is also fond of the little girl and is concerned about her.

Thomas, the second son of Lord Fellwood, happens across the gypsy camp and becomes besotted with Jane. However, Jasper Morris, the local miller, also has designs on the young gypsy, and inevitably, the two men do not see eye to eye.

Betsey is drawn into their rivalry for the attention of the beautiful young woman, and she finds herself promising to keep a dangerous secret for many years to come.

The Mazzard Tree

Book One in The Hartford Manor Series

1880 North Devon, England

Annie Carter is a farm labourer's daughter, and life is a continual struggle for survival. When her father dies of consumption, her mother, Sabina, is left with seven hungry mouths to feed and another child on the way. To save them from the workhouse or starvation, Annie steals vegetables from the Manor House garden, risking jail or transportation. Unknown to her, she is watched by Robert, the wealthy heir to the Hartford Estate, but far from turning her in, he befriends her.

Despite their different social backgrounds, Annie and Robert develop feelings they know can have no future. Harry Rudd, the village blacksmith, has long admired Annie, and when he proposes, her mother urges her to accept. She reminds Annie that as a kitchen maid, she will never be allowed to marry Robert. Harry is a good man, and Annie is fond of him. Her head knows what she should do, but will her heart listen?

Set against the harsh background of the rough, class-divided society of Victorian England, this heart-warming and captivating novel portrays a young woman who uses her determination and willpower to defy the circumstances of her birth in her search for happiness.

The Angel Maker

Book Two in The Hartford Manor Series

1884 North Devon, England

When carpenter Fred Carter finds a young woman in dire straits by the roadside, he takes her to the local inn, where she gives birth to a daughter. Charlotte Mackie is an unmarried mother and has run away from home, where she would have no sympathy from her strict parents. A few days later, Fred takes Charlotte to her aunt's house and does not expect to see her again.

When their paths unexpectedly cross, Fred finds that Charlotte is distraught as her aunt has arranged an adoption behind her back. Charlotte is desperate to find her baby, and Fred promises to help.

However, they are unprepared for the sinister discoveries that lie before them. Set alongside the absorbing detail of country life and budding village romances, dark forces are at work which ultimately test the bravery and resourcefulness of the whole community.

The Angel Maker is the sequel to The Mazzard Tree, and the second novel in a compelling series which follows the lives and loves of the villagers of Hartford. A rare treat for lovers of historical fiction.

The Rabbit's Foot

Book Three in The Hartford Manor Series

1885 North Devon, England

Mr Edward Snell was more than a little curious when Robert Fellwood, the heir to Hartford Manor, and Lady Margery, his elderly aunt, begged an audience on a Saturday morning. However, being such valued clients, the solicitor was happy to oblige. As his clerk showed the visitors in, he was intrigued to see them followed by an older man who, though respectably dressed, had something of a vagrant about him. The crisp suit in which he was attired could not disguise his weather-beaten face or his missing teeth.

Robert introduced his Uncle Sam and explained he had come to claim his inheritance. The solicitor was old enough to remember the extensive search for Thomas Fellwood when his father, Ephraim, died in 1840. However, that was some forty-five years ago, and the young man had never been found. Yet, here was Sam, who claimed to be Thomas Fellwood's son, and even more surprising was the fact that the Fellwood family appeared to have accepted him as such.

The Rabbit's Foot tells the tale of how an old man who has spent his life with barely a penny to his name suddenly finds himself rich beyond his wildest dreams. However, there is only one thing that Sam Fellwood truly wants, and that is to be reunited with his son, Marrok, whom he abandoned at the age of five.

Millie's Escape

Book Four in The Hartford Manor Series

1885 North Devon, England

It is winter in the small Devon village of Brampford Speke, and a typhoid epidemic has claimed many victims. Millie, aged fifteen, is doing her best to nurse her mother and grandmother as well as look after Jonathan, her five-year-old brother. One morning, Millie is horrified to find that her mother, Rosemary, has passed away during the night and is terrified that the same fate may befall her granny, Emily.

When Emily's neighbours inform her that Sir Edgar Grantley has also perished from the deadly disease, the old woman is distraught, for the kindly gentleman has been their benefactor for many years, much to the disgust of his wife, Lilliana. Emily is well aware that Sir Edgar's generosity has long been a bone of contention between him and his spouse, and she is certain Lady Grantley will evict them from their cottage at the first opportunity.

As she racks her brain for a solution, Emily remembers her father came from Hartford, a seaside village in North Devon and had relatives there. Desperate and too weak to travel, she insists Millie and Jonathan leave home and make their way to Hartford before the embittered woman can cause trouble for them. There, she tells them, they must throw themselves on the mercy of their family and hope they will offer them a home.

With Emily promising to follow them as soon as possible, the two youngsters reluctantly set off on their fifty-mile journey on foot and in the harshest weather conditions. Emily warns them to be cautious, for she suspects Lady Grantley may well pursue them to seek her revenge.

A Woman Scorned

Book Five of the Hartford Manor Series
1886 North Devon, England

Lady Lilliana Grantley has been seriously ill with typhoid, a disease that recently claimed her husband Edgar's life and that of his long-time lover, Rosemary Gibbs. Now recovering at last, the lady wastes no tears on her husband but is determined to wreak revenge on his two illegitimate children.

Embarrassed for years by his affair with Rosemary, a childhood sweetheart living nearby, she has falsely accused Sir Edgar's daughter, Millicent, of the theft of a precious brooch and wants to see her jailed or hanged.

Fortunately for Millie and her little brother, Jonathan, their granny, Emily, insisted they leave home as soon as she heard of Sir Edgar's death, for she knew his widow would seek revenge. The old lady was soon proved right, and Lady Lilliana, furious that the two youngsters were nowhere to be found, evicted the old woman despite the fact that she, too, was dangerously ill.

After a long and hazardous journey to North Devon, Millie and Jonathan were united with some long-lost family members who made them welcome and gave them a home. However, aware that Lady Lilliana has put a price on Millie's head, they know they are not yet out of danger. Despite this, they are determined to find their granny, Emily, who seems to have disappeared.

Aided by her long-time lover, Sir Clive Robinson, Lady Lilliana is determined to find Millie and Jonnie and get them out of her life once and for all, but how far will the embittered woman go?